Pra

"*Sanctuar* [barcode] y
by a crack i-
fully told g
the healing power of love."   —Susan Wiggs,
                              #1 *New York Times* bestselling author

"I didn't read this book, I inhaled it. An incredible story
of love, forgiveness, healing, and joy."

                                        —Debbie Macomber,
                              #1 *New York Times* bestselling author

"A heartwarming, emotional, extremely romantic story
that I couldn't read fast enough! Enjoy your trip
to Sanctuary Island! I guarantee you won't want to
leave."   —Bella Andre,
                              New York Times bestselling author
                                      of the Sullivan series

"Well written and emotionally satisfying. I loved it! A
rare find."

       —Lori Wilde, *New York Times* bestselling author

"Fall in love with Sanctuary Island. Lily Everett
brings tears, laughter and a happy-ever-after smile to
your face while you're experiencing her well-written,
compassionate novel. I highly recommend this book,
which hits home with true-to-life characters."

                                        —*Romance Junkies*

"Redemption, reconciliation, and, of course, romance—
Everett's novel has it all."   —*Booklist*

ise for the Sanctuary Island serie

ary Island is a novel to curl up with and enjoy
ng fire or on a sunny beach. It's a beauti
ory of hope and forgiveness, celebrati

ALSO BY LILY EVERETT

Sanctuary Island
Shoreline Drive
Homecoming
Heartbreak Cove

AVAILABLE FROM ST. MARTIN'S PAPERBACKS

Home for Christmas

A Sanctuary Island Novel

LILY EVERETT

St. Martin's Paperbacks

NOTE: If you purchased this book without a cover you should be aware that this book is stolen property. It was reported as "unsold and destroyed" to the publisher, and neither the author nor the publisher has received any payment for this "stripped book."

This is a work of fiction. All of the characters, organizations, and events portrayed in this novel are either products of the author's imagination or are used fictitiously.

HOME FOR CHRISTMAS

Copyright © 2015 by Lily Everett.

All rights reserved.

For information address St. Martin's Press, 175 Fifth Avenue, New York, NY 10010.

ISBN: 978-1-250-07404-1

Printed in the United States of America

St. Martin's Paperbacks edition / October 2015

St. Martin's Paperbacks are published by St. Martin's Press, 175 Fifth Avenue, New York, NY 10010.

10 9 8 7 6 5 4 3 2 1

For my husband, Nick,
who makes every season bright

Chapter One

Libby sat with her fingers poised over her laptop keyboard, her deadline looming over her shoulder like a stern, demanding schoolteacher.

You could excel if you'd work a little harder, she imagined Mrs. Deadline saying. *Are you stupid or just lazy, Ms. Leeds? Why don't you apply yourself?*

Libby sighed in the dark silence of her small home office. Another week, another column for *Savor* magazine . . . another shame spiral.

Imaginary Mrs. Deadline was right, Libby told herself firmly. Why did she put herself through this every time? She ought to buckle down, grind out a few sentences, and see what she came up with. If it sucked, she could fix it later! She wasn't curing cancer, here. All she was doing was describing a Thanksgiving feast—and that should be easy! The main course was predetermined. It had to be turkey! So what was she waiting for?

Nothing. She was going to start typing. Libby rested her fingertips on the smooth keys and took a deep breath in. The blank white page glared back at her, painfully bright in the dim room. Any second now . . .

Without conscious thought, Libby's right hand twitched and her pinky hit the button that maximized her internet browser. Before she could get her rogue fingers under control, they'd clicked her mouse and re-started the video that she—and more than a million other people—had been watching on repeat since the clip first aired on the *Good Morning Show*.

"And how are you recovering from your ordeal?" The talk show host's platinum blonde bob quivered with sympathy as she leaned over the hospital bed's railing.

Libby held her breath, her gaze eating up the details of this image she'd already viewed at least fifty times. The man being interviewed didn't shift a single hard muscle. Copper glinted from his short-buzzed hair under the fluorescent lights. His broad chest was barely contained by the plain white hospital gown, his muscular shoulders straining the material where he sat propped against several flat pillows.

Even with his right leg in a cast and raised slightly in traction, he sat at attention, looking ready to spring from the bed and into action at the first sign of danger. His left arm was in a sling that held it immobile across his chest, the tanned skin dark against the pristine fabric.

Next to the hospital bed was a small open box framing a bronze medal hanging from green and white striped ribbon. It was the Army Commendation Medal for distinguished service and valorous conduct, usually awarded to those who had risked their lives above and beyond the normal duties of combat.

Libby knew, because she'd looked it up yesterday after the first time she'd watched the video.

When Sergeant First Class Owen Shepard finally spoke, it was with quiet authority, his rough voice stroking over Libby's skin like a callused palm. "Recovery is slow but steady."

Rhonda Friend, the premier network morning show host, blinked big blue eyes at him. "And was it just awful?" she asked in hushed tones. "The explosion that nearly took your life?"

It was only because Libby had basically become a PhD-level expert in Sgt. Owen Shepard's facial expressions that she caught the miniscule tightening of his sharply angled jaw.

"I can't speak about that," he said, clipped but polite.

"Of course, of course," Rhonda rushed to reply, still simpering. "An active military operation—we wouldn't want you to compromise it. But you can share a few teensy little details with us, can't you?"

Something shifted behind Sgt. Shepard's blue-green eyes, and suddenly he smiled. Bright, charming, effortless—but Libby's gut told her it was fake.

"I'd rather talk about the future," he said. "Rehab is hard work, but I'm committed to getting back on my feet and going back to my men. They tell me it might not happen, but I'm not good with accepting limitations. I'll get there, even if it takes a few months."

Rhonda, who hadn't seemed to notice anything off about her interview subject's easy smile, gave him another smile dripping with sympathy. "It will be won-derful to have some time off, I'm sure! Time with your family, to reconnect, before you return to your unit over-seas to fight for our freedoms back home. And speaking of home, where is that for you?"

For the first time in the interview, a hint of something real and joyful warmed Sgt. Shepard's weary eyes. "My sister, Andie, and my daughter. Caitlin. Wherever they are, that's home."

Libby's heart skipped ahead two beats, the way it had every time she'd watched the clip.

Obviously sensing the nearby presence of gold, Rhonda dug deeper. "Your sister is a small-town sheriff, isn't that right? Heroism must run in the family."

"I don't know about that—but Andie is pretty great. Her town is lucky to have her standing watch over them."

"And what about your wife? Is there a Mrs. Shepard waiting for you at home?"

Something flickered through Sgt. Shepard's gaze, and his smile dimmed a bit. "No. Caitlin's mother passed away . . . almost a year ago, now."

"Tragic," breathed Rhonda, clearly delighted. "I'm so sorry for your loss."

"All that matters to me now is Caitlin." A muscle ticked in the wounded soldier's jaw, and he glanced past Rhonda's startled face to stare directly into the camera as if making a vow to his little girl. "All that matters is getting home to her in time for the holidays. I want to give my daughter the perfect Christmas."

The moment held, intense and riveting. Libby's lungs seized, her throat tightening and eyes burning. He was so intent, his fierce need to be there for his young daughter was almost palpable.

With a jerk of her chin, Rhonda gestured for the cameraman to re-focus on her tight smile. "I'm sure you will."

Sgt. Shepard shrugged, sinking back into the pillows. "Thanks for the vote of confidence. The doctors tell me I'll be recovered enough to get out of the hospital and down to Sanctuary Island in time—but whether I can manage anything approaching a good Christmas is less certain. I'm not even sure I'd know a good Christmas if it ambushed me in the desert, much less how to make sure Caitlin . . . well. I'll figure it out."

"There you have it, ladies," Rhonda purred, turning back to the camera and flicking her hair back. "He's single, handsome, and a real-live hero—and he needs you. Send us your holiday ideas and help a genuine American hero give his daughter the Christmas she deserves."

With only seconds left on the video, Libby ignored the talk show host's babble in favor of staring at Owen Shepard's handsome, angular face. There was a bone-deep confidence to him—not arrogance, exactly, but a deep assurance in his own strength. The only hint of vulnerability was the way he softened over his daughter . . . and the pain that hardened his mouth when he shifted his weight against the hospital bed.

Libby noted the sharp slash of his cheekbones as he glanced down, one hand dropping to massage the muscle above his leg cast. Even partially veiled by his dark chestnut lashes, his eyes were an extraordinary color, a blend of blue and green that she'd spent way too long trying to come up with the perfect word to describe.

And when he looked up, Libby paused the video right before it cut out, her breath catching in her throat at the way his gaze burned through the screen and into her soul.

She stared, caught up in the unfamiliar feeling of connection. For a girl who spent most days hiding out in her living room in yoga pants, not speaking to anyone other than her impatient editor and the coffee shop guy on the corner who supplied her caffeine needs, what she felt when she looked at Owen Shepard defied understanding.

Libby wanted to know him. Everything about him. And she wanted him to know her, the way no one had since . . .

Enough. Huffing at the silly fantasy, Libby determinedly clicked out of the video and shut off her internet connection for good measure. It was time to get to work. This Thanksgiving piece wasn't going to write itself. Unfortunately.

Libby rested her fingertips on the keyboard and stared at the blinking cursor at the top of the screen. This was good. She was working.

She sighed, her mind as blank as the page in front of her. When she closed her eyes, her imagination betrayed her with visions of Owen Shepard's strong, weathered face. Cracking her knuckles in frustration, Libby forced herself to focus. She started typing.

I sometimes think I must have done something especially wonderful in a past life to deserve the riches of this one. Not the material things—although I'm grateful for every stick of furniture and every crumbling brick holding up the walls of this old house—but our wealth is in the air. So sweet and clear it almost sparkles in the morning sun.

Our wealth is in the deep blue of the ocean stretched under the horizon and the swaying boughs of the pine-wood trees leaning over our back porch.

Our wealth is in the warm, friendly community of Sanctuary Island, where wild horses thunder across the sandy beaches and autumn shades everything in tones of russet and gold. This Thanksgiving, I'm grateful for so many things, especially—

When the phone rang, she jerked in surprise. Cursing silently at the distraction just when she'd been getting into a good rhythm, Libby didn't even check the caller ID before answering. She knew who it had to be. No one but the sweet, caring nurses at Uncle Ray's assisted living center ever called her.

Bracing herself for bad news from Sunnyside Gardens, Libby was startled by the brisk masculine voice asking, "Is this Elizabeth Leeds?"

"Yes," she replied cautiously. "May I ask who's calling?"

"This is Hugo Downing."

Libby's blood froze. The publisher of *Savor* magazine.

"Your boss," Hugo continued, as if Libby might not recognize the name. "And first of all, I want to say how glad we are to have you at *Savor.*"

Keeping her voice calm and pleasant, Libby tried to contain her panic. "Thank you so much, Mr. Downing. I appreciate that more than I can say."

Clearly having had enough small talk, Downing cleared his throat and barreled on like a jovial, speed-talking Santa Claus. "An incredible promotional opportunity has fallen into our laps, Elizabeth. May I call you Elizabeth? Ha, ha, ha, at any rate, I'm thrilled, absolutely thrilled, to inform you that you and your family will be hosting an extra guest at your holiday table this year. A famous guest, no less."

Libby nearly fell off her ergonomic desk chair. "But Mr. Downing! I couldn't possibly!"

The cheer dropped out of his voice, leaving only steel. "You can and you will. This is not a request, Ms. Leeds. I've already committed you."

Mouth dropping open in shocked horror, Libby groped for the upper hand. "Mr. Downing, I'm so sorry but I must decline. My family, my privacy—"

"Are nothing," Downing declared, "when weighed against the need of a true American hero."

A true American hero. The phrase echoed in Libby's swirling brain, familiar as her own name. Her fingertips prickled, and blood rushed to her head so quickly she felt faint. He couldn't possibly mean . . .

"Sergeant Owen Shepard," her boss said. "You've seen the video? Yes, you and everyone else in America. Well, it turns out that the man's daughter and sister live . . . guess where? Sanctuary Island! Small world, eh? You can imagine how your many readers reacted when they made the connection. My assistant sifted through an avalanche of fan mail, and each one contained the same plea—that you and your husband host the Shepard family for Christmas. I know you would not want to disappoint your loyal readers, so obviously, you must give Shepard and his daughter the perfect Christmas."

Or you will be fired.

He didn't say it, but Libby heard it anyway. Loud and clear. There was just one problem . . . the truth.

Squeezing her eyes shut, Libby scoured her mind for a way out, any other option, but there was none. This was it. The moment she'd been dreading for two years was breathing down her neck.

She opened her eyes and stared around her. Instead of the spacious and homey living room she envisioned as she wrote her column, with handmade quilts draping comfy couches and a handsome husband contentedly tying fishing lures in the corner by the crackling fire, Libby saw her cramped, empty studio apartment. Outside, instead of the whisper of wind through pine boughs, she heard the loud rumble of the 7 train passing practically beneath her feet on its way to Flushing.

Libby thought of all the reasons she'd started this terrible deception in the first place—well, the one, single reason, actually. With a quick and silent prayer for her uncle Ray, who'd taken in a grieving orphan girl and raised her with love, Libby took the plunge.

"Mr. Downing. I have something to tell you. And you're not going to like it."

Chapter Two

Libby was right. Mr. Downing *didn't* like it. He shouted a bit, then seethed for a while and when he was finally calm enough to listen, Libby tried to explain.

He cut her off before she'd gotten out more than a few words. "I don't care about Uncle Ray's medical bills! I care about this magazine's reputation. This could ruin us. If word gets out . . ."

"Can't we just back out? Tell Sergeant Shepard that something came up? It's a little rude, I know, but . . ."

"It's gone beyond that," Downing said grimly. "I posted the invitation on the home page of the web site—and he accepted. Publicly. News outlets are reporting on it. There's no graceful way out of this."

"I'm so, so sorry." Libby wanted to bang her head against the desk. "I know that's not enough. I know it doesn't mean anything to you now, but I couldn't see another choice at the time."

"There's always another choice," Mr. Downing

spat out. "For instance, not lying to millions of readers every month about your life. That's a choice. Where did you get your material? Have you ever even been to Sanctuary Island?"

Familiar pain shot through Libby's heart, and she breathed around it the way she'd learned to at eight years old. "I spent part of my childhood there, until my parents died."

There was a pause, then Downing said, "So. Do you still have family on the island, by any chance?"

"Just a grandfather, my dad's father." Drowning in guilt, Libby tried to apologize again. "Listen, Mr. Downing, I can't tell you how much I regret putting you in this position. I'll take full responsibility, obviously—I'll make sure no one blames the magazine for what I've done."

The tips of her fingers felt numb and tingly with fear. This was going to be bad. But whatever the consequences, she would face up to them. Her stomach churned, but another part of Libby was actually a little relieved. To have the truth come out, finally—it was like being able to take a full breath again after two years of gasping for air.

"No," Mr. Downing said, decisive and curt. "You will not take responsibility for anything."

Her breath caught. "What?"

"There's always another choice," he said again, but this time his tone was all smug satisfaction. "We can salvage this. It's simple. You will go to Sanctuary Island and convince your grandfather to host the holidays for Sergeant Shepard and his family."

Libby sat up so fast, her desk chair scooted sideways

and nearly dumped her out on the floor. "I can't do that! I haven't spoken to my grandfather in years, he and Uncle Ray are estranged—"

"Irrelevant." She could picture the man waving away her objections like they were a swarm of irritating gnats. "We need a house on Sanctuary Island—he has one. Problem solved."

Trying to inch back from the edge of the fiery pit opening up at her feet, Libby scrambled to present other objections. "Okay, but, you promised them we'd have the perfect Christmas . . . which means a big feast, right? I can't cook!"

"That's a lie, too?" Poor Mr. Downing sounded like he might be literally tearing his hair out. "But the way you write about food . . . it all sounds so good."

"My mother was a wonderful cook. When I write about a meal, I draw on my memories of how she cooked." Libby swallowed around the lump in her throat. "But I don't even have her recipes to follow. I wish I did."

Downing made a thoughtful noise. "This can still work—we'll provide you with some recipes and you'll be fine. If you can read, you can cook."

"No, I really can't." Desperation made her words rush, tumbling out of her. "The last time I tried to make myself a cup of tea in my apartment, I got caught up researching how to describe learning to churn my own butter for the column, and all the water boiled away. I scorched the bottom of the teapot so badly, I had to order a new one. I set off the smoke alarm! You know what that means? I literally *burned water*."

"So pay attention," Downing growled impatiently. "For the love of—it's not rocket science. Figure it out."

Tears of frustration prickled behind her eyes. "You don't understand—"

"No," Downing broke in. "You are the one who doesn't seem to understand. This is not a request. I am not asking you to do this. I am telling you, *you are doing this.* You have no choice."

The arrogant command in his tone had Libby's spine straightening. "But according to you, there's always another choice," she said quietly. "Right?"

She could actually hear him grinding his teeth. "Fine," Downing spat. "Put it this way—your other choice is to be sued for fraud. Who's going to pay Uncle Ray's medical bills if you go to prison?"

Everything in Libby's whirling brain suddenly stilled, giving her a light-headed feeling of vertigo. "Prison."

"Public disgrace, financial ruin, and potential criminal charges on the one hand," Downing enumerated as if he were making a pro and con list, "or you can do this one little thing for me, show a wounded war veteran and his motherless daughter a good time on Sanctuary Island, and then I'll let you retire quietly from the column and we all go our separate ways with the public none the wiser."

Retire! Libby shook her head reflexively, her heart clenching. Despite how hard it could be, she loved writing. Her stories about Sanctuary Island and the fake life she'd created there were all she had. She couldn't bear to lose them. "You mean, you'll fire me and I'll go quietly or you'll carry out your threat to sue me."

"I'd say an employee who lied about who she is to get her job deserves to be fired. Wouldn't you? You're lucky I'm giving you the chance to walk away clean. And it all hinges on Owen Shepard."

Of course, it had to be Owen Shepard. She'd meet him, get to know him in person. The idea was too strange and thrilling to entertain for longer than a single shivery second. Just the idea of being in the same room with him, much less around the same holiday table, made Libby go flushed and hot with embarrassed longing.

"I don't understand why you're willing to go to such lengths for one story." Libby stalled for time, her mind racing, trying to figure a way out—some way to keep the job she loved, the salary that paid for Uncle Ray's care, and herself out of prison.

"This Sergeant Shepard is a hot commodity," Downing said. "Everyone wants a piece of him, and we're lucky enough to have our most popular columnist living in the same town where the man is spending the holidays. I'm not passing up this chance for free publicity—and I'm certainly not trading the free publicity for the public humiliation of the world finding out our star columnist is a fraud."

The determination in his gruff voice gave Libby the glimmer of an idea. Taking a deep breath for courage, she said, "I have a counterproposal for you."

"I'm not sure you're in a position to negotiate, but go ahead."

Stung by the amusement in his voice, Libby gripped the phone tightly. "I'll do it. I'll go home to Sanctuary Island and ask for my grandfather's help in hosting

Christmas for Sergeant Shepard and his family, and I'll figure out how to cook and throw a great party—and when I do, you'll let me keep my job."

In the long pause that followed, Libby listened to herself hyperventilate and thought about how insane it was for her to make any demands in this situation. She did deserve to be fired! She probably deserved prison, too—but Uncle Ray needed her. And she needed this job, not only for the money, but because writing about her fantasy life in her hometown was as close as Libby ever got to feeling truly alive.

"You want to keep writing the column," Hugo Downing said slowly, all traces of amusement erased from his tone. "Even though you admit you can't cook and haven't lived on Sanctuary Island in years."

"It hasn't slowed me down so far," Libby pointed out. "And after this Christmas, I'll have more material and experience than ever. My columns may not be strictly factual, Mr. Downing, but they're good stories. They make people happy. I've got the fan mail to prove it."

She held her breath, going light-headed when Downing said, "Fine. I'll consider it. But put me down as one of your guests for Christmas dinner—I'll want to judge how you do for myself."

Nerves and adrenaline roiled in Libby's stomach, turning her queasy. She couldn't believe she was agreeing to this crazy scheme. "I'll do my best, Mr. Downing. I promise. Although . . . I'm still not sure I can pull off the perfect Christmas. Not to mention that, well, you might not believe this, but I'm not actually a very good liar."

"I've always found that employees rise to challenges,"

Downing said, cheerful again now that he was getting his own way. "It's amazing what people can do with the right motivation."

And that's how Libby found herself boarding a ferry headed for Sanctuary Island, almost before she knew what was happening. Once she gave in to the inevitable, everything came together shockingly quickly. One final trip out to Sunnyside Gardens to visit with Uncle Ray—it was a good day, too, he actually recognized her—and one hideously awkward phone call to the grandfather she barely knew, and here she was.

Libby clutched her pink puffy coat's collar closed and huddled her neck down into the thick turtleneck of her sweater. Even on the bottom floor of the ferry, indoors and mostly protected from the biting December wind, she was cold.

Or maybe that was the chill of terror at the thought of setting foot on the island that was home to her happiest memories . . . and her darkest grief.

At least I'll have a couple of weeks to get over whatever emotions this trip brings up, Libby comforted herself. Sergeant Shepard was scheduled to be released from the hospital on December twentieth, so Libby's plan was to settle in at her grandfather's house, get the lay of the land, and practice cooking.

Once he'd gotten over his evident shock at hearing from her, Libby's grandfather had been surprisingly eager to open his home to an unknown relative. She'd forced herself to explain the circumstances of her visit— he deserved the chance to turn her away if he didn't want anything to do with this deceitful charade. She'd told him she only planned to impose on him for the week of Christmas. But to her shock, he'd immediately jumped in with both feet by ordering her to get on the next flight to Virginia. Before they'd even gotten off the phone, he'd gone online and bought her a ticket for the first week-end of December.

Something told her Dabney Leeds was a man who was used to taking charge and being obeyed.

It was just as well since, now that she'd committed herself and made her deal with the devil, Libby found herself at a loss as to how to go about setting up this whole fake Christmas thing. Luckily her grandfather, Dabney Leeds, didn't seem to require her input. He'd launched into planning mode, ignoring equally both her worried apologies and her stammered thanks.

Libby burrowed her mittened hands deeper into her coat pockets and leaned her head against the cold Plexi-glas window. Her breath fogged a circle blocking her view of the water as the ferry carried her relentlessly to-ward her destiny.

She was out of practice at sticking up for herself, she knew. If she didn't find her backbone soon, the forceful men in her life were going to keep running roughshod over her. It was hard, though. She'd always preferred to live in her sweet dreams of the past rather than the real world. Libby had spent most of her life alone, but she'd never been lonely. Not with her books, her memories, and most importantly her imagination for company.

Letting the rhythmic chug of the ferry's engine lull her into a doze, Libby pictured Sergeant Owen Shepard as he'd looked in the video. Her vivid memory lovingly recreated every line and angle of his shadowed face . . . then promptly got sidetracked into a fantasy of what it would be like when she met him for the first time.

He would smile, and it would be a real smile that lit his gorgeous eyes from within. And she would be gracious, poised, welcoming him into her stately home decorated with greenery and red velvet ribbons. Light would glow from fat, cinnamon-scented pillar candles, and in that flattering candlelight, Libby would be pretty. She would be confident and friendly, able to converse with her guests easily, no hesitation or shyness at all. She imagined the music of laughter and the clink of heirloom silver on precious, hand-painted china.

And she had two whole weeks to prepare. Two weeks to make that fantasy a reality. If that was enough time, it would be a miracle.

Sighing, Libby sat up straight and rubbed at the cold spot the window had left on her forehead. With her sensitive skin, she probably now sported a red mark the size and shape of a Ping-Pong ball front and center. She leaned over, bracing herself on her roller bag to dig through the zipper pocket for her wool cap.

Without warning, the wheels on her brand-new suitcase unlocked, sending both the case and Libby shooting forward. She squawked, off balance and arms trembling with the effort of keeping the case from crashing into the passenger across the aisle.

She gasped, wrenching herself upright while keeping a grip on her runaway bag. But she didn't have the hang of it quite yet, and when she wobbled, the bag squirted sideways and banged into a man making his way up the aisle.

Mortified, Libby ducked her head and grabbed for the stupid bag. The man reached down to steady her, wrapping hard but gentle fingers around her wrist.

"Oh! Sorry, sorry," she babbled, her downcast gaze catching on the cane hooked over the man's wrist. There was a walking cast encasing his leg from foot to thigh. "Did I hurt you?"

A warm thrill of premonition shook Libby's frame as she let her gaze travel up the length of his strong, denim-clad thighs to the fitted black T-shirt stretched over the impressively broad and muscular chest that even a loose, open flannel shirt couldn't hide. One of the man's arms was in a sling, and Libby closed her eyes briefly.

Why? Why here, why now, like this? It had to be punishment for living a lie—a punishment she probably deserved, but that didn't make it any easier to look up and meet Sergeant Owen Shepard's amused gaze.

"Don't worry," he told her with a hint of a smile. "It looks worse than it is."

Libby didn't think that was true. From the news reports she'd read, he'd been seriously wounded in the explosion that took out half his team. But the locked-down control he exhibited in every efficient movement as he pulled her carefully to her feet told Libby that he was not a man who wanted or needed coddling.

Which didn't mean she could stop herself from apologizing. "Oh my gosh, I'm *so* sorry. I feel awful. Your leg . . . it's amazing you're up and about, Sergeant Shepard! They said on the *Good Morning Show* that you wouldn't be released from the hospital for another couple of weeks. Are you sure you're okay to be out already?"

Until his eyes went cool, she hadn't been aware of

how warmly he'd been regarding her. "I'm fine. I heal fast. And believe me, if you were trying to finish me off, you'd have to come at me with something more dangerous than a rolling suitcase."

Libby realized he was still holding her wrist. She felt her cheeks go hot at the same moment he let go and took a hitching step back. "I'm sorry. Should I not have mentioned the *Good Morning* video? But I recognized you from it. I mean, I saw it."

"You and four million other people," he muttered, jaw clenching before he shook his head. "Don't worry about it, ma'am. Have a safe trip."

Panic clutched at her throat. This whole first meeting hadn't gone at all the way she'd imagined. "Do you want to sit down? You must be tired. There's an empty seat next to me."

He looked almost as taken aback by her boldness as she was, but he recovered quickly. "I was looking to get out of the wind, but I guess everyone else had the same idea."

The lower deck was full of people in thick coats and hats with earflaps. The two rows of chairs running along the center of the ferry were all taken, as were the two-person tables set by the windows. As Libby glanced around, she noticed that most of them were openly watching her exchange with Sergeant Shepard. Cheeks and ears burning, she ducked her head again. At least they were all undoubtedly looking at him. Handsome and soft-spoken, he nevertheless had a presence that commanded attention. He made you want to lean in to catch every word he said.

"Please," Libby mumbled, gesturing at the table behind her. "It's no trouble. I mean, I'd love to share my table with you. I promise I won't talk about the video—or anything! We can sit in silence if you want. That's probably best."

Making a face at her own rambling, Libby almost missed the slight twist of humor that warmed Owen's face. "Something tells me that might be a problem for you."

"No, it won't!" Libby tried to project earnestness. "I promise. I spend most of my time not talking to people. I'm great at not talking to people. Sorry."

Owen laughed. He actually laughed, rusty but appreciative, and Libby felt her insides melt like marshmallows in a cup of hot cocoa.

"What if I want to hear you talk?"

Chapter Three

The pretty blonde woman blinked her big eyes as if she'd never heard anything so crazy. Owen stood his ground. He wanted to hear more.

This woman . . . there was something about her. A softness that made him want to sink into her, like coming home after years of wandering.

Except Owen had never had a home like that—not really. And at this point in his life, he was pretty sure he'd missed his chance. He wouldn't even know how to come home anymore.

The woman opened her mouth, then shut it again, ironically struck dumb by his request that she speak. Taking pity, Owen propped his cane against the free chair and lowered himself into it. After five months in the hospital and rehab, it was second nature to keep his expression free of the grimace of pain his stressed body wanted to make, but even after all this time, it still surprised him.

He'd relied on his body and what it could do for a long time. He couldn't get used to not being at peak physical condition. Thankfully, it was a temporary situation. It had to be.

"Come on," he invited. "Sit with me. I'll help you keep your luggage under control."

That got a tiny, embarrassed smile out of her. She tucked her caramel-blonde hair behind her ears, her gloved fingers clumsy, leaving her hair mussed in staticky wisps. "Okay. Um. Thanks."

She slid into the seat on the other side of the wobbly round table and stared down at it like it held the secret to cracking a coded message. Owen already missed the nervous babble from before. Even when she'd brought up that stupid video, it hadn't bugged him as much as it should have. Maybe because her voice was so nice, light and clear as a set of silver sleigh bells.

Or maybe it was just a good distraction from the chaotic brawl of his thoughts and the constant background throb of pain in his still-healing body.

"I got myself transferred to Sanctuary Island for the second half of my physical rehab work," he offered. It was against his training to give up info so easily, but he was half afraid if they sat any longer in that embarrassed silence, the pretty blonde was going to fake a seizure or something to get away from him.

"Oh!" Her face lit up, lovely and animated, nothing like the bleak blankness he saw in his own features staring back from the mirror every morning. "Are you going to be working with the Windy Corner Therapeutic Riding Center?"

"That's the idea." He thumped his cast right over the

spot where it velcroed around his lower thigh. "This thing comes off in a couple of days, and I guess there's some kind of way the horses help a guy learn to walk on his own two feet again. I don't really get it, but they tell me it works."

And, more importantly, it would get him to the island where his daughter lived in time for the holidays.

"So you'll be one of the first to participate in their pilot program, partnering with The Hero Project!"

Owen blinked, a little surprised. But he guessed it was a small island, and people would notice something like their local therapy riding center getting hooked up with a major national nonprofit that helped people wounded in the line of duty.

Still a little uncomfortable with being classified as a "hero," Owen gritted his teeth against the need to point out that he was only doing his job. No more and no less than the thousands of other soldiers and support staff overseas. Instead he said, "Yes, ma'am. I'm looking forward to it."

She cocked her head as if she'd heard a whisper of words he hadn't said, her dreamy eyes suddenly going laser sharp. "Sorry, but . . . are you really?"

Letting his spine touch the back of the plastic chair, Owen worked up a wry smile. "Okay, you caught me. I'm not really looking forward to it—I have a feeling it's going to be kind of touchy-feely and woo woo. But I know if I put in the work I'll get back to combat condition, so the program doesn't matter that much. It's mostly an excuse to get to Sanctuary Island."

Her gaze softened. "For your daughter. You must

miss her so much every time you're deployed. I'm sure she can't wait to see you."

A strange clutching sensation invaded Owen's throat. "I wish I could be so sure of that. But the situation is . . . not ideal."

He planned to leave it there—he wasn't used to "sharing" or talking about what was going on in his personal life. He wasn't used to having a personal life, period. Not since he decided to go out for the Ranger program. But something about the way she leaned in, propping her pink-jacket-clad elbows on the table and leaning her head on one red-mittened hand had Owen opening his mouth.

"Caitlin's mom . . . I think I mentioned in the interview that she'd died, but that's not the whole story."

Owen paused, the words backing up in his chest, but she didn't seem impatient. She gave him a slow, sweet smile and said, "Well, I love stories. You can tell me the whole thing if you want, and I promise not to get too touchy-feely or woo woo about it. I'll just listen, Sergeant Shepard."

"It's Owen," he said. "If you're going to hear all my secrets, you can call me by my name."

"Owen," she repeated, her smile brightening until she glowed like the star at the top of a Christmas tree.

"And you are?"

She hesitated briefly, then stuck out her hand. "I'm Libby."

Owen clasped her slender fingers through the wool of her mittens, sparing a brief moment to wish they were skin to skin. "Well, Libby, I'm not sure what it is about you that's making me chatty. When you invited me to sit with you I said I wanted to hear *you* talk—you kind of outflanked me there."

Cheeks going red as cranberries, Libby tucked her chin down so that a sheaf of wheat-gold hair swung forward to shield her face. "You don't have to talk," she said anxiously. "Not if you don't want to. I'm sorry."

Protectiveness warmed his chest. "Don't apologize. Ask anyone in my unit—it's pretty damn hard to make me do something I don't want to do."

That got her to look up at him through her lashes. Her eyes were a complicated light brown color, with flecks of gold and a ring of deep green around the iris. Owen couldn't stop staring at them, trying to decide what that color was called. Hazel, maybe.

"Okay. I'm sorry, I'll stop apologizing." Her eyes got big as she obviously replayed what she'd just said. She cringed. "Oops, sorry! I mean, not sorry. I mean . . . help?"

Owen couldn't help it. He laughed, the sound rusty and unfamiliar after months of pain and recovery. The moment broke some of the building tension, untwisting the tangle his guts got into every time he thought about what it would be like to lay eyes on Caitlin. "I'm going to start keeping a tally of how many times you apologize to me—we've got to be getting close to double digits here."

"Sor—" Libby grimaced, cutting herself off. "I told you, I'm not great at talking. Like, to other people."

Owen quirked a smile. "But you do okay when you're talking to yourself?"

"It's sort of like talking to myself, actually. I'm a writer."

Owen began to put some pieces together. The dreamy quality to Libby's smile, the far-off look in her eyes that told him she regularly traveled to distant lands in her imagination. "You said you like stories. Do you write fiction?"

The twist of her mouth went flat as she nodded, her hair shadowing her expression.

"Are you . . . working on a novel?" Owen struggled for the right terminology. "Or have you got a book out already?"

"No, I don't know if I could ever really write a book." Libby met his gaze, her eyes lighting up again. "I mean, I have a thousand ideas! But the hard part is sitting down and actually writing it, believing I have a story to tell that anyone else might want to read. I'm still working on that. "

She was a dreamer. Owen, who lived his life firmly mired in the harshest of cold realities, felt a deep swelling of protectiveness for Libby and her dreams. That's what he did it for—what he and all the other people he fought alongside did it for. So that the ones back home, like Libby, could follow their dreams in peace and freedom.

"You'll write that novel one day, I bet." Owen smiled at her, knowing the men in his unit would be making catcalls and wolf whistles if they could see him now. But Libby brought out a side of him those guys had never seen.

"Thanks for the vote of confidence. But we weren't talking about my story—you were going to tell me yours. Unless you don't want to anymore?"

A pang shot through his thigh right where several

metal pins held his bone together, telling him he'd unconsciously tensed his muscles. Making a deliberate effort to relax, Owen glanced away from Libby's searching
gaze to stare out the foggy window. Condensation clung
to the fiberglass, misting over his view of the choppy,
gray-green Atlantic Ocean as the Virginia coastline
receded in the distance.

The monotone hum of the ferry's powerful engine
was a cocoon of sound, wrapping around Owen and
Libby's table, making him feel like they were alone
on the ship. He couldn't hear the conversations taking
place around them—if he wanted to hear Libby, he had
to focus and lean in close. It was as if they were the
only two people on board.

"I'm just not sure where to start," he finally admitted.

"That's always the hard part! Half the books I read
seem like they start in the wrong place. It's part of what's
keeping me from getting going with *my* book."

Owen gave her a half smile. He appreciated the out
she was handing him—the understanding, and the tacit
offer to change the subject back to her writing. But the
moment, the place, the woman . . . they were all com-
bining to give Owen one of the strongest feelings he'd
had since the gut-deep dread that had warned him right
before the explosion.

In combat, Owen had learned not to discount those
gut feelings. His gut had saved his life, and the lives of
his men, more times than he could count. And right now,
it was shoving him at Libby so hard, he felt an almost
physical push against his shoulder blades.

"I'm pretty sure my story starts ten years ago, when

I met Caitlin's mother. Jenna was a party girl—which tells you something about who I was back then. Young and stupid, fumbling around trying to figure out what I wanted to do with my life, and in the meantime, I met this girl at a bar and we . . . dated. Only for a few weeks, but it was long enough for me to start to see that she was into some heavy stuff. Jenna was halfway down a bad road, and there was a moment where I thought about following her."

Owen dropped the thread of his narrative for a second, flashing back to Jenna's slim, dark beauty and the infectious temptation of her wicked smile. She'd been so young, so dramatic, so lovely, and so full of life—even for Owen, who'd seen more than his share of senseless death, the knowledge of how Jenna's life turned out gave him a brief moment of vertigo.

"But you didn't follow her," Libby said with a touching certainty. "You couldn't."

Grimacing, Owen palmed the back of his neck. "It wasn't as simple as that. It was touch and go there . . . but in the end, I enlisted in the army instead. When Jenna found out, she was spitting mad, throwing things and screaming—and that was it. I left and never looked back. And I never heard from her again."

Libby sucked in a breath, and a red-mittened hand came up to cover her mouth. "You mean, when she got pregnant, she didn't tell you?"

It was a gut punch every time Owen thought about it. "No. I don't know if she even tried. If she hadn't died, I'd still probably have no idea that I have a daughter. And now I'm about to meet Caitlin for the first time, and

I just . . ." He shook his head. "After everything I've seen and done, you wouldn't believe how terrified I am of one little girl."

"She's going to love you." A shy smile peeked out from behind Libby's mitten, and for the hundredth time, Owen wondered why he was sitting here spilling his guts to a complete stranger. Maybe it was easier that way, somehow. He could work through some of this crap before he got to the island and came face-to-face with the sister whose life he'd disrupted and the daughter he'd unknowingly abandoned.

And Libby, who knew his secrets, would go back to her life and he'd never see her again. Oh, maybe they'd run into each other in the grocery store or pass each other on the sidewalk—Sanctuary was a small town, Owen knew.

But this would be their only intimate, intense conversation. Owen would make sure of it, because a woman as sweet as Libby deserved better than a broken-down wreck of an Army Ranger with an eight-year-old kid he didn't know and a boatload of issues.

The best thing he could do for Libby in return for her listening ear and wide, sympathetic eyes, would be to never talk to her again.

Why did the prospect of that make him feel like he'd swallowed a lump of coal?

Chapter Four

Libby's heart couldn't decide whether it wanted to clench in empathy with the pain shadowing Owen's ocean-blue eyes or race like a runaway horse every time a smile teased at Owen's firm mouth. Her entire body felt so attuned to him, she could hardly remember to breathe without matching her inhalations to his.

For a woman who'd spent much of the last twenty years feeling isolated from the rest of humanity, this immediate connection was overwhelming. Libby hardly knew what to do with herself. She bit her lip against the urge to apologize yet again, this time for being such a tongue-tied goony idiot, but the memory of Owen's grin when he said he was keeping track of her apologies helped her control the impulse.

Although if it would make him laugh again, she'd happily apologize all day long. Anything to lift the veil of sadness that had dropped over his handsome face.

She wished she could explain that she understood

some of what he was going through. Libby, too, was about to meet several close relations for the very first time, and she was scared spitless.

"Your daughter—Caitlin?—she knows you didn't have a choice about not seeing her until now, right?"

Owen rubbed his jaw. "I think so. I'm pretty sure my sister would have explained it to her, even if Jenna didn't. Andie's been taking care of Caitlin ever since I found out about her. I was deployed at the time, couldn't get leave."

"So, it could be worse," Libby pointed out. "I mean, you might've been about to meet someone who knows you stayed away on purpose. That you chose not to meet them . . . for whatever reason."

Nervousness jittered under Libby's skin as she remembered making that phone call to her grandfather. After one long, pregnant pause when she'd said her name, he'd moved briskly forward as if they'd known one another all along. But she couldn't help wondering if he was saving up his recriminations to deliver face-to-face.

"That's true enough." Owen glanced aside, the weak winter light filtering through the window silvering his strong profile. "It still feels like I should've known, though. About Caitlin. How can there be a part of me alive in the world, for years, and I had no idea? She needed me, and I wasn't there for her."

Libby's heart ached. "You can be there for her now."

Owen didn't pretend to be comforted. A muscle clenched in his jaw, and his good hand tightened in a spasm. "I'm not sure I know how. I'm going to need help."

Everything in Libby yearned forward. The words "I'll help you" were on the tip of her tongue when Owen rolled his shoulders to loosen them and said, "That's why I said yes to that magazine publisher's invitation, I guess. Caitlin deserves a perfect Christmas. And I'm going to give it to her, even if I have to ask for help to do it."

The words dried up in Libby's mouth. He didn't know who she was—or, who she was pretending to be. She had to tell him, but the whole truth was getting tangled with the partial truth, turning everything into a huge mess.

Libby steeled herself, drawing in a breath to explain—whatever she could . . . just as the ferry made a slow, grinding noise and lurched, as all around them the other passengers got to their feet and began making their way toward the exits.

"We're here," Owen said, standing and offering her his good hand.

"Wait—Owen, there's something I have to tell you," Libby tried, desperation making her voice shake.

The rush of people toward the exits got Owen's heart hammering with anticipation. He was about to see his daughter for the very first time.

Shoving to his feet, he balanced on his one good leg while he got his cane braced. "Can you manage your suitcase?" he asked distractedly. "I'd help, but it's about all I can do to carry myself off this boat without pitching over the side."

"I can get it." Libby surged up from the table and grabbed at her wheeled packing case's handle. "Owen, did you hear what I said? I have something I need to tell you."

"I heard. Come on, walk and talk. My daughter is waiting for me down there on the dock."

Libby responded to the note of command that had snuck into his voice, falling in step beside him as he made his slow, halting way through the line of disembarking passengers. "That's what we need to talk about."

"Caitlin? Hey, you want to see a picture—I've got a bunch on my phone that my sister sent me when I was in the hospital."

"Oh," Libby said, taking the phone and swiping through a few images with a slow smile curling the corners of her kissable mouth. "She's beautiful."

He knew what Libby was seeing. He'd long ago memorized every line, every shaded angle, of those photographs.

Owen called up the image of his small, fine-boned daughter astride a horse who looked big enough to crush her. But Caitlin sat tall and proud in the saddle, a look of serious concentration on her face. Wisps of carroty red hair escaped from beneath the black helmet, and something about the way Caitlin's elbows stuck out as she grasped the reins always squeezed Owen's heart with tenderness.

"She looks like my sister, and our mother," Owen confided. "And her mother, too, a little."

Libby's soft gaze lifted to his. "She looks like you."

A chill of dread raced down Owen's spine. He shook his head once in instinctive denial before he got his reaction under control, but Libby's dark-gold brows had already drawn together in a perplexed frown.

"Yes, she does," Libby insisted, and Owen broke their gaze to stare grimly ahead at the approaching door.

"So long as her looks are the only thing she inherited from me," he muttered.

Before Libby could ask him any questions that might prompt even more uncharacteristically emotional confessions, they'd made it to the door and stepped out onto the metal ramp that led down to the pier. A chill breeze off the water stole Owen's breath, and he felt more than heard Libby's sharp gasp at the sudden shock of cold.

The railing along the dock was twined about with greenery and old-fashioned strands of fat multicolored bulbs. A shaft of sunlight broke through the pale gray clouds, illuminating the hand-painted sign welcoming visitors to Sanctuary Island's Christmas Village. Owen wasn't a hundred percent sure what that was, but maybe it explained why the ferry had been nearly sold out when he snagged his last-minute ticket.

At the foot of the pier, people were swept up in joyous reunions punctuated by shouts and laughter, squeals of happiness and long hugs as families and friends reunited. A big bear of a man, dressed in the green tunic and tights of one of Santa's elves, shouted greetings and waved visitors in a stream up the hill toward the town.

Owen looked for the bright flash of his sister's auburn hair amidst the chaos, his eyes hungry for the sight of a little girl standing next to her, but he didn't see them. "Come on," he said, glancing over his shoulder at Libby. "Let's find my family. I want you to meet my daughter."

"That's what I'm trying to tell you," Libby said,

sounding agonized. She hung back, causing a bottleneck on the pier as the wave of ferry passengers behind her were stopped.

With an apologetic look at them, Libby moved to the side of the pier to let them pass while Owen schooled his body not to reflect his impatience. "What's going on, Libby?"

"I'm going to meet Caitlin," Libby told him urgently as the stream of passengers brushed past them, adding to the boisterous crowd.

"I know, I want you to. Wait. What do you mean?"

She bit her lip, white teeth sinking into the plush pink cupid's bow and zeroing Owen's focus in like a heat-seeking missile. "I mean, I'm—"

"Elizabeth! There you are!"

Libby's head jerked up and her eyes went wide as she stared at something over Owen's shoulder. He turned to see a tall man plunging through the line of ferry passengers like a sleek salmon swimming upstream. The stranger's eyes were fixed on Libby, but when Owen's gaze swiveled back to her, she looked more shocked than anything else.

Before Owen could do anything but register the surprise on Libby's face, the stranger had reached them. Without hesitation, he swooped down on Libby and wrapped her up in his long arms, swinging her around. She made a muffled "oh!" into the man's shoulder, and every muscle in Owen's body tensed for battle.

The pain of his injuries drowned under the tidal wave of adrenaline flooding his system, and Owen changed his grip on the cane, turning it from support to weapon. "Put her down," he said, his voice lethally quiet.

It was the tone his men knew meant they'd better hop to, and quick, or someone was in trouble—and this guy seemed to understand that Owen meant business. Letting Libby's feet touch the dock but keeping his arm around her shoulders, the tall stranger faced Owen with a polite, if wary, smile.

"What's the problem, friend?"

Instead of snapping that he was no friend of Owen's, Owen ignored the guy to focus on Libby. "Who is this man? Is he bothering you?"

"Who am I?" The guy laughed, easy and relaxed. "Why, I'm Nash Tucker! Elizabeth's husband."

Did most people get seasick after getting off a boat? Libby couldn't catch her balance. Her legs were as wobbly as a newborn colt's and her stomach roiled with tension.

She'd come so close to telling Owen everything; she'd been right on the cusp of just spilling it all and damn the consequences, when she'd heard her name shouted by a man she'd never met.

After that, everything happened almost too fast to follow, but she held onto the words he'd whispered in her ear when he'd picked her up and twirled her into a hug.

"I'm your cousin, Nash. Nice to meet you! Just play along," he had said.

And then he'd introduced himself to Owen as Libby's husband while Libby gaped in shock. What was going on?

Owen's gaze shot to her face, making Libby instantly aware of what a crazy—or possibly moronic—expression she must be sporting. Closing her mouth with a snap, she looked up at the man still holding her clasped to his side. Nash. Her cousin.

"N-Nash," she stammered. "I wasn't expecting to see you here."

"You weren't expecting your husband to meet you at the ferry?" Owen murmured, a chill settling into his tone as he looked Nash up and down as if scrutinizing an enemy for weaknesses.

Thinking fast, Libby blurted out a version of the story she'd intended to give for the absence of her fictional husband. "I thought he was going to be out of town, away on business."

"I couldn't miss the holidays with my best girl," Nash boomed cheerfully, giving Libby a careful squeeze as if in warning.

Her cousin's brown eyes crinkled appealingly at the corners, as if he spent a lot of time laughing in the sun. Despite the scruff of beard and the tousled, over-long waves of his brown hair, there was something essentially clean cut about Nash. With his broad shoulders filling out his chunky cable-knit fisherman's sweater, he looked like an ad in a men's magazine about outdoor sports.

Libby couldn't help but cringe at how badly she matched him. Slight, timidly hunched, and with the pasty paleness that came from living like a hermit, Libby knew she didn't make a very convincing wife for this strapping picture of all-American masculinity.

As if to prove it, Owen's eyes narrowed slightly as he studied them. Putting out his good hand, Owen said, "Sergeant Owen Shepard. I met your wife on the ferry. She was kind enough to find me a place to sit down and keep me company for the trip."

And she hadn't mentioned any husband. Owen didn't say it, but Libby knew he must be thinking it. This whole thing was already going so wrong. How had she ever thought she could pull this off?

Okay, to be fair, she actually *hadn't* thought she could pull it off, and she'd said so, but no one listened. It was less gratifying to be proven right than Libby might have hoped.

"That's my Elizabeth," Nash was saying, maintaining his firm grip on Libby's shoulders as he turned and began to lead their little group down the dock toward the parking lot. "The soul of friendliness. And of course I know who you are, Sergeant Shepard. Welcome to Sanctuary Island!"

The corner of Owen's mouth twisted. "You saw that video too."

"Well, sure." Nash shrugged. "Who didn't? But I know who you are because I understand you're to be our guest this holiday season. You and your daughter?"

Even though he was behind her, Libby felt the instant Owen's steps faltered. She glanced back to find his eyes narrowed intently on Nash. "*Your* guest," Owen said sharply. "I thought you said your last name was Tucker."

"Oh, it is," Nash said smoothly. "Elizabeth started writing before we were married, though, so she kept her maiden name for publication."

Libby risked another glance over her shoulder, her gaze tangling with Owen's intent stare at once. "Elizabeth Leeds," he said, quiet and sure.

"I'm sorry," she burst out. "I was going to tell you on the ferry. I wasn't trying to trick you, I just—"

Just couldn't resist getting to know you as my real self, even if only for an hour or two.

Libby broke off, the lump in her throat squeezing the words back down into her chest, but Owen was already shaking his head.

"That's ten," he said, with a ghost of a smile, and Libby felt the top of her head go hot and light as she smiled back. Even now, Owen didn't want her to apologize. With that one, simple reminder, Libby knew she was forgiven.

Her smile faded as she contemplated how much more there was for Owen to forgive. If she had any sense, she'd stop Nash and face Owen, tell him the whole truth now before this web of lies got any more tangled.

But then who would take care of Uncle Ray? If she lost her job, if Mr. Downing sued her as he'd threatened, then there would be nothing left to pay for the round-the-clock care Uncle Ray needed.

The memory of her gruff, but loving, uncle got Libby moving down the dock again. She had to see this through. It was only for a few weeks, then she'd be free and able to clean up the mess she'd made of her life. That was a worthy goal . . . she had to keep her heart set on it.

"Come on," Nash said as they reached the end of the pier and stepped onto the gravel of the dockside parking lot. "I parked at the top of the hill. It's a madhouse down here today."

"Wait." Libby set her heels. "We can't just leave Owen here."

"I'm sure my sister is around somewhere," Owen said, scanning the crowd.

"I think I saw the sheriff's SUV pulling in after me," Nash contributed. "I guess she was running late."

"We should stay until we're sure Owen has a ride," Libby said stubbornly. But it occurred to her suddenly that Owen might not be as eager for his daughter to meet her now, and she finished with a quick, "I mean, if you want us to. We don't have to."

Owen gave her a small, but real, smile. "If you don't mind, I'd like you to stay. You could meet my sister, and Caitlin."

Nerves fluttered under Libby's ribcage, but she smiled back. "That sounds wonderful."

Through the crowd of people, she heard someone calling Owen's name. His face lit up when he heard it, too, and he turned just in time to catch a leggy redhead up in his arms. The woman was dressed in a tan uniform and had a sheriff's badge clipped to her belt, and when she blinked back tears to grin up at Owen, Libby saw that her eyes were his same shade of stunning ocean blue.

The sister, Andie. Had to be. Libby watched, her heart in her throat. She could read the love and joy in every line of their fast, hard embrace. But where was Caitlin?

"It's good to see you," Owen was saying.

"Me!" The lady sheriff sniffled and whacked her brother gently on his good shoulder. "You're the one who's been home, stateside, for months and wouldn't let anyone come visit."

"I didn't want to meet my daughter for the first time all bandaged and bruised, looking like a monster," Owen protested, stepping back. "I wanted to wait until I wouldn't scare her just by standing here."

"You didn't wait long enough," Andie said, eyeing him critically. "You've still got the same face."

The handsome face in question went shocked for a half second before it creased in a wide grin. "And you've still got the same mouth on you, sis. I can't believe I missed you."

Libby saw the way Andie's lips trembled and her eyes filled, even as she smirked mischievously up at Owen. "You did miss me, though. And I missed my bratty baby brother."

Clearing his throat gruffly, Owen glanced over and met Libby's gaze. He gestured them over, and Libby started forward eagerly, only remembering her so-called husband when Nash twined his fingers with hers and swung their linked hands between them as they walked.

Oh, right. She was supposed to be married. Moderating her pace, Libby shoved down the urge to shake off Nash's grasp and worked up a tentative smile for Sheriff Andie Shepard . . . who didn't smile back. In fact, her aquamarine eyes were narrowed suspiciously as she took in Libby and Nash's joined hands.

"Mr. Tucker," the sheriff said coolly. "Nice to see you, as always."

It looked to Libby as if there were more Andie would like to say, but it might not be quite so friendly. As if sensing the tension, Owen interrupted with introductions.

"Hey, Andie, guess who I met on the ferry?"

Blinking, Andie took in Libby's pale-pink wool coat and poppy-red mittens.

"I give up. Who?"

Owen frowned. "Don't tell me you don't know Elizabeth Leeds. How many famous magazine writers live on this tiny island? I was sure you two must already know each other. That's part of why when she invited us over for the perfect family Christmas, I took her up on it."

"Um." Libby barely stopped herself from apologizing, her heart drumming in her chest at having to come up with something plausible on the spot. "I don't go out much! I told you that. Writing is a very solitary job."

"Nice to meet you. Kind of amazing what a small town this is, and yet it's still impossible to know every single person." Andie gave her a polite smile, but her brows drew down as she looked over at Owen. "But about Christmas, I don't know. This year, with Caitlin and you here, and Sam moving in . . ."

Libby's breath caught. If Owen were the one to back out of this Christmas deal, surely Mr. Downing wouldn't punish Libby for that. Or would he?

"Speaking of Caitlin," Owen said, looking past her. "Where is she?"

Libby wondered if anyone else could see the nerves sparking below his calm, confident demeanor. Maybe she was seeing them because she knew they were there, but it seemed so obvious to her that Owen was barely listening to any of this conversation. At least ninety per cent of his concentration was spent on watching out for his daughter to suddenly appear.

Only Andie was biting her lip and looking unhappy. "She . . . well, she had a riding lesson this afternoon, and she didn't want to miss it. I said she could still go. I hope that's okay—there's plenty of time to meet her tonight, right?"

The disappointment that darkened Owen's eyes was hard to look at. Libby tensed, wanting to go to him, to say something or do something, but Nash's grip tightened on her hand and kept her in place. Not that there was anything to say or do, in any case.

"Of course, that's fine." Owen straightened his shoulders and smiled at his sister. "I know the two of you have a good routine. I don't want to do anything to mess that up, or to upset her."

Libby wanted to protest—how important was a routine, when it came to introducing a child to the father she'd never met?—but it wasn't her place. Andie seemed to know, if her worried face was any indication. Clearly torn between the niece she'd taken in and the brother she loved, Andie said, "I'm sorry, Owen, I wanted her to come, but she's just like you. Stubborn. She'll need you to be patient with her until she adjusts."

She tried to smile, and Owen shrugged back, looking intensely uncomfortable. "It's a tricky situation. I get that."

At Libby's side, her cousin leaned down and whispered in her ear, "I think that might be our cue to vamoose."

Startled, she bit back her instinctive denial. She didn't want to leave Owen, not when he looked like he'd just been dealt a worse injury than the wounds that landed him in the hospital. But he glanced up and saw Nash trying to pull her away, and Owen nodded. "Right. No Caitlin for you to meet—sorry about that. And about Christmas . . . I guess we'll have to talk about it and see."

Impulsively, Libby grabbed a pen from the assortment she always carried in her purse, along with a spiral notebook for jotting down ideas and observations. "Here, give me your arm."

Bemused, Owen stretched out his good arm and Libby shoved up the sleeve of his jacket. She was proud of herself for not lingering over the electrifying contact of skin on skin when all she wanted was to explore the crisp copper hair lining his hard, muscled forearm. Instead, she uncapped her pen and quickly wrote her cell phone number on the smooth tanned skin on the underside of his wrist.

"Call me," Libby said, unintentionally fierce. "Any time, if you need anything."

Owen looked directly into her eyes, and she got lost for a second in the fathomless ocean depths. "Thanks," he said slowly, curling his arm back to his body slowly, as if he were as reluctant to give up the contact as Libby was.

"I mean it," she insisted, not caring that Nash and Andie were both watching her with varying degrees of perplexed confusion. This was one of those social situations that made her the most uncomfortable, the most aware that she was doing things wrong, but for once, she didn't care. She wasn't even embarrassed. "Really, Owen. Call me. I don't make friends so easily that I can afford to let new ones slip away."

He nodded, and the last thing she saw before Nash grabbed her bag and led her away was the glint of warmth she'd kindled in Owen Shepard's weary eyes.

Chapter Five

"I hate to rush you out of there," Andie said, shifting her sheriff's department vehicle into gear and maneuvering them around a crowd of red-cheeked townspeople heading for the square. "But I've got to get back to work. This weekend is insane."

Owen's mind was still wrestling with the problem of his daughter and what he was doing to her by crashing into her life like this. And when he managed to take a break from worrying about that, he was remembering Libby Leeds and her bright eyes and blushing smile. She hadn't exactly acted like a married woman on the ferry—but what would Owen know about how married women behaved? His and Andie's mom had died when he was just a kid, and since then, most of his experiences had been with women who were very definitely *not* married.

"The ferry was packed," he commented absently. "What's going on this weekend?"

"Tonight is the opening ceremony for our annual Christmas Village," Andie explained as she eased the SUV onto a side street that took them away from the worst of the crowds. "Every December, Sanctuary Island transforms our town square into a holiday-themed village. A ton of local businesses take part, there are games and contests, sleigh rides and pictures with Santa, and a parade—it's a pretty big deal. People come from all over to see it, and all the money the village brings in goes toward caring for the wild horse sanctuary on the island."

"Sounds like a good cause."

Andie sighed. "It is. And it's a good time—kids love the Christmas Village, of course, but the whole town really gets into it. It's something to see."

Owen knew that exhausted tone. He grew up with a cop, too. "But for y'all in the sheriff's department, the Christmas Village isn't all fun and games," he guessed.

"Lots of permits, lots of logistical support, lots of headaches," Andie confirmed. "Plus, a huge daily influx of strangers who need food, water, medical attention—all kinds of stuff. I thank God every day that there's no place for all these tourists to stay overnight on the island, or I swear, we'd never have a moment's peace."

Owen shifted in the deep seat, grimacing at the lance of pain through his lower back where he tensed it as he walked with the cane and the air cast. "I wish I could pitch in and help out, but I'd probably be more of a liability."

And didn't that grate on him? The knowledge that the army had been right to place him on the Permanent Disability Retired List, though he'd wanted to fight it.

He couldn't help, couldn't fight, couldn't *serve*, until he was back to peak physical condition. His men deserved him at his best, and that's what they would get.

"How are you doing?" Andie asked, a little tentative.

Remembering the way their father had tended to bite the head off anyone who asked him a question like that, Owen worked up a quick smile for his sister. She deserved his best, too. "Better every day. And I'm sure the good folks at the Windy Corner Therapeutic Riding Center will get me back on my feet again."

"Windy Corner is where Caitlin has her lessons with Sam," Andie told him. "He works there."

Protectiveness stirred in Owen's chest, but he throttled it back. Andie had been taking care of herself for plenty of years without any help from Owen after he enlisted. "Tell me about this Sam guy. You're pretty serious about him, I take it? If he's moving in with you."

Andie sent him a wry look out of the corner of her eye. "Caught that detail, did you? Yeah, Sam is . . . well, he's it for me. I can't explain it any other way but that."

Something pressed, tight and aching, against the back of Owen's breastbone. "You love him."

"I really do."

"When you smile that way, you look like the pictures we have of Mom on her wedding day."

Andie's soft, glowing smile faded. "I hope not. Or at least, I hope Sam and I have a longer happily-ever-after than Mom and Dad got."

The anger that clenched Owen's stomach at the thought of their father was so old and familiar, it was almost comforting. "Dad didn't have to turn from the hero of the story into the villain when Mom died. That was his choice."

"I used to agree with that, but now . . ." Andie shook her head. "I can't be sure how I would react if anything happened to Sam. I know that it would change me."

"That's hardly a convincing advertisement for being in love." Staring out the window, Owen automatically tracked the turns they took, estimating distances and clocking landmarks. "I worked damn hard to become the man I am now. Not perfect, by any stretch—but I'm not interested in starting over from scratch as a whole different person if I lose someone I love."

In his sharp peripheral vision, Owen saw Andie give the signature Know-It-All-Sister Smirk. "Oh, sweetie. It's cute that you think you'll get to decide whether or not to be in love. In my experience, love doesn't require your permission to come right on in and change your whole life."

Privately, Owen disagreed. Intimacy—emotion—was never a tactical advantage.

For some reason, the soft, dreamy prettiness of Libby Leeds flashed through Owen's mind. Her pink coat and pink cheeks made her sort of pink all over, like a frosted sugar cookie.

Owen frowned at his wavering reflection in the SUV's window. She was married, he reminded himself. And even if he'd disliked her grinning husband on first sight, that didn't mean Owen had the right to think about whether Libby would taste as sweet as she looked.

His forearm tingled where she'd scratched out her number. Palming it absently, Owen thought about calling her up, asking her to meet him for coffee—or hot cocoa, which seemed more her speed—to talk about why she'd seemed so surprised to see her husband meet her at the ferry. She'd listened to all Owen's problems. He owed her an ear in return.

Owen clamped down on the idea. Dangerous. What he ought to do was call her up and politely decline her invitation to spend Christmas at her house. That would be the smart play.

He promised himself he'd do exactly that as the SUV pulled off the main road onto a bumpy graveled driveway. Andie slowed way down, giving Owen plenty of time to appreciate the view of the big white barn perched atop the hill, surrounded by maritime pines.

"Nice place," he commented, taking in the glimpse of paddocks and training rings out behind the barn. A curious horse poked its large chestnut head out of one of the windows lining the side of the barn and whinnied a shrill welcome.

Andie parked beside a few other vehicles and hopped out. She made it all the way around to his side of the SUV before he'd managed to wrestle his sling free of the seat belt. Already on edge, Owen glared at the red and white twinkle lights outlining the double-wide barn doors. "Is this whole island crazy for Christmas?"

"Yes." Andie raised her hands in surrender and stepped back to let Owen struggle down from the car on his own. "You might as well get used to it. And when did you turn into such a Grinch, anyway?"

"I don't hate Christmas," Owen groused, grabbing his cane from the backseat and ignoring the twinge of soreness in his muscles. "I just don't see what the big deal is. It's a day, like any other."

He expected Andie to laugh at him, or guilt him with reminders of how special their mom had made the whole holiday season when they were kids. He didn't expect the hard grip of her hand on his bicep, or the deadly serious glint of steel in her eye when she said, "Do not let me catch you talking like that around Caitlin. I mean it, Owen. She's been through a lot and she's already playing down how excited she is about Christmas. I mean to give her a good one this year if it kills me."

Twin spikes of anger and guilt jabbed at Owen. "You think I don't want that for her? That's why I agreed to the magazine idea. A great Christmas with a great family."

"We're her family," Andie argued. "We're all she needs."

Owen snorted, her words cutting deep into the most vulnerable part of him. "Right. Because we're so good at being a family."

Andie sucked in a breath, and for a second, Owen felt the cold satisfaction of a direct hit. But it was followed swiftly by the regret he never let himself feel while on a mission.

"At least I'm trying," she choked out, the temper they both inherited from their father flaring bright. "While you were hiding in your hospital bed, too afraid to meet your own daughter, I've been raising her."

Talk about a direct hit. Owen fought not to flinch at the raw truth of Andie's accusation. Time to retreat. "I don't want to fight with you, Andie. And despite what you think, I am trying. And I'm well aware that the best I can do is nowhere near good enough for any kid."

"Caitlin isn't just 'any kid,'" Andie fired back. "She's your daughter. Your little girl, who spent nearly a year asking me every single night if her daddy was coming home tomorrow."

Gritting his teeth against the pain that wanted to gut him and leave him bleeding out on the ground, Owen said, "For most of that year, I was deployed overseas. I couldn't be here, and I'm sorry for that. I know it was an imposition to ask you to take her—she's not your responsibility."

"No, she isn't my responsibility. She's my family. My joy. My *privilege*, to get to know her, to be here for her." Andie shook her head, clearly despairing of making Owen understand. "And I know you couldn't be that person for her before, when you first found out she existed. I don't want to guilt you about that—you were fighting for your country and you almost made the ultimate sacrifice. But since then, since you were wounded . . . Owen, you've been back in the states for weeks now. Worse, you've been on TV. Caitlin's classmates have seen you, they ask her about your video, they want to know why you haven't come home yet. But you know what? She's stopped asking me."

"That's good, right?" Owen gripped his cane hard. "She's learning to be patient."

Andie's glare had a pitying edge. "Owen. Every night since she came here, without fail, she's asked about you. Until you showed up on TV and then didn't show up here. For her. The way I'd been promising."

Cornered, Owen lashed out. "What are you angry about—that I haven't been here for Caitlin, or that I made you look bad?"

He expected a fiery explosion, the kind of knock-down drag-out they'd had in their teens when their tempers were spiked with hormones and fresh grief—or even later, when Andie had tried to convince Owen to come home for a visit, and he'd refused, unwilling to step foot in his father's house. But sometime in the last few years Owen's older sister had learned control. Self-mastery. Restraint.

Andie's eyes softened, her shoulders dropping out of fighting stance and slumping slightly with sympathetic exhaustion. "Let's not. Okay? I love you. However long it took you to get home to us, you're here now, and I'm glad."

She'd learned more than self-control. She'd learned how to forgive.

Forcing himself to back down was one of the harder things Owen had ever done, but he'd learned a bit in the last few years, too. For instance, he knew how to defuse a situation with honesty. "Look, Andie. I'm glad to be here too, and I want to do what's right for Caitlin. But the fact is, I'm only here until I get combat-ready again. Once I'm cleared for duty, I'm going back to my unit."

Andie's eyes widened in shock, and Owen frowned. He couldn't believe this was news to her. But then he noticed that her agonized gaze was directed slightly behind him, and he turned with a sense of inevitability to see a huge bearded man in a plaid flannel shirt holding the hand of a small, carrot-topped girl. The kid was staring up at Owen with her serious face as set and pale as stone.

"Caitlin, honey," Andie started, moving toward the pair, but before she got two steps, the girl wrenched her hand away from the big guy's grip and took off running.

Owen watched the red flag of her hair streaming behind her as she disappeared over the hill and down to the paddock behind the barn, his every muscle locked in place and thrumming with tension. He would've given anything for the ability to toss aside his crutch and sprint after her—and at the same time, the idea of catching Caitlin up and staring into her hurt eyes, having to figure out the right words to say, the right thing to do to make this all okay for her, was the most daunting tactical challenge Owen had ever faced.

As it was, he couldn't do anything but lean helplessly on his walking stick and watch his daughter run away from him as if she were trying to outrun a snarling monster.

"Well," said the big guy calmly, putting his arm around Andie's trembling shoulders. "That could've gone better."

Chapter Six

The drive from the ferry dock to her grandfather's house was a blur. Libby stared avidly out the windows, craning her neck to peer up through the windshield, trying to get every angle she could on the island she barely remembered.

"It's been so long," she murmured, staring at the imposing brick house at the end of the long drive. Memories shimmered just below the surface of her mind, like reeds waving under a frozen lake.

The house was much bigger than she'd expected, and grander somehow. Libby shifted uncomfortably as Nash brought the car to a stop, noticing for the first time that the car was a very high-end model with polished burled wood accenting the dash and buttery soft leather seats. How much money did her grandfather have, anyway?

"Don't worry." Nash grinned as he grabbed her suitcase from the backseat and started up the steps to the stately wraparound porch. "Nothing much has changed. Nothing ever does, on Sanctuary Island."

Libby hurried to catch up with him. "You grew up here?"

He paused at the front door to give her a look over his shoulder. "You really don't remember me, do you?"

Oh no. "Have we . . . met before?"

"We're cousins," Nash pointed out. "We were both born here. Of course we've met."

Feeling like an idiot, Libby reached out and plucked at the loose sleeve of Nash's leather jacket. "I kind of blocked out a lot of my memories of this place," she admitted. "I missed it so much, for a long time it was easier to never think about it at all."

Sympathy, deep and genuine, turned her cousin's magazine-ready perfection into something more human and relatable. "I get that. You got a raw deal. I was only ten or so when your parents passed away, but I remember them well. Your mom gave the greatest birthday presents—they were always weird, off-beat things I never would've thought to want, but once I tried them, they turned out to be the best things I got."

Libby gazed up at him hungry for more. "And my dad?"

"Taught me how to throw a ball," Nash said promptly, nostalgia and fondness warming his light gray eyes. "My own father was . . . not around much. But Uncle Phil made up for a lot."

Nash's smile crinkled the sun-tanned skin at the corners of his eyes, and Libby let herself smile back at him, feeling put at ease for the first time since she walked away from Owen Shepard.

"Thanks for telling me that. My uncle Ray—I guess he's your uncle, too!—never talked much about the family when I was growing up. I'm afraid I'm pretty in the dark about how we all fit together."

A shadow crossed Nash's classically handsome face. He set down her suitcase and glanced over his shoulder at the wide, heavy door with its shiny brass knocker. "There are maybe a few things I should have told you before we got here. About . . . the family."

A frisson of unease skittered over Libby's skin, and she wrapped her arms around her torso against the chill. "Okay."

"So, Grandfather and Grandmother had three children," Nash explained. "Ray, the oldest, then your dad, Philip, and last, my mom, Susan. The Leeds family was one of the first families on the island, several generations back. We have a long and storied history here, as Grandfather will be happy to tell you."

Curious, Libby said, "I know Ray left home pretty young after some kind of fight with his parents. He never would tell me what it was about."

Nash's mouth tightened. "We have a long and storied history—but not all the stories are happy ones. Or ones that Grandfather can be proud of. For instance, my mother got pregnant with me while she was still in high school."

"That must have been hard." Libby tried to imagine it, the very public shame in such a small town, the abrupt change from carefree teenaged girl to mother. "And your father? You said he wasn't around much."

"Oh, he married her. Grandfather made sure of that." Nash smiled, so tense and tight it was more of a grimace that pulled at his mouth. "But even Grandfather couldn't make my mom and dad magically ready to be spouses and parents. Dad took off when I was still a baby."

"I'm so sorry."

Nash shrugged. "Don't be. I don't remember him. I don't remember Uncle Ray, either, because he fell out with Grandfather over that forced-wedding business. I guess Ray didn't think Mom should have to marry Dad just to keep me from being born out of wedlock. And he was right, in the end. The marriage didn't last, and Mom moved to the mainland as soon as I left for college. "

Libby's head spun, the bare facts of Nash's story— her family's history—playing through her mind like a film. She could see it all, the forcefulness she'd noticed in her brief conversation with her grandfather prevailing on the frightened young woman. Her bull-headed Uncle Ray taking a stand and sticking to it, to the point of leaving his family and everything he knew behind for a solitary life in New York City.

And her father, caught in the middle. Her heart ached for all of them, and right then and there, Libby decided that if there were a way to manage it, she would do her best to put the broken pieces of her family back together. She owed her love and loyalty to the man who'd taken her in and cared for her as if she were his own daughter— but she couldn't help feeling that Dabney Leeds deserved at least the chance to reconcile with his son before Ray's terrible disease erased every scrap of the person he'd once been.

"Your mother left home," Libby mused. "And so did Uncle Ray. It sounds as if my parents—"

"Were the only ones who could stand to live in

such close proximity to Grandfather?" Nash smiled faintly.

Heart squeezing, Libby reached out and rested her hand on the gleaming polished brass of the doorknocker. It was in the shape of a bulldog's head, pugnacious and morose, and she couldn't help wondering if her grandfather had chosen it as a symbol for his own stubborn, outsized personality. "What is he like? Grandfather, I mean."

A funny look came into Nash's eyes as he scrubbed one big hand through his tousled dark gold hair. "That's what I wanted to warn you about. Grandfather is . . . he can be difficult."

Unease prickled across the back of Libby's neck. "He did seem a little, um, bossy. When I talked to him on the phone."

"Bossy, huh?" Nash laughed. "Let me guess. You told him you had a problem and before you knew it, he was laying out a plan and expecting you to fall in line. No arguments, no discussion, no input from you required."

For the first time since she met this catalogue-model cousin, with his perfect hair and movie-star looks, Libby felt the spark of kinship. She gave him a half smile. "You too, huh?"

With a lift of his broad shoulders, Nash communicated the same helplessness Libby had felt when dealing with her grandfather's schemes. "You know how in movies, grandpas are always wise, kindly old men with big, friendly bellies and maybe a fluffy, white beard? Yeah, not our grandfather. Whatever image you have in your head, I can almost guarantee it's wrong."

Libby, who'd started revising her imagined vision of her grandfather the minute he answered his phone with a terse and crabby "What now?" glanced up at the flawless façade of the plantation-style house. Pristinely white, as if it were repainted every two years like clockwork, the house was impressive. Imposing. Stately, even.

But it wasn't very welcoming.

"I don't know," Libby murmured, wrapping her arms around the chill that settled in her chest. "I think I'm getting a pretty clear picture. But if he's so awful, why did you come back here?"

Nash hesitated, a strange expression flitting over his face. Sensing a story, Libby waited breathlessly. But before Nash could say anything else, the front door swung open soundlessly on well-oiled hinges, revealing a slight, stooped figure in a crisp dark suit. Libby jumped at the sharp rap of a brass-handled cane on the hardwood floor of the foyer.

"Well?" The voice was creaky and petulant, sharp with impatience. "Stop standing around out here in the cold before you catch your death of darned foolishness. I would never have thought any grandchildren of mine could be so idiotic and lacking in consideration."

Shocked, Libby took a step back and nearly tripped over her large suitcase. But Nash grimaced apologetically. "Sorry, Grandfather. We were just—"

"Gossiping like a couple of biddies at a quilting bee," Dabney Leeds grumped, his faded blue eyes narrowed in disapproval.

To Libby's surprise, her tall, confident cousin ducked his head like a shamed little boy. And for some reason, the sight of Nash's chagrin overcame her normal shyness. Taking hold of her courage with both hands, Libby lifted her chin and said, "We were getting acquainted. That's what I'm here for, after all."

His bushy white brows went up, as if he'd expected Libby to cower before him. "Hmm. To get acquainted, and to pull the wool over your boss's eyes by making a show of the perfect family Christmas."

Reminded of her less-than-noble reasons for coming to Sanctuary Island should've deflated her. Nothing about this trip was going the way she'd imagined. But the glimpse of vulnerability she'd seen under Owen Shepard's calm strength made it impossible for Libby to give up now. "Yes," she agreed. "At your invitation, Grandfather. Thank you again for that, by the way. It means a lot to me that you would open your home to a relative you haven't seen in years."

Maybe it was naive, but Libby chose to view that invitation—which had honestly been more like a royal proclamation—as proof of Dabney's generosity of spirit rather than a desire to control his family. And for a moment, she thought she detected a slight softening in the harsh lines of his weathered face.

But in the next instant, he was scowling and turning away with a harrumph. "Quit letting all the heat out," he said, stomping further into the house. "Despite what you may think, I'm not made of money, and I don't intend to waste what I do have by trying to warm up the whole outdoors."

Nash gave Libby a sympathetic glance as he brushed past her, carrying her bag up the wide, winding staircase. Heart sinking, Libby turned to close the door behind them. The solid thunk of heavy wood meeting the doorjamb sounded incredibly final to Libby's sensitive ears. Slowly, she let out the breath she'd been holding as the still, chilly silence of the big house settled around her.

She gazed around the empty foyer, the gleaming hardwood floors smelling of beeswax and pine-scented polish, the unblemished expanse of white walls hung with framed paintings whose subjects Libby could barely see through the gloom.

Where were the lights? The pine boughs festooned with red ribbons and the clusters of mistletoe hanging from every doorway? Where was the homey smell of baking cookies? The warm, smiling family to welcome Libby back to the island she'd loved and lost so long ago?

Nowhere but in your imagination, she scolded herself as she started to follow her cousin up the stairs. Once again, she had let herself spin a fantasy, a vision of home and love and family that existed only in her own head and heart. Ever since she could remember, Libby had found the differences between the world of stories she made up and the real world to be disappointing at best. Heartbreaking at worst.

She had a chance here, though. Maybe a slim chance, but a real chance all the same. With some hard work, perseverance, and yes, a good imagination . . . she could turn this drafty old mansion into the warm, welcoming home she'd always wanted for Christmas.

Hope flooded her chest. Libby marched up the steps with renewed determination. She would unpack and take a quick tour of the house to see what decorations they needed—maybe there were some things stored in closets or an attic waiting to be dusted off and admired.

But if it took hiking into the forest with a saw and chopping down a tree with her bare hands to get this house looking festive, she'd do it. Because this time it wasn't just about Libby and her dashed hopes and crushed dreams. And it wasn't all about keeping her job and providing for her uncle.

There was a little girl out there who deserved a great holiday. And if the memory of that little girl's father smiling, slow and warm, sent a thrill all through Libby's body . . . well. Owen Shepard deserved a perfect Christmas, too. And somehow, Libby had the honor of providing it. She refused to disappoint them. It was all going to work out. She was sure of it.

After all, Christmas was a season for miracles, right?

Chapter Seven

The Christmas Village was one of Nash's favorite memories of growing up on Sanctuary Island, and he couldn't help straining for his first view of it as eagerly as any kid. But the first thing that hit him as he parked in Grandfather's reserved spot behind the Town Hall was the noise.

The merry jingle of silver bells chimed under the music of laughter and childish shrieks of joy, shouts of "Ho ho ho!" and "Merry Christmas!" ringing through the simple symphony. Scents of roasting sugared nuts and apple cider spiced the air, and Nash breathed in deeply, transported back to his childhood for one bright moment.

He opened his eyes and smiled at his cousin's rapt, upturned profile. Libby wasn't exactly what he'd been expecting when Grandfather informed him that Nash was to play husband to the cousin he hadn't seen in more than a decade. Nash had pictured a schemer, the sort of hard, beautifully brittle woman who would run a con like this to keep her job. Not that he could judge her— he had his own reasons for agreeing to take part in this charade, after all.

But instead of being hard and sharp-edged, Libby turned out to be soft. Soft spoken, soft eyed, with softly rounded cheeks and a tentative smile that made him want to tickle her to see if he could make her laugh the way she used to when they were little kids.

For some reason, Nash didn't think Libby laughed a whole lot these days.

But she was happy tonight, if the starry look in her hazel eyes was any indication. Nash remembered that her mother's eyes had been that exact same changeable color, like sunlight through the leaves in a deep, ancient forest, and the wave of nostalgia almost knocked him over.

Coming back to Sanctuary Island hadn't worked out quite the way he'd thought it would, but there was no denying the power of the memories he'd buried here. They routinely snuck past his defenses and ripped him open when he least expected it.

"Tonight should be fun," he said as he got out of the car. He leaned over the roof for a minute, waiting for Libby to grab her puffy pink coat from the backseat. "It's the Opening Ceremony to welcome everyone to the village. There's a parade and everything, and we can walk around and check out the stalls."

"Will there be any place selling nativity sets, do you think?" Libby asked keenly.

She'd spent the entire afternoon rummaging through the attic, opening unlabeled boxes and sifting through

tissue-wrapped treasures looking for Christmas decorations. She'd unearthed enough ornaments to trim at
least four eight-foot fir trees, and enough lights to get
her started. But she hadn't found Grandmother's hand-
painted nativity, even though Grandfather swore it was
up there somewhere.

Nash had helped in the futile search, but Grandfather
refused, saying his bones were too old and creaky to be
dragged up the attic stairs. But Nash had a sneaking sus-
picion that the old man couldn't bear to see the memen-
toes of the family he'd pushed away. Grandfather had
been morose, in his own cantankerous way, all day. It
was a relief when he had his chauffeur take him down
to the Christmas Village early to run through his part
in the Opening Ceremony . . . and, presumably, to drive
the festival organizers crazy with his contradictory or-
ders and petulant demands.

Even Libby, who seemed determined to find the good
in their difficult grandfather, had visibly relaxed a little
once Dabney was out of the house. But she still hadn't
managed to find the nativity and now she was determined to replace it. Maybe she thought a replacement
set would disperse the gray clouds that permanently
hovered over that sad old house, but Nash had his doubts.

"I don't think any of the stalls sell nativity sets," Nash
told her apologetically.

"It's been a while since you came to one of these
though, right?" Libby zipped up her coat with a flourish and plopped her red knit hat over her messy blonde
hair. The pom-pom on top bobbed merrily at Nash as
they slipped into the crowd of festivalgoers streaming
toward the town square. "Maybe there are some new

vendors since the last Christmas Village you went to," Libby continued hopefully.

"Maybe." Nash couldn't help the skepticism weighing down his tone. "The stalls are set up by the businesses that line the town square, and I don't think there's been a new one or a change of ownership in the last two hundred years."

"Gosh. Well, keep your eyes peeled anyway. This is amazing!"

She bounced, reminding him briefly of the little girl he used to tease and torment. "You don't remember any of this, do you?"

Craning her neck to try and see over the shoulders of the people in front of her, Libby shook her head. "Not exactly. I have . . . flashes, I guess? Little moments that might be memories, or they might only be pretty things I dreamed up. It's hard to tell the difference, sometimes."

Before Nash could ask what kind of things, they'd reached the blockades keeping vehicular traffic off of Main Street. The sheriff's department had people out, lining the streets and keeping the crowds in check until the parade was over and everyone was allowed to rush across the street and swarm the town square.

Nash caught a flash of jet-black hair out of the corner of his eye, and his heart, which had quickened at the first sight of the khaki uniforms of the sheriff's department, took off like a runaway reindeer.

"Come on," he said, grabbing Libby's mittened hand and tugging her through the throng of people. "We need to find a good spot to watch the parade. It'll be starting any minute."

"Not so fast," Libby panted along at his side, cheeks

as red as the apples Miss Ruth draped in caramel and nuts and sold from a stand like the one where she offered homemade ice cream in the summertime.

Feeling guilty, Nash moderated his pace. But he couldn't stop scanning along the barricade for a glimpse of the woman he hoped to see.

"Nash, Nash, it's starting." Libby tugged against his grip as the high school marching band struck up the first chords of what sounded like a version of Tchaikovsky's *Nutcracker Suite,* heavy on the trumpets and drums. The garland-wrapped street lamps shone down, glinting off the brass instruments as the kids marched down the street. And that's when Nash saw her.

Ivy Dawson. The one who got away. Dressed in a sheriff's department uniform that clung to her pin-up girl curves in a way that ought to be illegal and leaning one rounded hip on the do-not-cross barrier with a half smile on her red-lacquered mouth.

Nash had kissed that mouth. He'd seen that mouth kick up at the corners in a flirtatious smirk, he'd seen it open in a loud, generous laugh. He'd seen it thin and trembling with anger and suppressed hurt.

"This way." Nash plunged into the crowd. With Ivy in his sights, he cut through the pile of parade watchers like an alpine skier through fresh powder. Within seconds, he and Libby were at the front of the audience in time to see Ivy waving to the first float to follow the marching band down Main Street.

It was the volunteer firefighters who manned Sanctuary Island's lone firehouse. Their float was a flat platform built to look like a fire truck, decorated with red tinsel and plenty of silver garland. The firemen were dressed in their turnout gear—or at least, their bottom halves were dressed in flame-retardant pants and heavy black boots, but their suspenders stretched up over tight white T-shirts.

One of the firemen, Nash noted with a hot feeling of possessiveness cramping in his chest, had foregone the white shirt and was giving a dazzled Ivy a quick wink while flexing his overdeveloped pecs in everyone's faces.

"Aren't you going to cite him for public indecency?" Nash snarled into Ivy's ear, relishing the way she sucked in her breath at his sudden closeness.

When she tilted her face up to his, however, there was no trace of surprise or embarrassment on her perfect features. "More like give him the keys to the city for self-lessly devoting himself to beautification of our fair town," she purred. "Yummy."

"It's idiotic," Nash pointed out, crossing his arms over his own chest, which was sensibly covered in multiple layers of shirt, sweater, and coat. "The temperature is dropping below freezing tonight. He'll be lucky if he doesn't get pneumonia."

"Hmm. Somehow I doubt a man like that is going to stay cold for long." Ivy tapped her lower lip with a long, glittery red fingernail, as if contemplating the many wicked ways she'd be willing to help warm the fire-fighter up, and Nash's guts coiled into a knot.

This was why he'd agreed to help Libby. Ever since he followed Ivy back to Sanctuary Island, she'd been acting like he didn't exist. Or worse, that Nash existed only to annoy her. Every time he tried to apologize or explain what happened back in Atlanta, she shut him down.

But when she thought he wasn't looking, he'd caught an expression on her face that shredded his heart and choked his lungs—a look of longing so intense, it matched his own.

Not that it stopped her from paying attention to every guy on the island who wasn't Nash Tucker. Seeing her laughing and flirting with other men gave Nash the same sinking feeling he'd had in college during the tackle that had ended his football career forever—everything about it was wrong.

Well, maybe if Ivy saw him with another woman, she'd get the same feeling of bad wrongness in the pit of her stomach, and she'd have to admit that there was still something between them. At least, that was the plan—okay, it was a dumb plan, but he was desperate—until Nash actually got face to gorgeous, uninterested face with Ivy Dawson.

At that point, all plans flew out of Nash's head. Instead of suavely introducing Ivy to his new lady love—carefully omitting the fact that Libby was his cousin, obviously—Nash had to get all jealous and act like a big, dumb caveman about it.

"That firefighter is acting like a moron, and you're encouraging him," Nash growled.

Ivy rolled her eyes, making him notice the sharp wings of her black eyeliner. "That was always your problem, Nash. You were never willing to put yourself out there, to do or look or say anything that might let the world in on your little secret."

She leaned in conspiratorially, and Nash couldn't help it . . . he leaned in too, breathing in her cinnamon honey scent. "What secret is that?"

Her red lips curved in a smile that held surprisingly little humor. "You are not perfect," she whispered, the words coming in puffs of warmth against his cold ear.

"Believe me," Nash said hoarsely. "I know I'm not perfect. But at least I'm trying."

A flash of something crossed Ivy's face, but as her gaze flitted away from his intent stare, her eyes widened and then narrowed until she looked like a suspicious cat. "Who is your friend, Nash?"

Oh, right. The plan. Tugging Libby awkwardly to his side, Nash wrapped an arm around her shoulders. "This is Libby. My wife."

If he hadn't been scrutinizing Ivy's perfectly made up face for her reaction, he might have missed the way she went still and blank for a half second, as if she'd been struck on the back of the head with a hammer. But she recovered in time to take the hand Libby held out, murmuring how nice it was to meet her and starting up a quick patter of small talk without ever once meeting Nash's eyes.

Frustration burned in his gut. Even now, when he knew Ivy must want to tear him a new one, she was ignoring him instead. It drove him crazy . . . which she surely was aware of. She knew him, after all. Better than anyone else alive.

Lost in his thoughts, Nash turned his blind gaze on the parade while the stilted conversation between Ivy and Libby ground to a halt. He barely took in the floats, decorated with streamers and twinkle lights and pulled by tractors and pickup trucks. The charms of the high-school color guard were lost on him. He couldn't even muster up a smile for the band of farmers who showed up every year in kilts, wailing "Auld Lang Syne" on their bagpipes.

Cheers and shouts from the kids around them startled Nash out of his funk. The huge antique sleigh loomed into view, majestic as ever. Since there was no snow, it sat on a wheeled flatbed platform pulled by four brown horses whose bridles sported lightweight fake antlers. And at the reins was the most convincing Santa Claus that Nash had ever seen.

A huge white beard covered most of the man's face, and he wore little round spectacles under his fur-trimmed red cap. His rotund body was covered in a red velvet suit edged in more white fur, and when he boomed out a laugh and shouted "Merry Christmas!" his big belly shook.

"That's one of the things I remembered," Libby gasped, pulling Nash down to speak into his ear. Her eyes were wide and amazed, fixed on the vision of Santa Claus. "I thought it must have been because I was a kid, but I was sure that the real, actual Santa came to Sanctuary Island every year—and now I see why! Who is he?"

"No one knows," Nash told her, enjoying the mystery. "It's the same guy every year. The parade organizers leave the horses hooked up to the empty trailer at the end of the staging grounds, and somehow, the sleigh and Santa appear every year to close out the parade. And then he disappears again."

"Like magic," Libby breathed, clasping her hands under her chin.

"Doesn't anyone ever try to stalk the guy down and find out who he is?" Ivy asked, her head cocked as she took in what must seem like a crazy spectacle to an outsider. For the hundredth time, he wondered what on earth made a city girl like Ivy move to a tiny town on an isolated island that she'd only heard about from an ex-boyfriend she clearly still hated.

"Oh, no." Libby was shaking her head. "That's not any fun. Finding out how the trick works would take all the magic out of it, like letting the air out of a balloon."

Ivy shrugged, frowning a bit as she scanned the crowd of grinning, waving, shiny-eyed children and their parents. The adults looked only slightly less entranced than the kids as the wonder and joy of the scene swept everyone up into the holiday spirit.

"I don't know," Ivy said. "Mystery is overrated, in my experience."

Libby bit her lip, looking torn between arguing her point and fading into the background, where she liked to be. "But . . . mysteries make the best stories. There's mystery in everything we do, because we never know for sure how it's going to turn out."

Ivy arched her perfect brows. "And you like that?"

"Sometimes." Pink burned across the tops of Libby's cheeks, but she didn't back down. "I mean, not every story has a happy ending. Believe me, I know that. But doesn't the suspense make a happy ending even better? Well. I'm not sure what we're even talking about anymore. This metaphor has maybe gotten a little over extended. All I wanted to say was that I love this town's mysterious, secret Santa—and I bet if you look around and see the happiness he's bringing to this town, you'll see a reason to love him too."

Ivy blinked, bowled over by the barrage of words, as

Santa's sleigh disappeared down the street and into the darkness beyond the lights strung around the town square. That signaled the end of the parade, and the crowd around them began to surge forward, pressing against the barricade in their eagerness to cross the street and be set loose in the winter wonderland awaiting them on the village green.

While Ivy turned her attention to enforcing what order she could on the stream of amped-up, bouncy kids and their only-slightly-less-excited parents, Nash gave his cousin a squeeze and said, "I like our secret Santa too."

She gave him a brilliant smile that turned into a wide-eyed expression of discovery. "Nash! Look! A sign for a nativity!"

And with that, she was off, ducking around the barricade and joining the flow of foot traffic stampeding into the Holiday Village. Craning his neck, Nash peered over the heads of the townspeople and caught a glimpse of the signpost that set Libby off. At the entrance to the Holiday Village stood a candy-cane-striped pole hung with hand-painted signs pointing the way to the various attractions. Santa's Toy Shop, Mrs. Kringle's Kupcakery, and the Polar Express kiddie train whose tracks circled the square—and right there in the middle was a sign that read NATIVITY.

"I'd better go after her," Nash said as Ivy waved through a few stragglers.

"Wouldn't want her to get kidnapped by a rogue elf," Ivy agreed snidely, then she grimaced. "Sorry. What I meant to say was congratulations. She's really sweet, Nash. What on earth is she doing with you?"

Nash grinned, as he knew Ivy intended, but the joke fell flat between them. There was a look in Ivy's china-blue eyes that he didn't like, and he hated himself for putting it there. This was the dumbest plan of all time. "Don't apologize. I'm the one who's sorry. I shouldn't have sprung her on you like this."

"Why not?" Ivy tossed her head. "It's not like I care who you marry."

This woman, above all others, had the ability to make Nash want to tear out his hair. "Fine. And I don't care if you sleep with the entire Sanctuary Island Volunteer Fire Department."

Her eyes flashed. "Maybe I will."

"Maybe you should!"

"Maybe you should be glad I'm not writing you a ticket for being a dickhead!"

Nash threw his hands up. "Maybe you should just admit that things aren't over between us!"

Her mouth dropped open and she took a step back from where they'd somehow ended up standing toe to toe, leaning into each other's space and breathing each other's breath.

It was rare enough to catch Ivy Dawson speechless that Nash couldn't help himself. "Also, you're a dispatcher, not a deputy. You can't write tickets."

Her jaw shut with a snap, anger crackling around her head like static electricity. "And you are a married man. So whatever you think is going on between us is definitely, officially, completely and in all other ways *over*."

Damnation. This wasn't going at all the way he'd hoped. Trying to backtrack, Nash lowered his voice.

"Look, the marriage thing—it's not real. I mean, Libby is great, but she's not the woman I . . ."

"Stop right there." Ivy held up her hands as if she were warding off an over-enthusiastic dog. "I don't want to hear this. I can't believe you're standing here, trying to tell me you don't love your wife so it's okay to flirt with me."

"We have an understanding," Nash tried, knowing even as he said the words that they sounded lame.

Ivy clearly agreed. "Does Libby know that?"

"Actually, she does," Nash declared, relieved that truth gave it some weight. "It's complicated, but I promise you, Libby doesn't love me either. Not that way."

"How sad for you. But none of that means you and I are going to pick up where we left off in Atlanta. We broke up back then on purpose, Nash. And if your *marriage* isn't a good enough reason to stay away from each other now—which it *so totally is,* by the way—I still wouldn't be masochistic enough to risk my heart on you again."

With that shot through the chest, she slipped past the barricade and crossed the street, stepping over the train tracks just as the kid-sized Polar Express rounded the curve. Ten open-air cars full of smiling parents and clapping children stopped Nash from going after her, even if he could have thought of anything to say that might change her mind.

Sighing, he stuck his hands in his pockets and wondered if a hot chocolate might help take the edge off this disaster of an evening.

Owen flipped up the collar of his sturdy field jacket and circled around the back of the miniature train, mind reeling from what he'd just overheard.

Sweet Libby Leeds, a woman who clearly trusted too easily, was in over her head with her jackass of a husband. That loser's wandering eye could get her hurt. Beyond the emotional fallout, there was the threat of sexually transmitted disease. It was Owen's responsibility to tell her the truth about her philandering husband. Right?

Or maybe that was just a convenient excuse to talk to Libby once more, this time without any pesky guilt over desiring a married woman. And he had to ask himself: Did he really have the right to focus on anything other than getting to know his own child, for the first time in her life?

Chapter Eight

Libby followed the signs for the Nativity, hoping she'd find one of the vendors she passed in adorably decorated stalls selling local hand-crafted goods. There were people dressed as Santa's helpers selling everything from embroidered tree ornaments to homemade marshmallows, but when she finally found the Nativity stall tucked away at the far end of the town square, it was . . . an actual stall. Like, a barn stall with live animals, all gathered around an empty manger. A low wooden fence encircled the enclosure.

Instead of porcelain figurines of sheep and camels, there were actual sheep munching patiently on the hay littering the floor of the stall. A bored-looking llama smacked its lips in the shadows behind the unlit manger.

Libby blinked. She didn't remember a goat—not to mention a llama—in the original nativity story, but tethered to the manger stood a black-and-white spotted goat with only three legs.

"Looks like we're a little early. Or everyone else is late."

The deep voice from behind her should have made Libby jump in startlement, but her body recognized Owen Shepard's rough rasp before her mind did. Whirling around, she realized there was no one else nearby. "Hello again," she stammered, cheeks heating even in the cold night air.

Owen smiled, but it didn't reach his eyes and faded fast, leaving him looking troubled. He checked his watch, and, afraid he might be about to make his excuses and run off, Libby blurted, "I thought they might be selling nativity sets. I didn't realize they'd set up a live one."

"Apparently it's also a petting zoo. My sister's boyfriend, Sam, is working with the local veterinarian to pull it off. They told me to meet them here, but I guess they're running behind."

"A petting zoo," Libby repeated, charmed. "What a great idea."

"I guess the kids are putting on a little pageant too," Owen told her. "My daughter is in it, supposedly. So it's good we're early, we should have the best seats in the house. I don't want to miss any more than I already have."

Heart clenching, Libby searched his shadowed face. She didn't want to pry, but curiosity and concern pricked at her more sharply than the frosty breeze off the nearby ocean. "What part is your daughter playing in the pageant?"

Owen blew out a breath and scrubbed one big hand over his face. Libby could hear the rasp of his leather glove against his stubbled jaw. "I don't know. She wouldn't even talk to me. Not that I blame her."

Libby's chest hurt at the resignation and pain in Owen's tone. "Give her time. I'm sure she'll come around."

"I've got until this leg heals and I can convince the army to take me back." Owen stared off into the darkness beyond the lights of the Holiday Village. "I don't know if that's enough time to make up for nine years of abandonment."

"Probably not," Libby said without thinking, "if you're planning to abandon her all over again as soon as you're fit for duty."

"I have to go back," he grated out. "My men depend on me. And it's not only that—we started something over there. We need to see it through."

Filled with remorse for her knee-jerk response, Libby put an impulsive hand on Owen's arm, feeling the flex of muscle beneath the layers of clothing. "I get that. And I can't begin to understand what it must be like for you, torn between family and duty. I don't know what choice I'd make, in your shoes. Well, actually, I do—I never would've had the guts to join the army in the first place, so that would eliminate that option."

"I don't buy that." Owen pinned her with an intense stare that felt as if it stripped away every secret Libby had. "You're stronger than you know. And courage comes in many forms. For instance, you were brave enough to take the plunge and get married. That's something I've never had the guts to do."

Libby's stomach twisted, but Owen's eyes were so serious and intent, studying her as if he knew there was more to the story of her "marriage." Trying not to squirm, she waved a vague hand in the air and peered down at the toes of her boots. "Oh, you know. Marriage isn't so bad."

She could practically feel Owen's interest sharpening, but at that moment the lights began to buzz, warming up and illuminating the quiet manger scene. Townspeople and visitors began to drift toward them, filling in the gaps around the fenced enclosure as a hush fell over the audience.

The crush of people pressed her close to Owen, and when someone on her other side jostled against her shoulder, Owen wrapped his free arm around her back and pulled her into the shelter of his large frame. It took everything Libby had not to lean into him, but he was still using that cane to brace his weight, and she wouldn't add to his discomfort for anything in the world.

A gate opened in the tall wrought-iron fence that surrounded the front yard of the large brick building across the street. Through it, Libby glimpsed a swing set and a slide . . . a playground. There was a sign arching over the gate, but it was hard to read in this light. Libby squinted, then giggled.

"What?" Owen's lips brushed her ear, making her shiver.

"They changed the sign." She pointed. "Sanctuary Elfementary School. How cute is that?"

A tall silhouette with a smaller one at its side appeared in the gateway. After a brief scuffle, a tiny little boy emerged swathed in white, wearing a pair of glittery wings with a crooked halo attached. The boy rubbed his fist under his nose and hitched up his trailing skirt before starting a solemn march across the school sidewalk.

"Billy!" The hissed voice came from the grown-up behind him. "You forgot something."

"Aw, geez." Turning on his heel, Billy scampered back to grab the big silver poster board star from his teacher's outstretched hand.

The soft huff of Owen's laughter ruffled Libby's hair and warmed her chest. "Look, here come the rest of them," she whispered.

First came a tall boy in a brown robe, carefully leading a gray-dappled pony. Sitting in the saddle was a petite redheaded girl, who kept careful hands on the reins and sat up in her seat as if she knew what she was doing on horseback.

Behind Libby, Owen went still. "That's Caitlin. My daughter. On the horse."

"She looks like a natural up there," Libby murmured, half turning to get a peek at Owen's bewildered, broken-open expression. He looked like he was seeing a ghost—or maybe the ghost of a dream he never knew he had.

"She's perfect," he replied, fierce and sure, as the stunned look faded. The openness stayed, though, as if the sight of his daughter wrapped in Mary's blue robes and quietly directing her mount's steps toward the manger had permanently dismantled Owen's defenses. Libby's heart swelled. She wanted desperately to help these two find their happy ending together.

The rest of the pageant was steeped in cuteness. Shepherds of varying ages and sizes jockeyed with the three wise men, who were of varying ages and genders, to get into the enclosure with the animals. A few teachers dressed as angels did their best to keep the peace, but it wasn't until a truly beautiful woman with curly dark hair under her glittering halo entered the manger that everyone settled down.

The prettiest angel carried an adorable toddler with a shock of black hair spiking from his head and a pair of inquisitive blue eyes. She whispered to him and he nodded very seriously before she set him gently down in the manger. She stood back to let Caitlin and the boy playing Joseph kneel down in the hay, but she didn't go far, and Libby's lungs squeezed at the look of tenderness on the young mother's face as she smiled at her baby boy.

Would Libby ever have that? Did she even deserve it?

One of the teacher angels, a slim young man with brown hair, stepped up, and all the children's eyes turned to him. He raised his arms and the kids breathed in, then started to sing. The slow, faltering notes of "Silent Night" drifted up into the sky, gaining strength and confidence as the children sang together, and Libby felt a shudder of pure joy rush through her.

"This is magical," she whispered, not even meaning to say it aloud but unable to hold back. Owen didn't reply, but his arm tightened in a quick squeeze that reminded her she wasn't alone, and she shivered all over again at the transcendent pleasure of his muscular strength pressed in a lean, hot line against her side. Libby breathed in the cold night air, tasting a hint of snow, and memorized this moment so that she could relive it over and over in her imagination.

After the song, the pageant broke up as the kids gave in to the excitement of being in a play with real live animals. A set of mischievous twins got into a mock fight with their shepherds' crooks while a stern-faced man stopped a little girl from putting her angel wings on the three-legged goat before scooping the giggling baby out of the manger and reeling the pretty mother angel in for a kiss.

At her side, Owen stepped away from her. His muscles went taut with expectation as he searched the chaos, probably looking for his sister or his daughter, who had ducked away from the manger as soon as the singing was over.

Released from the spell of the song and the moment and the nearness of the man, Libby swallowed around her desire for the kind of close, easy connection shared by the couple who'd contributed the live animals and the baby to the manger scene.

Instead, she had a fake marriage to a cousin she barely knew, and a heart-twisting attraction to a man she couldn't have.

"Come on," Owen said, setting off with his halting gait. "I want to find Caitlin and tell her how great she did. If she'll even talk to me."

Grateful to be jarred out of her small bout of self pity, Libby moderated her pace to match Owen's as they skirted around the fenced enclosure toward the back of the stall where the pony Caitlin rode had been tethered. "Do you really think she won't talk to you?"

"She ran away from me when I first showed up this afternoon," Owen confided grimly. "And then they had to come over here to the square to get ready for all this, so I stashed my stuff on my sister's couch and took a walk around."

Libby frowned. "You're sleeping on a couch? That can't be good for a man recovering from injuries like yours."

"Believe me, I've slept worse places than a soft couch." Amusement lightened Owen's tone for a moment, and Libby felt her heart lift just as they rounded the rear corner of the stall.

Beside the small dappled pony stood the miniature red-haired Mary in her blue robes, staring up at Owen's sister with such a heartbreaking look of fear that Libby stopped in her tracks.

"Oh, sweetheart," Andie was saying, kneeling down to put herself on Caitlin's level. "No one is going to take you away."

"But he's my dad," Caitlin argued, tears and a stuffy nose turning her voice thick. "I used to want him to come find me and take me away with him to somewhere else, but now I don't want to go."

Libby's heart cracked in two at the way the little girl's eyes filled with tears as she wailed, "I . . . I don't want to leave Peony!"

Throwing her thin arms around the pony's neck, Caitlin buried her face in Peony's mane while Andie got to her feet with a sigh. She caught sight of Owen and Libby hovering uncertainly by the stall, and hurried over to them.

"Hey! Owen, I'm sorry. She's just a little overwrought— too many candy canes, probably."

A muscle clenched in Owen's rough-hewn jaw. "The problem isn't a sugar overload and you know it."

Caitlin's sobs had tapered off and now she was watching them from over the back of her pony's neck. Her red-rimmed eyes darted from her father to her aunt, and landed on Libby. Libby's ribcage squeezed her heart like an orange, wringing every last drop of empathy out of her.

Libby had been that little girl, so lost and alone in an unstable world that she clung fixedly to anything that would hold still long enough. For Libby, it had been a book of fairy tales her mother had read to her. For Caitlin, it was the stolid, unconcerned pony tearing at the dry grass of the village green.

I was lucky, Libby remembered, picturing Uncle Ray's kind, weathered face and absent-minded smile. *Even if it took me a while to see it. Maybe I can help Caitlin see how lucky she is, even when things look bleak.*

Before she knew it, she was stepping across to the pony with her hand outstretched. "Hi, Caitlin. I'm Libby. I'm a . . . friend of your dad's, and I'm hoping to get to know you this Christmas."

Caitlin sniffled, not looking convinced. She didn't take Libby's hand, either. Casting a quick glance over her shoulder to where Owen stood, frozen with tension, Libby dropped her hand to pet her fingers through the coarse strands of Peony's meticulously combed mane.

"She's beautiful," Libby commented, searching for a way to connect. "And she did a great job in the pageant. Is she yours?"

From the way Caitlin's blue eyes lit up, Libby knew she'd hit on the perfect question. "No! She belongs to

Miss Jo at the stables where I take lessons. But Peony is almost like mine—she's my horse that I ride in every lesson, and I'm responsible for grooming her and picking out her hooves from stones if they get in there and for giving her peppermint candies because those are her favorite when she's been good."

Hiding a smile, Libby sorted through the jumble of information while her mind jumped forward a couple of steps. "I think Peony definitely deserves a treat after her performance tonight. And so do you! What would you think about coming to my house tomorrow to help me make a gingerbread house?"

Libby had no idea if Owen and his sister had yet had a chance to discuss where they'd be spending Christmas, but either way, Libby was determined to do what she could to make it special for Caitlin . . . and to give Owen a chance to get to know his daughter.

"By myself?" Caitlin asked, sneaking a glance at the other adults.

Libby kept her attention focused on Caitlin. "I was thinking we'd probably invite a few other people along. Like your aunt and your dad."

"And Sam," Caitlin said decisively. "Okay, I guess. Can we eat the gingerbread?"

A vague memory of research she'd done for a column a couple of years ago surfaced in Libby's mind. "Um, I don't think you would want to. The kind of gingerbread you have to bake that can stand up as a house isn't very good to eat. But there will be lots of candy to decorate with!"

Behind her, she caught Andie's soft groan and winced, wishing she'd thought a little faster and invited

Caitlin over for some sugar-free holiday activity, like
making snow angels or something.

But it was too late. Caitlin was running over to Andie,
telling her about the gingerbread houses and casting shy,
anxious glances up at her father whenever she paused for
breath. For his part, Owen had clamped his jaw tight
over whatever he wanted to say, but when Libby walked
back to his side, the expression he turned on her told her
everything she needed to know.

Thank you, his blue-green eyes said.

Libby nodded back and tried not to think about how
much she wished there were more than gratitude and
friendship behind Owen's smile.

Chapter Nine

Owen squinted his eyes open against the light pouring in the windows, sore and stiff, and unsure why he was even awake.

Situational awareness came back to him in a flash—there were no curtains because he was in his sister's living room, and he was stiff because her sofa was a diabolical torture device from the middle ages.

And he was awake because a nine-year-old girl was perched on the coffee table, staring at him.

Blinking to clear the sleep from his eyes, Owen braced a hand on the arm of the sofa and pushed himself up. He had to grit his teeth against a groan of pain at the way the move torqued his torso, but luckily he'd had a lot of practice at suppressing reactions to physical discomfort.

What he had a harder time suppressing were the feelings that gushed up in his chest like an oil rig exploding, sticky and terrifying. "Morning," he said.

His voice sounded like sand crunching under combat boots. Clearing his throat, he tried again. "How did you sleep?"

Caitlin shrugged. She had a poker face the guys on his team would've killed for. Owen, who'd never known what to say to kids, especially girl kids, even in the best of times, rubbed both hands over his face and prayed that somewhere in this house there was someone making coffee.

But he couldn't waste this chance to talk to his daughter.

"Listen," he started, leaning forward to rest his elbows on his knees, but then he paused. What could he say to this girl, whose entire life had been a secret to him up until a few months ago? "I know it's weird to have me just show up here, dropping into your life like a bomb. But I promise you, I'm not here to make things harder for you, or to upend everything you've got going with Andie and Sam and this island, and everything. School, the horse riding lessons . . ."

Owen trailed off, running a hand through his hair. Caitlin's expression hadn't wavered from stony staring. "Are you going to take me away to live with you?" she demanded abruptly.

Startled, Owen sat up straight as something like panic shot through him. "No! I mean, I don't think so. But I can't ask your aunt to look after you forever. It's complicated. And then there's my job. I haven't had a chance to talk it over with Andie yet, but she knows . . . and I guess you heard yesterday, that I'm hoping to go back to active duty when my leg heals up."

He massaged a hand down his cramping thigh, careful of the healing scars, and sighed. That was a crappy non-answer to Caitlin's very understandable question, and Owen knew it. But Caitlin's only response was a silent nod that Owen had no idea how to interpret. She could've been agreeing that she'd overheard his plans— or she could've been approving of the plan.

"All I want to say," he went on doggedly, "is that I know I'm late—years too late—and I don't know exactly where we're going to end up down the road. But I'm here now. And I want to get to know you. Can we do that?"

She shrugged and slipped off the coffee table, which Owen took as a yes. "Sam is making breakfast. I get to eat as much as I want. Even three pancakes, if I'm hungry," Caitlin announced.

"That . . . sounds good?" Owen blinked, hoping again that breakfast included coffee. "Should we go see if Sam needs any help?"

"Helping is my job," she said sharply. "You should brush your teeth. That's what we do when we first get out of bed, to wake our mouths up and get them ready for breakfast."

Hiding a smile at the echo of his own mother's words, passed down to Andie and filtered through his daughter's mouth, Owen gave her a nod of acknowledgment. "Good idea. Let me get on that."

Caitlin ran off toward the kitchen, leaving Owen to fumble through his duffel for his Dopp kit and troop down the hall to the bathroom. The counter was already cluttered with the detritus of two adults and a kid sharing space, and he went through his stripped-down morning routine as tidily and efficiently as possible. Andie's house was comfortable and cozy, but it was a tight fit with an unexpected adopted niece and a houseguest. Even family.

He worried about whether he was putting them out all through breakfast, while Caitlin chattered to Sam and Andie about people Owen didn't know who worked at the barn. Caitlin's eyes slid to Owen every so often though, so he smiled to let her know he was listening, but he didn't try to infiltrate the conversation. They'd made progress that morning, he thought, and he didn't want to push his luck.

A good leader knew when to forge ahead and when to hang back and let events unfold.

After breakfast, Caitlin was eager to get over to the Leeds' place and start her gingerbread house. Owen was ready in ten minutes—five longer than it would normally take him, but even without the air cast and with his arm out of the sling, his injuries slowed him down—and watched as the rest of them bustled around the small, confined space of the two bedrooms and one bathroom. Their smooth, choreographed moves reminded Owen of the way he and his guys operated in close quarters.

They had a routine that worked, a stable, organized way of doing things that Owen's presence was disrupting. Years in the military had given Owen a deep and abiding appreciation for order and routine, and he hated to be the extra variable that spun the whole careful construction off its axis.

That feeling of being extra and in the way intensified when they marched out to Andie's SUV and had to move a leather saddle and all its padding from the back passenger seat before Owen could get in. Apparently, caring for the saddle was one of Caitlin's jobs, and she fretted about leaving it behind at home the whole way to the Leeds' house.

"Okay, but just don't forget it when we go to the barn later," she was reminding Andie for the fifth time when the SUV pulled around a curve and emerged from a stand of tall evergreen trees in front of a huge white plantation-style house.

Two stories of white-painted brick gleamed under the late morning sun. Slim white columns supported the generous two-story porch, which looked as if it stayed shady and cool even in the swelter of summer with the aid of outdoor ceiling fans. Right now, as winter began to tighten its hold over the tiny coastal island, the porch railings were festooned with garlands made of glossy, green magnolia leaves studded with pinecones and scarlet pepper berries.

Framed by black wooden shutters, the windows glowed invitingly, and Owen felt his spirits lift. This was what he'd had in mind for Caitlin when he accepted the invitation to spend Christmas with America's Favorite Cook.

The front door opened just as Caitlin leapt up the porch steps, and Libby stepped out. Crossing her arms over the giant snowflake knitted into her sweater, she gave an exaggerated shiver as she grinned down at Caitlin's upturned face. "Quick, come inside before you freeze to death!"

"It's not that cold," Caitlin scoffed, waving her mittens in the air. "There's not even any snow."

"I know, it doesn't seem fair, does it?" Libby said.

"All this cold weather, but no snowball fights, no snow-men, no snow angels . . ."

"What's a snow angel?" Caitlin wanted to know, and Owen paused in his slow, painful trek toward the porch. *How can any kid not know what a snow angel is?*

Libby hesitated, her gaze flicking to Owen's before she said, "If we ever get any snow, I'll show you. How's that?"

That appeared to satisfy Caitlin, who slipped past Libby and into the house. Andie and Sam made their polite hellos and followed the little girl inside. But Libby waited for Owen, who ground his back teeth and made an effort to hurry it up even as his hip tightened with pain.

There was no trace of impatience on Libby's bright face, but Owen felt all twisted up inside anyway, and when Libby reached out a hand to touch his elbow as if to guide him over the threshold, Owen jerked away from her.

"I'm not a cripple," he growled, the clatter of his cane against the doorjamb punctuating the words and making him wince. "Fine. Maybe I am, for now. But I don't need help."

"Sorry," Libby apologized, then flinched as if she expected him to shout at her for apologizing.

All the angry heat drained out of Owen's muscles, leaving him tired and sore. "No, I'm sorry. I'm not dealing well with this injury. I'm used to being able to rely on my body, to give it commands and know I can trust myself to get the job done."

"We spend a lot of time apologizing to each other,"

Libby observed, her gaze still downcast and her cheeks paler than Owen liked. He couldn't help leaning in a little closer, breathing deeply to try and catch her elusive scent—warm and sweet, like vanilla.

"It's a shame," Owen said softly. "Since there are so many other things I'd rather be doing with you."

Her hazel gaze flew to his, her cheeks going as red as the holly berries in the wreath on her front door, and Owen cursed himself silently. He had to force his feet to move him back a pace, to get him out of her personal space, when all he wanted was to get even closer.

But Libby was married. To a jerk, but still. Owen hadn't decided what he was going to do about what he'd overheard at the Christmas Village between Nash Leeds and the sex kitten in the sheriff's department uniform, but making suggestive comments to the clueless wife was probably not the right or honorable thing to do.

"Sure," he said heartily, nodding toward the cozy interior of the house where he could already hear Caitlin exclaiming excitedly over the variety of candies and frosting colors. "Like make gingerbread houses, for instance. What gave you the idea?"

Was it Owen's imagination, or did a fleeting wrinkle of disappointment furrow Libby's brow for an instant? "Oh. I saw a flier at the parade last night advertising a gingerbread house contest!"

"That's right," Andie added, catching the tail end of the conversation as Owen followed Libby into a very formal dining room with heavy wood paneling. "They set up a whole gingerbread village laid out like the actual town."

"You're supposed to try and recreate your own home, in gingerbread form." Libby hurried to the head of the long table covered with white butcher's paper. On top of the paper sat bowl after bowl of brightly colored gumdrops and jellybeans, and stacks of pastel wafers and chocolate nonpareils interspersed with the jewel tones of fruity hard candies. There were bowls of red, white, and green frosting set beside slabs of dark, spicy-smelling gingerbread.

"I've got the pieces all patterned out," Libby was saying as she lifted her slender arms to tie back her tumble of blonde hair. "And I was hoping I could convince you to help me build the replica of the Leeds house. I promise I'll put all our names on the contest entry!"

"I don't understand," Andie said, shaking her head slowly at the overwhelming bounty laid out before them. "Did you already have plans to enter the contest on your own?"

Sam looked up from the platter of black licorice whips he'd been inspecting with interest. "She must have. How else could she have gotten all of this done?!"

Libby's gaze slid sideways before she clapped her hands together. "We should get started! Oh, good job, Caitlin. I was hoping you'd sample the peanut brittle for me. You know, the only rule of the contest is that everything on and around the house has to be yummy."

Caitlin hunched her shoulders guiltily while Owen gave Libby a sharp look. She was as beautiful as ever with her rosy cheeks and sparkling hazel eyes, but now that he looked, Owen saw purple smudges beneath those pretty eyes, and her skin was looking more pale than fair.

As Andie bent her head close to Caitlin's and Sam started constructing the main gingerbread structure, Owen limped to Libby's side and murmured, "You came up with this plan on the spot, talking to Caitlin after the pageant. You must have been working all night to get this stuff together."

She shrugged a little, avoiding his eyes. "It was nothing. I don't sleep much, anyway. With my deadlines, I'm used to being awake at all hours."

Something in Owen's chest swelled painfully, cracking his ribs open. He wanted to put his arms around her and draw her head down to his shoulder to let her sleep . . . and at the same time, he wanted to be the thing keeping Libby awake at all hours with kisses and touches. Throttling back his own needs, he took in her uncomfortable stance and the nervous way she was fumbling the silver tip onto a pastry bag.

She didn't want him to make a fuss. Owen got that, and he respected it. "Well, we appreciate this very much," he said, then paused. "I appreciate it. Thank you." And Libby finally met his gaze with a smile.

"If I have to stop apologizing to you, then you have to stop thanking me. I want to help. I'll do anything I can to help you."

The moment caught and held, as fragile as a blown-glass Christmas tree ornament. Libby's lashes fluttered as she blinked. "And Caitlin, too, of course. I know what it's like to struggle to make a new home for myself, far from everything I've loved and lost."

Owen frowned. He didn't like to think of Libby going through loss and hurt. "When was this?"

"Oh, a long time ago." She laughed a little, but sadness

hid in the corners of her mouth. "Both of my parents were killed in a car crash when I was . . . well, about Caitlin's age, actually. I was lucky, like her. I had family willing to take me in and love me like I was their own. But even though I know it could have been so much worse—I also know that it was a struggle. I got through it, and so will Caitlin."

Owen's breath caught in his lungs. He stared down at his daughter's squirming impatience as she waited for the icing between the gingerbread pieces to dry enough to start sticking candies to the walls.

"My mom died when I was a kid, too," he muttered. "And the only way I could deal with the person my dad turned into afterward was to run away. I left that house the minute I was of age and joined the army, and I've never looked back. But I don't want that for Caitlin. I want her to have the things I never had. Security. I want her to have fun just being a kid. I want her to have a home."

"Love?" Libby asked softly.

For some dumb reason Owen's throat had closed up, so he nodded.

"That's easy, then." Libby leaned into him, just enough to bump their shoulders together, and Owen felt the contact in every part of his body. "All you have to do is love her."

It was more complicated than that, and Owen knew it. The questions of his future in the armed forces, who would take care of Caitlin and where, were all still very much unanswered. And there was also the question of Owen's capacity for love—he'd lived without it for so long, he worried that maybe he'd lost the hang of it.

But as he turned his head far enough to brush Libby's temple with his lips, Owen could only smile. "You make me want to believe anything is possible."

Chapter Ten

Libby kept Owen's words cuddled close to her heart, locking them away to be taken out later and treasured. All through the afternoon of constructing their ginger-bread creation, Libby was achingly aware of Owen's closeness. Her heart throbbed when their fingers brushed while reaching for the same bowl of frosting, when his leg nudged hers under the table as he turned to consult with Caitlin on the best candy to line the sidewalk they'd made out of sticks of chewing gum.

Those stolen moments, along with Caitlin's wide smile and frequent laughter, made the sleepless night so worth it. Libby was glad Owen hadn't pressed her too much about what it had taken her to pull this impromptu gingerbread treat together. The patterns for the pieces based on her grandfather's house were in the attic, but it had taken her four screw-ups to get the actual gingerbread to come out right.

Nash had been in a funk all evening and had dragged

himself upstairs to bed the minute they got home, and Grandfather's version of helping had been to offer to have his driver buy pre-made gingerbread in the morning.

Libby was determined to do it herself, though, so she was on her own in the kitchen all night. She didn't mind, really—everything she'd told Owen about her nocturnal habits was the truth.

But the lack of sleep was making it harder to remember all the reasons she wasn't supposed to stare at Owen's mouth or close her fingers around his wrist to feel his strong, steady pulse.

She managed to hold herself back until the gingerbread house was done. It was slightly lopsided and in danger of caving in under the weight of all the jelly fruit slices Caitlin had decided would make good roof tiles, but Libby was unreasonably proud of it.

Caitlin beamed under the appreciative noises and congratulations of all the adults, almost seeming to unfurl like a flower facing the sun. "Do you think Miss Jo wants to do a gingerbread barn? I could make it for her. I'm good at making gingerbread barns, I think."

"I'm sure you would be," Andie told her, helping Caitlin stuff her skinny arms into her coat.

While Sam carefully carried the heavy tray holding their gingerbread house over to the sideboard to harden, Libby started folding up the butcher paper with the mess of broken candies, crumbled pretzel sticks, and smeared frosting still inside. "What's on the agenda for the rest of the day?" she asked Owen, who was getting to his feet with a slight grimace of pain creasing his handsome features.

"A nap for you, I hope," he said, arching his brows commandingly.

Libby fought down a shiver of pleasure and emphatically did not reply that she'd be happy to nap as long as Owen napped with her. She thought she probably deserved a medal for that.

"Sounds nice," she agreed vaguely, her mind already jumping ahead to the rest of her plans for decorating the house and getting ready for Christmas. "What about you?"

Before Owen could answer, they were both jolted out of their conversation by Andie's sharp, distressed voice. "Caitlin, what is this?"

In the act of pulling the mittens out of Caitlin's coat pockets, Andie had unearthed a hoard of candies. Some were wrapped, but most weren't, and they stuck together in a sad multicolored mass in the palm of Andie's hand.

"I wasn't stealing," Caitlin cried, panic flaring in her eyes. "I didn't mean to!"

Libby's stomach cramped in sympathy with the little girl's obvious distress. "It's okay," she said quickly. "Caitlin is welcome to as much of the candy as she wants."

But Andie was shaking her head, her concerned gaze never leaving her niece.

"You took that candy without asking," Andie pointed out, firm but gentle. "I know you know better. What's going on?"

"It was just in case," Caitlin said, almost pleading. "For later."

Andie closed her eyes, a look of terrible comprehension settling over her. "Oh sweetie. I thought we were past this."

Caitlin's tiny bow of a mouth trembled, then opened on a high, thin wail that shattered Libby's heart like glass. Beside her, Owen sprang into motion, heading toward his daughter as fast as his injured leg would take him. But Caitlin only sobbed harder and turned away, lifting her arms to Sam in a mute appeal that the big man answered by swinging her up and carrying her swiftly out of the room.

Owen started after them, but his sister put out a hand to stop him. "Let Sam get her calmed down," Andie said, her mouth drawn thin and tight with worry. "He's got a way with the wild ones—he'll get her settled."

Owen's reluctance was visible in every tense line of his rangy, muscular body, but he allowed his sister to hold him back so he could spear her with a glare. "What the hell is going on? What do you mean, you thought she was past this? Has Caitlin been in trouble for stealing?"

"Not exactly." Andie ran a shaking hand through her red-gold hair, obviously distraught, and Libby shifted her weight uncomfortably. She didn't want to intrude into what was clearly a painful family matter. She edged toward the door, about to offer to leave them alone to talk, but Andie startled her into pausing.

"I don't know all the details," Andie said baldly. "But we're pretty sure Caitlin was neglected by her mother, to the point where Child Protective Services was involved."

Owen's face . . . he looked as if his world had just been blown to pieces. His cane stuttered against the floor as his balance wavered, and Libby rushed to grab his elbow and steady him. He lifted his chin and firmed his stance, but instead of jerking away from her help the way he had before, Owen reached up with his free hand and covered her gripping fingers.

"Tell me what you know," he ordered, every inch the commanding officer, and Andie complied.

"Caitlin hasn't told me much—she doesn't like to talk about her mother or what it was like for her before she came to live here. But from the bits and pieces she's dropped over time, I believe that her mother was extremely self-involved and had a tendency to conveniently forget she had a child, especially when there was a boyfriend in the picture."

A grimace crossed Owen's face. "That sounds like Jenna."

"Specifically, I know there were frequent occasions when Caitlin climbed up on the counter to get cereal to feed herself, because there was nothing else in the house and no one to cook for her. She was hungry a lot of the time," Andie said, her voice low with suppressed emotion. "And I'm pretty sure she got into the habit of squirreling away food when it was offered, so she'd have something to eat the next time her mom forgot to feed her."

The muscles behind Owen's locked jaw flexed as he ground his teeth. Libby only realized she was still holding his hand when his fingers tightened on hers, squeezing as if he were holding on for dear life.

"Okay." Owen's voice came out clipped and emotionless, no trace of the anger Libby read in the tense lines of his body next to hers. "There's nothing I can do to change the past, and, luckily for her, Jenna is permanently out of my reach. So we focus on Caitlin. You said she'd given up her habit of hiding food since she came here. What does it mean that she's picking it up again now?"

Andie looked away, her brows furrowed. "I can't say for sure. It could be any number of—"

"Andie," Owen interrupted softly but firmly. "Your best guess, as the adult who knows her better than anyone else."

Pulling her shoulders back, Andie met her brother's gaze and didn't sugarcoat it. "I would guess that she's feeling a decrease in the stability and security of her world, and she's reacting the only way she knows how."

"Because of me," Owen said. "She feels less safe with me around. She's afraid of me."

Libby couldn't help the noise she made in the back of her throat, an instinctive denial that had both Andie and Owen glancing her way. She wished she could duck under the table and hide, but Owen was raising his brows in that expectant way, and Libby found herself saying, "She's not afraid of you. I mean, I know I just met her, but I know that's not it."

"I agree," Andie said, surprisingly. "She lived in an unstable and chaotic environment for the first eight years of her life. It's going to take us more than eight months to counteract that—and in the meantime, variations to her routine are going to affect her in big ways."

"Variations to her routine, like having her absentee father sleeping on the couch in the middle of her home," Owen pointed out, his eyes flat and resigned. "She's had it so rough already, and here I come along, making things worse for her. That's the last thing I wanted to do."

"Maybe, but Caitlin has to learn how to deal with change," Andie argued. "Especially when it's a good change. She needs her father in her life, Owen."

"There has to be a better way for me to figure out where I fit in my daughter's life. Something that doesn't involve unbalancing and unsettling her so much that she backslides into unhealthy coping mechanisms." He sighed, pinching at the bridge of his nose. "Maybe I should leave Sanctuary Island for a while. Give her some space."

"No!"

Libby blinked, terrified for a moment that she'd been the one to give the loud, emphatic negative, but Andie was sliding into the seat across the table from Owen's and leaning over the table to make her point. "You just got here. I'm not ready to lose you again. Caitlin will come around, she needs more time to get used to you and to see that you coming back doesn't mean you're going to take her away—even if that used to be her favorite daydream."

Owen sucked in a breath, like someone had thumped him hard right over his sutures, and Libby couldn't stand it. "I have an idea," she blurted without thinking. They looked at her, and she rushed to get the words out. "Why doesn't Owen stay here? We have plenty of room, and that would give Caitlin some space to adjust while keeping you all close by each other."

There was a pause, just long enough for Owen's expression to lighten a fraction as he considered the idea . . . and for Libby to realize what she'd done.

She'd invited the man she was supposed to fool into believing she was the perfect wife and homemaker into her house, where he'd have front-row seats to her every mistake and slip–up. She'd have to live the lie full time, with no breaks. This was the worst idea ever.

Except that Owen was smiling at her, the slow, sweet, secret smile that almost felt as though it belonged to Libby alone. "That's incredibly generous of you," he said. "If you're sure you don't mind having a virtual stranger in the house over the whole Christmas holiday."

Any sensible objections Libby might have been for-mulating melted away under the warmth of Owen's gaze. "I don't mind," she said, a little breathlessly.

"What will your husband have to say about it, I won-der." Libby flinched, her gaze darting to Andie's cool, watchful expression as the sheriff continued. "Not to mention his grandfather."

Andie's eyes dropped to where Owen and Libby's fin-gers were still tangled together, and Libby felt her cheeks go hot. She pulled free of Owen's grasp and gave them both a determined smile. "They won't mind, either of them. It's Christmas! The more the merrier."

"Hmm." Andie didn't look convinced as she turned back to her brother. "Are you sure this is what you want? I still think that we could help Caitlin through this together."

"We will," Owen assured her. "But I won't be in Cait-lin's face every minute, freaking her out. And even if I get woken up by your famous chickens every morning at dawn, Libby, at least I'll get to escape that monstros-ity my sister calls a couch."

Andie reached across the tablet to thwap his shoulder,

but Libby thought there was something like relief lurking behind Andie's grin. The warmth Libby felt at the idea that she was really helping made it easier to ignore the spurt of guilt over the imaginary chickens she'd written about in her column. Libby stood up and got back to clearing the table of their gingerbread mess. "The chickens are very quiet, I promise! You won't even know they're there. So it's settled! I'll get a room ready for you, just come on over with your things whenever you want. We'll be here."

"This is very kind of you," Andie said, getting up and gathering the rest of their things. "Please tell Councilman Leeds hello for me. And I guess this development means we'll also take you up on your kind offer to host us for Christmas. Apparently, I'll be asking Santa for a new couch."

Libby watched her go, unsure whether to be thrilled at the confirmation that her boss's scheme was going forward full steam ahead or terrified that now she was actually going to have to pull off the perfect Christmas.

"I'm going to go talk to Caitlin." Owen levered himself out of his chair and strode determinedly toward the front hall, where Caitlin's sobs had tapered off a few minutes before. "I can't just appear and disappear from her life at random. And I've got my first session at the therapy riding place in an hour, so I'll be back after that. In time for dinner! I'm looking forward to my first meal prepared by America's Favorite Cook."

He winked and slipped out the door, oblivious to the way Libby suddenly swayed on her feet. She felt as if all the blood had drained from her head. Groping for the table, she leaned over it and let out a piteous moan.

Dinner. Tonight.

It had taken her four tries over seven hours to master the simplest stir-and-bake recipe for gingerbread she could find online. And now she needed to figure out how to prepare a convincingly delicious dinner for Owen, and she only had the afternoon to work with. If she bombed dinner tonight, he'd start getting suspicious. All it would take would be one dangling thread and this whole blanket of lies would start to unravel.

Libby put her head in her hands and moaned again.

This was going to be a disaster.

"So they're finally gone." Her grandfather's querulous voice made Libby pick her head up. He rapped his brass-topped cane against the doorway imperiously. "What's the matter, girl?"

Another wave of disbelief swept over Libby's head, threatening to drown her. "I lost my mind, that's what. I invited Sergeant Owen Shepard to stay with us for the holidays. So now instead of cooking for him just the one time, on Christmas Day, I'll have to figure out how to put something edible on the table three times a day for the next two and a half weeks."

"Is that all?" Dabney's faded blue eyes gleamed with something that looked a lot like the enjoyment of the challenge. "I told you on the phone that I'd take care of everything, and I intend to. Leave it to me, girl. You just worry about putting on a good act with Nash. I've got a plan."

Men with plans. She was surrounded by men with plans.

Well, it wasn't as if better solutions were knocking on the door. She might as well let her grandfather try.

Libby picked herself up from the table and went back to cleaning. If they really were going to have a delicious dinner tonight cooked by someone other than Libby, they'd need someplace to eat it.

Chapter Eleven

Owen waved good-bye to his sister's boyfriend from the porch of the Leeds house. Sam, who had driven him over on his way to volunteer at the Christmas Village's nativity petting zoo, flashed his truck's lights in acknowledgment and drove off.

Alone in the gathering dusk, Owen allowed his shoulders to droop for a brief moment. It had been a long, exhausting day, and it wasn't over yet. He still had to make it through dinner at the same table with pretty Libby Leeds and her no-good skunk of a husband.

That was one of the advantages of staying at the Leeds house, Owen reminded himself. He could observe their relationship up close and personal, and decide how to proceed with regards to telling Libby the truth about her husband. The very fact that he wanted nothing more than to barge into the house and chuck Nash out into the cold was enough to give Owen pause.

He wasn't objective here. He needed more information.

Hitching his duffel higher on his shoulder, Owen braced himself to move again. After an hour of evaluation exercises with the physical therapist at the Windy Corner barn, Owen's entire right side was knotted with pain.

His spine snapped straight at the sound of the front door opening.

Libby poked her head out, an immediate smile brightening her face when she saw him. "I thought I heard a car! What are you doing out here?"

He couldn't say that he'd been taking a minute to drop the mask and acknowledge how much his body ached. The army wasn't the first place that taught him to never show weakness—his years there had only cemented those early lessons from his father.

Instead, Owen gestured to the darkening sky beyond the pinewood surrounding the gracious old home. "I was enjoying the night."

"Brrr." Libby rubbed her hands together and blew on them. "Enjoying the cold?"

Owen couldn't help but laugh. "This isn't cold. Midnight in the desert. That's cold. This is . . . brisk."

Interest sparked in Libby's eyes and she stepped outside to join him, pulling the door closed behind her. "I guess you can probably see a lot of stars out there, too."

Closing his eyes in memory, Owen pictured the black velvet expanse of the sky over Afghanistan dotted with pinprick diamonds so numerous, they lit the sand dunes below. "Yeah. A lot of the guys hated being over there, hated the sand and the heat during the day. They thought

I was nuts, but I kind of loved it. Afghanistan is beautiful, in its own harsh, unforgiving way."

"You sound as if you miss it."

"I do. And I don't." Owen shrugged, his shoulders heavy with the invisible weight of responsibility and duty that pressed down on him whenever he thought of his Ranger unit. "I miss the landscape and the people. I miss feeling useful—having a purpose. Readjusting to civilian life, especially with doctors telling me I might never walk right again . . . it's been rough."

Libby's sharp inhalation was audible in the cold, still night. "Owen. I'm sorry, I didn't know your injuries were that severe."

"Oh, don't worry," Owen assured her with a grim smile, and as he acknowledged silently that even if he made a good recovery, he might never reach Ranger standards again. "I don't intend to listen to the doctors. I'll be back to fighting fit in no time, if the physiotherapist I met with today has anything to say about it. And since she's in charge of my rehab for the next few months, I guess she does."

"I forgot you had your first appointment out at Windy Corner today! I want to hear all about it, but after you come inside and get settled in your room."

Owen followed her inside, breathing deeply in appreciation of the wonderful smells emanating from the back of the house where he assumed the kitchen must be. "Mmm. You can just point me in the right direction if you need to get back to cooking."

The back of Libby's neck went red, but she sounded perfectly composed when she said, "Don't worry, dinner is well in hand. Here we are."

She pushed open a door at the foot of the stairs and ushered Owen into a large, spacious bedroom. He could feel his brows climb as he took in the enormous four-poster bed hung with intricate lace drapes that matched the filmy floor-to-ceiling curtains at the windows. Tiffany lamps sat on slender-legged night tables in a gleaming, polished mahogany that matched the graceful sofa and chaise longue arranged in front of the—wow!—wood-burning fireplace.

Owen limped over to the marble mantelpiece that framed the fireplace and stared up at the huge portrait that dominated the wall above it. An elderly man sat in a wingback chair with a bulldog at his feet. Arrayed around the chair were a young woman and two young men, all with hair in varying shades of blond. The family resemblance was strong enough that Owen was sure this must be Nash's family.

Frowning, Owen studied the painting. It was funny he hadn't noticed it before, but Libby could almost have been born into the family instead of marrying in. She and Nash had such similar coloring, they looked more like brother and sister than husband and wife.

"We put you on the ground floor so you wouldn't have to deal with the stairs. Grandfather insisted. He's very big on supporting the troops, so he said he was glad to do it." Libby babbled, sounding nervous.

Owen halted in the act of setting his duffel down on the faded Persian rug. "This is your grandfather's room."

"Well, yes." Libby twisted her hands in front of her, obviously reading Owen's resistance. "But he insisted . . ."

Reshouldering his bag, Owen shook his head firmly. "I appreciate the thought, but I can handle the stairs. In fact, it'll be good for me."

"Oh, but . . ."

"Libby. I can't put an old man out of his own bed. *I* insist."

She hesitated longer than Owen would have predicted, and finally threw up her hands in amused annoyance. "Fine! But you get to be the one to tell Grandfather yourself. Heaven save me from men with opinions."

Stalking out of the room, Libby nevertheless waited for Owen at the foot of the stairs instead of leaving him in the dust. And she stayed by him, careful to pace him but somehow not giving the impression of hovering worriedly. Owen appreciated the way she managed to show she cared without making him feel like the poster boy for disabled vets.

The stairs were . . . more of a challenge than Owen had anticipated, but he gritted his teeth against the agony of lifting his right leg and pushed through it. He was never going to get better by babying the leg.

This is good, he told himself as sweat broke out along his brow line and Libby cast him a worried glance. It took far longer than it should have, but he made it to the top of the stairs eventually. And the rush of relief and accomplishment was almost as satisfying as the moment after a firefight when he counted heads and realized all his men had come through unscathed.

Okay, not quite that satisfying. But it was enough to let Owen grin at Libby when she held up her hand and said, "High five! You made it."

"Thanks for not trying to prop me up or make me lean on you," he said. "The nurses at the hospital were too quick to coddle me."

"Of course they were. You're a handsome war hero. I'm sure they were all half in love with you by the time you were discharged. They probably spent their coffee breaks fighting over whose turn it was to give you a sponge bath."

Owen blinked at Libby's back as she walked ahead of him to open the first door on the right. "Handsome, huh?"

She froze for a second before giving him a mock scowl over her shoulder. "You know what you look like. Quit fishing for compliments."

A warm glow almost like happiness suffused Owen's chest and relaxed him enough to take the pain in his hip down to a dull ache. "I like the way you come up with a story for everything."

"Occupational hazard of being a writer." Libby shrugged, leading him into a smaller but still elegantly appointed bedroom.

Owen dropped his duffel on the old-fashioned hooked rug with a sigh of relief. "But you have to know that the reality was pretty different. Aren't you a nonfiction writer? You're not allowed to make up whatever details you want when you write your articles."

Libby whirled to face him, her face pale and stiff. "Why would you say that?"

He blinked, his sixth sense for danger warning him he'd somehow wounded Libby without meaning to. "I just meant . . . what about that novel we talked about on the ferry? I'd read any book you wrote."

Tension seeped out of the air slowly as Libby visibly deflated. She shook herself, stepping briskly toward the door without meeting Owen's eyes. "Oh. I . . . that used to be my dream, but things don't always work out the way we imagine. I do know that."

"Sure," Owen said helplessly. He still had no idea what he'd stepped in with that thoughtless comment, but Libby obviously couldn't wait to escape his presence. "Thank you for the room change. I couldn't have felt comfortable knowing I'd displaced your grandfather."

"It's fine. I understand." She hesitated in the doorway, her face still turned away. "Nash and I are on this floor, right down the hall. If you need anything. I'm going to check on dinner."

Unable to let her go like that, Owen moved as swiftly as he was able to catch the door just as it was about to swing closed. Libby was already halfway down the stairs, but she glanced back when he called her name. "Libby. I mean it. Thank you for everything you're doing for me. I'm not sure what I've done to deserve your friendship, but it means a lot to me. I hope I can be as good a friend to you one day."

It was hard to read her expression in the shadowy hall, especially when she ducked her head and the silken fall of honey-colored hair hid her face. "You don't owe me anything. All I want is to know that you and Caitlin had a good Christmas. My family and I are proud to help."

Tightening his hand on the doorjamb until the wood bit into his fingers, Owen wrestled with what to say. Everything in him wanted to tell her the truth about her family—specifically her lying, cheating husband. But there was a reason he had resolved to get more information before butting into their marriage, and as he watched her descend the wide, curving staircase, the graceful glide of her slim body and the swing of her hair, he remembered what that reason was.

Owen wanted her. Badly. And that skewed his objectivity. He couldn't be sure he wasn't just seeing what he wanted to see when he looked at Libby's husband.

The ambush that resulted in Owen getting trapped in a collapsed building had been the result of an op based on faulty intel. He wasn't about to make that mistake again here, not when the stakes were Libby's marriage and happiness.

As soon as Libby was out of sight of the staircase, she broke into a quick jog. Heart racing faster than her steps, she hustled down the hall and skidded to a stop at the doorway to the living room.

Nash sat in the chair opposite their grandfather's favorite wingback, his long legs stretched out toward the fire and a cut crystal glass of amber liquid tilting precariously from one careless hand. He was still brooding, staring into the dancing flames with a bleak expression darkening his even features.

"Nash," Libby hissed, beckoning at him.

He looked up, but didn't make a move to get to his feet. "Why are you whispering?" Nash asked, without curiosity.

"Because we have company." Libby raised her eyebrows significantly, pointing up at the ceiling.

Nash's frown lifted a bit. "Right. The soldier. I thought he was staying in Grandfather's room."

"Change of plans," Libby said, reining in her impatience. "He didn't want to put Grandfather out."

"That's nice of him." Nash's attention drifted back toward the fire until Libby snapped her fingers in front of his face.

"Of course it's nice! But now he's going to be on the same floor as us. He's going to notice that we're not sharing a room!"

"Lots of couples don't."

"This isn't the nineteen fifties! We aren't Lucy and Ricky. These days, you know what separate bedrooms means. He's going to think our marriage is on the rocks!"

Nash tipped his head back and regarded Libby with a sudden light in his eyes that looked like hope. "Is that such a bad thing?"

"Of course it's a bad thing," she faltered. "I need Owen to believe that I'm who I said I was in all those magazine articles—the happily married stay-at-home wife who has dedicated her life to making her family happy through food."

"Or . . . do you need to give a soldier and his daughter a great Christmas so you can write a good final article about it?" Sitting up straight, a new energy seemed to infuse Nash's motions. "I mean, that's what your publisher cares about, right? He wants the publicity. He doesn't care about the details, right?"

"I don't know." A matching hope started to percolate under Libby's skin, fizzing like champagne. "It would be wonderful to get a little closer to the truth with Owen. I hate lying to him, especially about being married."

Nash smirked a little. "I see how it is. Soldier Boy must be hot stuff."

Heat flooded Libby's cheeks. "No, not because . . . I mean—"

"No, really. I shouldn't tease." Nash stood up and set his untouched whisky on the mantel. "I'm hardly one to talk about the perils of lying about being married."

"What is going on with you? Ever since last night at the Christmas Village, you've been acting like you were auditioning to play Heathcliff in an amateur production of *Wuthering Heights*."

When Nash gave her a blank look, Libby rolled her eyes and clarified. "You've been brooding. Which is what we call "sulking" when a grown-up man is doing it."

"I have not been sulking!"

"Uh, going to bed before dark, hiding in your room, avoiding the gingerbread party," Libby said, ticking things off on her fingers. "Sitting alone and staring into the abyss . . ."

"Okay, fine, maybe there's been a little brooding," Nash conceded, his mouth twisting. "Although I would more call it *thinking*. And trying to strategize."

"About what?" Libby perched on the arm of the chair he'd vacated, sensing a story.

Nash hesitated, and Libby tilted her head. "Come on," she coaxed. "You know everything about me, including, apparently, that I'm attracted to our houseguest. Which is incredibly inconvenient and a very bad idea, but still. That goes to show you what a mess I am. Nothing you have to say is going to make me judge you or think less of you."

"I agreed to pretend to be your husband partly to make the woman I love jealous as hell and convince her to give me another chance."

Libby nearly fell off the chair. *"What?"*

"I know." Nash sank into the opposite chair, obviously not caring that it was covered in white dog hair. "I am an idiot."

"You really are," Libby said with feeling. "I mean, I know I said I wouldn't judge you, but seriously."

Laughing, Nash lifted his head. "Okay, okay. I get it. Worst plan ever. But maybe I can salvage it if you and I had a trial separation from our fake marriage. I could tell Ivy . . ."

"Ivy! The gorgeous deputy you introduced me to last night?" Looking back, Libby thought she could see the sparks she'd missed in her excitement over the Christmas festival.

Nash nodded. "We were together when I lived in Atlanta, and I want her back. Letting her go was the biggest mistake of my life. There's no one like her."

The fervent passion in his voice struck a chord in Libby. "And you had a chance with her, until I showed up and embroiled you in my awful lie. Nash, I'm so sorry. Look—if you think it would help, and that we can trust her, you can tell Ivy the truth."

Nash looked glum. "Thanks. But Ivy's best friends with your soldier's sister, Sheriff Shepard. I don't think there's a chance in hell I could convince Ivy to keep a secret like this from her best friend. At least, not for me."

Rising from her chair and going over to put her arm around Nash's wide shoulders, she laid her cheek against the top of his head. "Oh, Nash. We are so bad at this love thing."

He sighed and circled his arm around her hips in a

quick hug before standing up. Pressing a kiss to her forehead, Nash said, "We're not so bad at it, Libs. Have I mentioned lately how glad I am that you're here with me?"

In spite of the messes she and Nash had both gotten themselves into, Libby felt her spirits lift. Standing on tiptoes, she threw her arms around Nash's neck and hung on tight. "Me, too. No matter what."

"No matter what," Nash echoed, and she knew he meant the same thing she did.

That no matter what happened with Owen, Libby's job, or Nash's heartbreak, at least they'd found connection—family—with each other.

That was worth a lot of heartache.

In the hallway, Owen let the door to the living room swing closed all the way. He had to stop lurking around overhearing things that were none of his business. For his own peace of mind, if nothing else.

His stupid brain wouldn't stop replaying the image he'd seen when he stumped down the hall and cracked the door open to ask about dinner.

Libby, embracing her seated husband and whispering that they were bad at love . . . and the way Nash had returned her embrace and obviously calmed her fears about their relationship.

Owen clenched his jaw against the surge of emotion. It wasn't seeing Libby in her husband's arms that drove him crazy—it was the fact that Nash seemed entirely sincere when he told Libby how glad he was to be with her. Nash loved his wife. Owen had seen it with his own eyes. Of course, he'd also seen Nash trying to convince another woman to give him a chance—so what was the truth?

The truth was that Owen ought to keep his nose out of it. He was a Christmas guest, nothing more. A traveler passing through Libby's life. What good could come of butting into the Leeds' marriage, rocky or not? What could Owen offer Libby?

Either he'd get better and be on his way, back to the fight, or he'd be forced to accept the doctor's prediction that he'd never walk without a cane again, in which case he'd be saddling Libby with a useless, crippled . . . no. Wasn't gonna happen.

Nothing was going to happen between Owen and Libby. He needed to keep that in mind and focus on his mission. Get to know his daughter. Make sure she knew he loved her and that he had her best interests at heart, no matter who ended up taking care of her. Get fit. Get back to the only thing he'd ever been any good at: fighting.

Chapter Twelve

The front door opened with a bang that made Libby jump. The sound of a cane thumping down the hall, accompanied by the plodding click of a bulldog's lumbering steps on the hardwood floor, were interrupted by a creaky voice demanding, "What the hell are you doing, loitering in my foyer?"

"Grandfather is home," Libby said, heading for the door.

"Just in time for dinner."

"Ugh, don't remind me," she moaned, nerves fluttering up into her throat. "This is going to be a disaster."

"Why? I thought Grandfather said he was taking care of it."

"Yes, but he refused to tell me what he has planned!" Libby tried to keep her voice low, but it was hard when anxiety kept pushing it shrill and way too loud. "I mean, what is he going to do? I think it would look pretty weird for the so-called favorite cook in America to serve Chinese takeout to her illustrious guest."

"Well, you're in luck, because there is no Chinese restaurant on Sanctuary Island. There's only the Firefly Café, and I'm pretty sure they don't do takeout . . . or Chinese."

"You're missing the point," Libby said, aiming a withering look at her cousin.

Nash followed along in her wake, not seeming especially withered. "Am I? What was the point?"

"Disaster," was all Libby could say, as she pulled open the living room door and saw Grandfather sizing up Sgt. Owen Shepard in the front hallway.

"Nice cane," Grandfather was saying, in what passed for polite for the cranky old man.

A muscle ticked in Owen's jaw, and Libby winced, knowing how much he hated to be reminded of his injury. But all he said was, "Not as stylish as yours. I like the topper. Was this handsome guy the model? Hey, buddy."

Owen leaned down to scratch behind the droopy ears of Grandfather's pet bulldog, Pippin. The usually morose dog opened his mouth in a wide, panting grin, tongue lolling out hilariously as he pressed his head up into Owen's touch. Relaxing a little, Libby had to admire Owen's keen grasp of tactics—making a big deal over Pippin was the surefire way into Grandfather's good graces.

Emerging from the living room, she smoothed her sweaty palms over the thighs of her corduroy slacks and wished she'd packed something sexier. She wished she *owned* something sexier, but even when she used to care what she looked like, she hadn't really understood how to dress to set off her own looks. And without a mother to help her figure it out, Libby eventually gave up on the whole thing.

One of the advantages of an isolated career working from home meant that she could wear sweatpants and ratty T-shirts every day, and no one minded—but it turned into a disadvantage when it came time to go out in public and the nicest clothes in her closet were jeans and sweaters.

Not that it matters, she reminded herself as she walked over to greet her grandfather with a kiss to the papery thin skin of his cheek. *Owen isn't here to take me out on a date. He's here for his family, nothing more.*

Still, the combination of how intensely he'd looked at her, the way he'd leaned in close back in the upstairs guestroom, and Nash's idea about letting Owen believe their marriage was in bad shape made Libby's pulse quicken with possibility.

But Owen didn't even look at her when she smiled and said, "I see everyone is already getting acquainted!"

"I came down to ask if there's anything I can do to help with dinner," Owen said, more to Grandfather than to Libby, and before she could blurt out anything unfortunate in her panic, Grandfather shook his head.

"Come have a predinner cocktail with me in the library," Grandfather commanded. "I want to get to know you. Libby can handle dinner."

"Of course," Owen replied, with a bare hint of a smile. "And she has her husband to help her. How are you, Mr. Tucker?"

Owen held out his free hand, and Nash reached around Libby to shake it. "Call me Nash," he instructed with an easy smile that Owen didn't quite return.

Straightening his shoulders with military precision, Owen dipped his head in a nod. "Thank you for having me to stay for the holidays, Nash. It's very generous of you and your wife."

Was it Libby's imagination, or did Owen place the slightest emphasis on the word 'wife'? Maybe that's where it came from, this sudden chasm she felt opening up between Owen and her. Maybe he'd sensed her crush and was trying to remind her that she was married.

It was hard not to stiffen up when Nash threw a casual arm around her shoulders. "Don't thank me. It's all Libby. When she heard you were coming to Sanctuary Island, she wouldn't rest until we'd extended the invitation."

A muscle ticked in Owen's jaw. He still hadn't met Libby's eyes. "It's very kind of you all."

Nash squeezed her shoulders, and Libby glanced up at him. He was watching Owen with a speculative stare. "What can I say? My wife is a patriot. Come on, honey, let's go finish up with dinner."

"Good," Grandfather said, harrumphing and starting off toward the living room. "Come on, Sergeant, let's leave them to it."

When Owen moved forward to pass him and hold the living room door open, Grandfather took the opportunity to give Libby a shooing motion behind Owen's back. Waggling his bushy gray eyebrows, Grandfather scowled ferociously and jerked his head toward the kitchen.

Not sure what else to do, Libby went. Nash paced her and once they were out of earshot, he immediately punched her lightly in the arm. "Libby! That guy is hot for you."

Shocked, she froze with one hand on the swinging kitchen door. "What? No he isn't."

"Trust me. I'm a man, I know what it looks like when a man is into a woman. And Sergeant Shepard is into you, in a big way. Did you see how he was when I shook his hand? He doesn't like me at all."

"That's hardly proof of anything," Libby said tartly. "Maybe he just has good taste."

Nash laughed. "He obviously does have good taste, if he's into you. Which he is."

Libby's heart wanted to believe it, but years of being basically invisible and alone—not entirely by choice— kept her from getting too excited about the idea. "Maybe there's something between us, but it's more likely friend-ship than anything else."

"Sure, because he thinks you're happily married," Nash pointed out. "And he's obviously a man of honor, or whatever. I'm telling you, Libs, you've got a shot with him if we can be convincing about this whole rocky marriage thing. I say we go for it."

"You just think *you've* got a shot with *Ivy* if we 'go for it,'" Libby argued. "Which is reason enough for me. But leave Owen out of it. The poor man has enough on his mind. And God knows, so do I. It's going to take all my concentration to make it through the holidays—I can't be worrying about my love life."

"Or lack thereof."

Stung by the truth, Libby wrinkled her nose at him.

"You don't know that. I could be going out with a different man every night of the week back in New York."

"You could," Nash said seriously. "You are beautiful and sweet and fun. And yet I have this funny feeling that you haven't been on a date in . . . I'll say a year."

More like four years, but who was counting? "I've been busy," she muttered.

"Yes, building a fake online persona who has come to represent the best of traditional American womanhood to thousands of magazine readers."

"Too bad I didn't use any of that time learning how to actually cook, huh?" Libby pushed open the swinging door and stuck her head into the kitchen, unsure what she'd find. Without time to confer privately with her grandfather, she didn't even know what to expect, but it wasn't this.

The kitchen was full of amazing smells, steam billowing from various pots and pans on the six-burner range, and piles of mixing bowls and chopped ingredients littering the marble countertops. At the center of it all was a petite and very round woman wearing a black French maid's costume and a ferocious scowl. She was moving so quickly she was basically a blur of short black skirt, tiny white apron, and brown hair in a messy topknot.

"Um, hello?" Libby tried, exchanging raised eyebrows with Nash as they entered the kitchen.

The woman didn't even pause as she bustled from the marble-topped kitchen island to the stove to dip a wooden spoon into a cast-iron pot. She tasted whatever she'd spooned up, her expression never wavering from the ever-present scowl. Grabbing a lemon from the bowl in the corner with one hand and reaching for a wickedly sharp-looking knife with the other, she cleaved the citrus in two and squeezed a few drops into the pot in one smooth motion. Spooning up another taste, a brief look of satisfaction displaced the frown before she whirled to face Libby and Nash. "Get out!" '

Libby took a quick step back, bumping into Nash's chest. Keeping her wary gaze on the knife being brandished in her face, Libby said, "Um, I'm Libby. I think my grandfather hired you?"

The woman tsked once, then flew back into motion, peeling and dicing an onion with fast, sure strokes of her knife. "Yes. To cook and serve zee meal, not to entertain. So you will please leave."

Behind her, Nash was struggling manfully not to laugh, but Libby didn't think it was funny. "I promise I won't get in your way, Miss . . . ?"

"Robie," the woman said, her accent as French as her stiff, starched costume. "Chef Genevieve Robie."

"Yes, of course. Hi. I mean, it's nice to meet you," Libby started, wondering how much her grandfather had told this woman before hiring her.

"*Enchantée*," Genevieve said, dry as toast. "Now please to get out. I must have complete privacy and freedom for my art."

"Oh. Right." Libby frowned repressively at Nash, who was biting the inside of his lip. "But the thing is, well. I'm not sure how to explain this, but it's kind of important that it look like I did the cooking tonight. So it would be weird for me to not be in the kitchen while dinner is being prepared. Right? My grandfather did explain all this to you, didn't he?"

"He explain," Genevieve muttered darkly, sweeping her perfectly uniform cubes of onion into a sizzling sauté pan and giving them a quick stir. "It make no sense to me—why hire famous French chef and not tell anyone? But he eez rich, no? The rich do not have to make sense. Only have to pay. So I say, okay. I come, I cook, I wear dress, I serve."

Libby blinked rapidly. "Great. Then I guess we'll leave you to it. We'll just be in the corner over here, out of the way."

"And no interference!" Genevieve snapped, her attention already back on her battery of pots and pans.

Nash pulled Libby off to the side, still looking far too amused.

"What was Grandfather thinking?" Libby wrung her hands together. "This will never work!"

"Are you kidding? This is a classic Dabney Leeds plan," Nash declared. "Wave around a giant stack of cash, hire the very best in the business, and assume the universe wouldn't dare to defy him by allowing things not to work out."

"I mean, it does smell incredible in here," Libby said, inhaling the aroma of onions caramelizing in butter.

"Oh, it'll be delicious. I have no doubt about that. But this time, Grandfather may have bitten off more than he can chew."

A chill of premonition ran down Libby's spine. "What do you mean?"

Nash gave her a look. "You really don't get out much do you? Or read your own magazine, for that matter. Genevieve Robie was named the top chef in New York last year."

"That's good, right? Since I'm supposed to be such a good cook, it makes sense to have someone who's famous for her cooking do it for me."

Nash dropped his voice to a whisper. "She's not famous only for her cooking. According to the stories, she's one of the most temperamental chefs in the business. Do you remember that book that was all over the bestseller lists last year? *Hotter Than Hell*?"

"I read that! About the new cook just starting out who ends up being mentored by a woman chef who turns out to be . . . completely crazy . . ."

Nash nodded. "It was a barely fictionalized memoir, written by a line cook who used to work for Genevieve Robie."

Remembering some of the more dramatic episodes in the book, Libby felt her blood run cold. "Oh no."

"Oh yes. This time, Grandfather's need to always have the best may come back to bite us."

Libby watched the intense woman whirling around the kitchen like a miniature tornado and sent up a brief prayer that they could all make it through the evening with a minimum of broken crockery and shrieking.

Granted, it had been years since Owen last sat down to supper around a table full of family, so he was no expert. But was it supposed to be this tense?

He wasn't helping, he knew. The only way he could be sure to keep his new resolution to remember that Libby Leeds was off limits was to shut down, which did not make him sparkling company for a dinner party. Not that this felt anything like a party, with Libby pale and subdued across the table, her jackass of a husband ignoring her to talk to his grandfather, who was presiding over the table with a calculating look in his deep-set blue eyes. Owen hadn't been able to get much of a handle on the old man over a glass of Scotch, but it appeared that he owned the house. Owen wondered why Nash and Libby lived here instead of getting a place of their own, but maybe he was biased. After all, he'd left home as soon as he was of age and hadn't been back since.

The kitchen door swung open and the maid marched in carrying an ornate silver soup tureen. Owen tried not to stare, uncomfortable with the overt display of Mr. Leeds' wealth. Was it really necessary to make the poor woman wear that ridiculously clichéd uniform? It looked like a Halloween costume. And if she bent over, she was going to be showing all of them London *and* France.

"Here eez soup," she announced, dropping the tureen on the table so abruptly that a few drops of bright orange liquid sloshed out. "Butternut squash. You will enjoy eet."

With that, she marched back into the kitchen, leaving Libby to stand and grasp the ladle with a bright blush reddening her cheeks. "Er, I'll serve, shall I? Pass me your plates."

"Wow, this is delicious," Owen said when he'd tasted his. He stared down at the bowl and inhaled the steam rising off the soup. "Seriously. It's going to be damn hard to go back to army food after eating your cooking, Libby."

Her blush intensified, but the smile she gave him was wide and glad. "I'm so happy you like it."

"I love it," he corrected, closing his eyes to better savor the complex flavors. "What else is in there besides squash?"

"Oh," she said, looking down at her husband's bowl while she filled it. "You know. Stuff."

"Secret recipe," Nash put in, winking at him.

Owen did his best not to frown. What kind of grown man went around winking at people? "Is this one you're working on for the column? I'd say it's ready, if you ask me."

Libby sat down, having dished up her own bowl last, and spread her napkin in her lap with exaggerated care. "I don't know. It's possible I might . . . well. To be honest, I'm thinking about taking a break from writing the column."

She gave Nash a grateful smile when he put his hand over hers where it lay on the table, and Owen fought the urge to grit his teeth.

"That's too bad," he said. "My men love your columns. Private Fisker's wife sends the magazine overseas as soon as there's a new issue out, and you wouldn't believe the squabbling over who gets to read it when he's done. On second thought, maybe it's good you're taking a break. Less dissension in the ranks."

"Really?" Libby took back her hand from Nash and used it to tuck her hair behind her ears, looking equal parts embarrassed and delighted. "I never would have imagined . . . that is, I didn't know you'd read my columns."

"Sure, we all read 'em," Owen said, shrugging and trying to ignore the kernel of satisfaction that she and Nash were no longer touching. "The way you write about your house and your community and your family life, even your chickens. The saga of Sweetie Pie, the hen, gets the guys going like you wouldn't believe. It's the next best thing to getting a letter from home, for most of them."

"And what about for you?" Libby asked.

Owen hesitated, feeling strangely exposed. But these people had opened their home to him, at Christmas, no less. The least he could do was open up a little in return. Wiping his mouth on his napkin, he met Libby's hopeful, interested gaze. "I don't really have a home. Haven't since I was a kid. So for me, I guess I'd say your columns are like a fairy tale. A pretty fantasy about what it might be like to have a home like that. Reading it is an escape from reality, for me."

Recognition flared in Libby's eyes, and once again Owen felt the tug of connection between them. It didn't make sense and it wasn't a good idea, for either of them, but he could no more turn it off than he could stop breathing.

Chapter Thirteen

Whatever Libby might have said in response was interrupted by the kitchen door slamming open again. Owen sat back in his chair as the maid swept in and removed their soup bowls with more efficiency than courtesy—in fact, she grabbed Nash's bowl out from under his nose as he was leaning in to spoon up the last bit of his soup. He barely had time to sit back and avoid getting clocked in the face with his soup bowl.

"Next course," the French maid declared, dispensing plates around the table. "Poached skate with warm oysters and a bacon and Brussels sprouts mignonette, served with Dijon mustard sherry emulsion and potatoes roasted in duck fat. *Bon appétit.*"

Owen stared down at the plate in front of him. It looked like modern art, as if it belonged in a museum. Every element the maid had described was perfectly balanced in a precarious tower on top of a brushstroke smear of something sticky and rusty red across the center of the plate. "This is . . . very pretty."

"Tasty too," Nash said cheerfully, tucking into his plate as if he was used to getting served stuff like this. Well, of course he was. He was married to the cook.

"Um, thank you." Libby had her lips pressed in a tight line as she stared down at her plate. "Dig in, everyone."

The silence that fell around the table should've been warm and companionable—the happy quiet of a group of people coming together to enjoy good food. But instead, there was a thin wire of tension running through the atmosphere, like the fuse of a bomb. Owen took a few bites, and it was good. Of course it was. But the more he ate, the more he wished it were a little less fancy and a little more like the homey, hearty dishes Libby had described in her column.

The maid banged into the room again, hands on her hips and an expectant frown on her face. "Well? How you like?"

Libby darted a glance at Owen before he could smooth away his confusion about why the maid would be asking if they liked the food. Cheeks burning red, Libby said, "Um, Genevieve helped me. In the kitchen. With the cooking."

"Everything has been wonderful so far," Owen said to Libby, with a nod of thanks at the maid, who harrumphed.

"Next course is *poulet au vinaigre*."

While the maid went around the table grabbing plates and balancing them on her arm, Owen cleared his throat awkwardly. Was he the only one who felt uncomfortable? He was more used to chowing down on MREs in the front seat of a Humvee than being served by an actual French maid, but he didn't think that was it. There was something weird going on here.

He looked to the head of the table, where Mr. Leeds sat. That odd, calculating gleam Owen had noticed when he was introduced was back. Noticing Owen's scrutiny, Mr. Leeds lifted his wine glass in a toast. "Welcome to our humble home."

Of course, Owen thought, relieved. All this extra fancy food was meant as a welcome for him. Which he appreciated, but . . . "I hope you don't feel you have to go to this much trouble on my account. Tonight has been great, don't get me wrong, but honestly, I'd be just as happy with the fried chicken dinner you talked about in your last column, Libby. Maybe even happier. "

She smiled, twisting her napkin between her fingers. "Oh! That would be . . . I'm sure we could have fried chicken tomorrow."

The crash of a china plate on the floor made everyone at the table jump. Adrenaline surged through Owen's blood and he was on his feet before he'd registered moving, his hypervigilant senses scanning the room for the threat.

But all he saw was a livid French maid sneering at them with lips white with rage. "Fried shicken," she hissed. "You dare compare that garbage to my *poulet au vinaigre*! Insult. Outrage! I cannot work like thees. I quit!"

"That was my great-grandmother's china," Mr. Leeds bellowed, rising shakily to his feet and brandishing his cane at the maid like a baseball bat.

"Oh, no," Libby moaned, darting out of her chair and

scurrying to gather up the shattered pieces of porcelain, as if she might be able to fit them back together, jigsaw style.

"Grandfather, keep calm," Nash cautioned, hurrying to the old man's side. "Your heart."

"My heart is fine! And if this French floozy thinks she can commit property damage . . ."

"I am not floozy, I am world-class chef! But I cook for you no more. Philistines!" With that, the French-woman turned on her heel and marched back into the kitchen, presumably to gather her things.

Libby jumped up and ran after her, crying, "Oh, please, Genevieve! Don't go! We can work something out . . ." while Owen sat staring at the commotion and wondering what the hell just happened.

"Why would you hire a world-class chef when you have America's Favorite Cook in your house already?" he muttered, mostly to himself, but Nash looked up from resettling his grandfather in his chair.

"She's not a chef, she's a maid with delusions of grandeur," Nash insisted as he fished a bottle of pills out of Mr. Leeds' coat pocket and palmed a couple.

"I need to splash some water on my face," Mr. Leeds said, reaching an imperious hand for his grandson's arm. Nash helped him stand up, a little shaky on his feet. Owen wondered if it was old age or fury that had given him the shakes. From the way he bared his teeth at his grandson, who was only trying to help, Owen had a good idea it was the latter.

Libby reappeared in the doorway between the kitchen and dining room just as Nash escorted his grandfather out into the hall toward the bathroom. "Is he okay?"

"Don't worry," Owen said. "I'm pretty sure he's not about to go into a rage coma. And Nash gave him some pills—hopefully for his blood pressure."

Slumping against the wall, Libby wrapped her arms around her torso. "I couldn't talk her out of leaving," she said, her breath catching in something like a sob, and Owen couldn't restrain himself.

He stood and rounded the end of the table to stand beside her. Everything in him wanted to take her in his arms, but he was intensely aware that her husband and grandfather-in-law might return at any moment. All Owen could do was to put a hand on her shoulder and say, "Let her go. You don't need her help—you're a better cook without her."

Libby's face screwed up like she couldn't believe her ears, and Owen huffed out a laugh. "I mean it. I'd rather eat your old-fashioned family style food any day of the week. I don't know why you hired that crazy French-woman in the first place."

"I wanted to impress you," she admitted, staring down at the floor.

"You don't have to do anything special to impress me. I'm already impressed. I was impressed the minute I met you."

It was nothing more than the truth, but the way it lit Libby up made Owen feel like he'd suddenly developed a knack for epic poetry.

"That's kind of you to say." Libby tucked a piece of hair behind her ear, exposing the delicate pink shell and making Owen's fingers itch to trace it. "I'm not used to being impressive."

"That can't be true. You have thousands of fans, readers who love what you do and the way you write. You must get dozens of letters—they publish at least one in every issue of the magazine."

"Strangers I'll never meet, who don't know the real me," Libby dismissed, a complex spasm of emotion twisting her pretty mouth.

"It can be tough, showing your true self to people and trusting them to accept what they see. I know a little something about that."

"Right, you have fans, too," Libby said. "After that interview on Rhonda Friend's show, and all the others. But you managed to be so . . . authentic. Even when I watched that interview, before I ever met you, I felt as if I knew you."

All those probing questions, the shallow sympathy and equally shallow admiration for his so-called heroism. . . . Owen grimaced, his stomach churning. "Trust me. Nothing about those interviews was authentic. Rhonda Friend didn't want to hear the truth about what happened, about what's still happening, over there in Afghanistan, Iraq, and places like it—the real price of freedom. No one does."

"I do."

Owen studied her solemn expression. All the fluttery softness and anxious fear had disappeared, swept away by the force of her conviction. Owen looked into her steady eyes and, for the first time since he woke in that hospital bed, he thought he could tell someone the whole story. Libby was strong—stronger than she even realized. She could take it.

But Owen couldn't afford to open up to her. To another man's wife, a woman who could never be his.

Telling her would be giving her a piece of his soul. And the thing was fractured badly enough as it was—he couldn't go leaving pieces of it on Sanctuary Island when he went back into battle.

So he smiled at Libby and dropped his hand from her shoulder. "I appreciate that. It's nice to know not all civilians want to stick their heads in the sand and ignore the sacrifices military men and women are making."

It was a surface answer, and Libby obviously knew it. She dropped her gaze, soft and anxious once more. "I, for one, am eternally grateful. And I'm sure you're right. We can get along without Genevieve's help, as long as our guests are all as understanding as you."

"Don't think of me as a guest," Owen suggested. "Think of me as . . ." *A lover. No! Dammit, Shepard.* ". . . a friend of the family."

A bittersweet smile flickered across Libby's face, making Owen's gut clench. "I'll try," she murmured, drifting ever so slightly closer as if she had no idea she was moving. "But it's hard. I'm not that used to having that."

"A friend? Or a family?" How recently had she and Nash gotten hitched, anyway? Owen tried to remember how long he and his team had been fighting over those columns, but he couldn't. More than a year, less than five, maybe.

"Either. Both." Libby shook her shoulders like a she had a chill. "Sorry, ignore me. I'm not complaining. I know how lucky I am."

"It's not luck. You're a good person. You deserve to have good things in your life."

Instead of reassuring her or comforting her, Owen's words seemed to hit Libby like a slap to the face. She actually flinched and squeezed her eyes shut for a second, and Owen's protective instincts overrode every other consideration. He lifted his hands to frame her face, frowning at the cool chill of her skin and rubbing gentle thumbs over her pale cheekbones. "Why is it so hard for you to believe me?"

A nameless fear was growing in Owen's chest, gripping tight and refusing to let go. Libby's lack of self confidence, her constant apologies as if she felt guilty for any momentary happiness.

"I'm not the person you think I am," she said, her hazel eyes wet with unshed tears.

Owen dropped one hand to her shoulder and used the other to tip her chin up, forcing her to meet his stare. "Libby. If you're in trouble, I hope you know you can come to me. I'll help you, no questions asked, no strings attached."

For a moment her expression cleared, like a strong ocean breeze blowing clouds away from the sun, but a sound from the hallway startled her and she jumped. Her gaze darted toward the door, and Owen tightened his grip on her unthinkingly. Maybe he was way off base, but he had to at least ask . . .

"Libby, if your husband is hurting you, if you're afraid of him—"

Her eyes widened, tears trembling in her lower lashes, but the look on her face was complete and genuine shock. "What? Nash? No, no, he's never laid a hand on me. I swear, Owen. Please don't think that."

Now that he'd started down this road, Owen was grimly determined to see it through. "But things between you aren't perfect."

She squirmed in his grasp, awkward and embarrassed, but Owen didn't let her off the hook. He had to know what was going on here, before he got in any deeper.

"There's no use pretending," said Nash from behind them.

Libby squeaked in surprise, but Owen refused to leap away from her as if they were a couple of teenagers caught necking. Nash leaned in the doorway and regarded them thoughtfully. He didn't look much like a jealous husband, but people could be unpredictable.

"What do you mean?" Owen demanded, angling his body to keep Libby slightly behind him.

"You've obviously figured out that Libby and I are having problems," Nash said lightly even as Libby made a vague, protesting noise at Owen's back. "In fact, we're separated. We'd be divorced already if it weren't for Grandfather's health. I'm afraid it would be too much for him."

Owen's mind was racing, putting together details and making connections the way he did in the midst of battle. He turned to Libby. "Not just for Mr. Leeds—the magazine, too. Your image as a blissfully married woman is part of what they're selling, and you think they wouldn't like it if you were divorced. That's why you said you might not be writing for them much longer."

"I'm trying to be realistic about the future. But all I

want is to tell the truth." Libby didn't meet Owen's eyes—in fact, she seemed to be pleading with Nash, who shook his head regretfully.

"You can't. Not yet," Nash said, and at least he sounded truly sympathetic about it.

At his side, Libby's shoulders slumped in weary resignation. Owen hated to see it, but what could he do? Push her to blow her life to pieces on his account . . . and then ditch her to go back to the Rangers?

So he kept quiet as Libby stepped away from him and joined Nash at the door. He watched them conferring together over Mr. Leeds, who'd gone to bed, and Owen wondered how he hadn't seen before that they acted more like friends than husband and wife. Owen kept his mouth shut, even when they all trooped upstairs and Libby cast him a sidelong glance as she slipped into a separate bedroom, one not shared with Nash. Owen clamped his jaw shut and said nothing.

They were still married, after all. And lots of marriages foundered on rocky shores but managed to keep afloat.

But the knowledge that Libby wasn't as far out of his reach as he'd thought gave Owen a heated sense of promise that followed him into sleep and infused his dreams.

Nash typed out a quick text to Libby—*That went well!*— and plugged his phone in on the nightstand. It was a little stupid to text, since she was right next door, but he'd wanted to make the point that they had separate bedrooms.

His phone dinged, and he grinned down at Libby's reply. *I could kill you. Can't believe you sprang that on me.* There was a short pause, then another text popped up. *Thank you.*

Nash wondered if she was thanking him for unraveling their fake marriage, or for reminding her that she couldn't come clean completely. *Thanks for going along w/ it,* he texted back. *Especially after you'd just defended me to Owen.*

I couldn't let him think that about you, was Libby's immediate response. *You've done so much for me. You're not the villain of this story. You're the hero.*

Amused and touched, Nash unbuttoned his shirt and shrugged out of it while contemplating what to say. *I wish someone would tell Ivy that,* he finally wrote back.

Happy to, Libby texted. *But it would work better if you showed her.*

Nash finished getting ready for bed and slid between the sheets of the queen-sized four-poster that had seemed so enormous when he was a kid. He didn't know what it said about him that he was thirty years old and had never managed to find anyplace that felt more like home than the house he'd lived in as a child. Even when he'd sworn never to return to Sanctuary Island, this house, this room, this bed had been the standard against which he'd judged every other place he'd laid his head.

The closest he'd come to making a new home had been in Atlanta, with Ivy—and of course, he'd screwed that up. But Libby was right. He could still fix this. He could show Ivy he was a good guy, not a bad guy. Maybe if he rescued some kids from a burning building, or cured cancer, or . . .

His phone dinged, alerting him to a new text. Nash propped himself up on an elbow and squinted at the lit screen.

And I don't mean you should come up with some elaborate scheme, Libby had sent. *I mean talk to her honestly about whatever went wrong before. Then tell her you love her and let her make up her own mind.*

Nash thumbed the phone to silent and lay back down, staring up at his darkened ceiling and thinking about what Libby had said. It would never work.

Would it?

Chapter Fourteen

"Thanks for the ride to the barn," Owen said, giving Libby another one of those careful smiles.

She'd seen a lot of those in the week since she and Nash had let Owen in on the cracks in their so-called marriage. A lot of careful smiles, distant nods, and polite conversation while they took turns volunteering at the Holiday Village, hung stockings and mistletoe, and hiked into the woods to find the perfect Christmas tree.

She'd kept them so busy that there honestly hadn't been time to cook, other than cereal for breakfast. They'd eaten at the Firefly Café every single day. At this point, Libby could recite the menu by heart.

It was all fun—about the most fun Christmas Libby could remember having. But she missed the man she'd met on the ferry. The man who had opened up to a stranger. The man who had made that stranger feel closer to another person than she had in years. But Libby didn't know how to reach him, now that Nash's plan had somehow had the opposite effect from what they'd intended.

"No problem," she said helplessly, clenching her fingers around the steering wheel to keep from grabbing at Owen's wrist and begging him to please talk to her for real. "Have a good time at physical therapy. If that's not weird to say. Sorry, it's probably not a lot of fun, is it? My uncle's rehab after he fell and broke his hip was pretty brutal."

Stop babbling, she ordered herself, but Owen actually grinned at her for the first time in days.

"You know what? This particular rehab is the most fun one I've ever been involved with. Not that it isn't hard work, because it is." He opened the car door and levered himself out. She noticed he was already using his cane more for balance than support.

"It seems to be doing you some good," Libby observed. "You'll be back on your feet in no time, at this rate."

"I look forward to every session, to the progress I can see and feel." Owen's left hand dropped to his injured hip and rubbed at the muscle as if unconsciously. "I can't wait to get rid of this stupid cane. And then I can get out of your hair, and head back overseas."

Libby's throat tightened. "No rush," she managed to choke out. "You're welcome here for as long as you'd like to stay."

Forever would suit me fine, she added silently.

Owen glanced to the side, as if he'd heard her thoughts and wanted to spare her the embarrassment of acknowledging it. "You're too good to me," he said quietly.

Libby pressed her lips together, then pulled up a

determinedly pleasant expression. "So! What time should I come back to pick you up?"

Before he could answer, Libby was distracted by a small fist knocking on her closed car window. She looked down to see Caitlin's breath fogging up the glass. The girl stepped back far enough to draw a heart in the fog, smiling proudly, then she waved.

Absurdly pleased, Libby cracked the door open so she wouldn't have to roll the window down and erase Caitlin's heart. "Hey there, Caitlin! I haven't seen you for a while, but your dad told me you've been showing him around the island."

Every afternoon, Owen disappeared for a few hours to spend time with his daughter and sister. His mood when Andie would drop him back at the Leeds' house was usually quiet, reserved . . . but Libby thought it must be going fairly well, since he kept with it.

"What are you doing here?" Owen demanded, rounding the front of the car to frown down at Caitlin. "You should be in school."

"School is out." Caitlin didn't roll her eyes, but the "duh" was heavily implied in her tone. "It's winter break. I don't have to go back for a whole year!"

Libby grinned at Owen's bewildered face. "I think you mean, you don't have to go back until *next* year. Because by the time school starts up again, it'll be next year instead of this year."

"That's what I said," Caitlin claimed, her brows beetling in an expression that matched Owen's perplexed scowl perfectly. Libby swallowed her laughter into a quiet cough.

"Winter break, huh?" Owen stroked his chin. "We'll have to come up with some fun things to do, won't we?"

He was still a little stiff with the child, hesitant in a way Libby was unaccustomed to seeing him, but the warmth in his face when he looked down at Caitlin was real and sincere.

"I have a riding lesson today," Caitlin informed them. "You should come watch."

"I'd love to"—Owen's mouth pulled down at the corners regretfully—"but I've got physical therapy right now."

Caitlin shrugged, short and sharp, as if she didn't want to admit she was disappointed. "Miss Libby can watch me, then. Please, Miss Libby?"

Melting a little, Libby said, "I'd love to!" at the exact same moment that Owen said, "She can't."

Ouch. Owen didn't want her here?

Caitlin looked back and forth between the adults like a spectator at a tennis match. Shaking his head, Owen said, "We can't take up so much of Miss Libby's time. She's got other things to do than drive me around and hang out at Windy Corner."

"But nothing I'd like to do more," Libby declared stoutly, unable to stand it when Caitlin shrugged again, clearly hurt and trying not to show it. If Owen didn't like it, well, he could yell at her later, Libby decided as she climbed out of the car. "Come on, Caitlin, lead the way! Can I say hello to Peony before your lesson starts?"

"Yes. I have to groom her now." Caitlin raced off, her scuffed brown leather paddock boots skidding on the gravel driveway. "Hurry up!"

"You don't have to do this," Owen started, but Libby cut him off by starting after Caitlin.

"I want to. Your sister is probably at work. Caitlin is obviously proud of what she's learning at Windy Corner, and I'm curious to see how she's doing. Besides, it's good for kids to have someone to show off for, every now and then."

Owen's grip on his cane went tight and white-knuckled for a moment as he stared after his daughter, and Libby debated whether to say anything. Maybe it wasn't her place, but in the end—did that matter? All that really mattered was Caitlin and Owen, and their slow, cautious progress toward a relationship.

"The person Caitlin truly wants to impress is her father," Libby said, keeping her tone carefully light and nonjudgmental. "But I'm happy to step in as a poor substitute, since you'll be busy with your physical therapy."

She knew what Owen was struggling with as he walked silently at her side toward the barn. He was a man of honor who felt he had a duty to finish what he and his brothers-in-arms had started, and every day he spent hovering around the fringes of civilian life, he felt like he was shirking that duty. Libby understood that, and she respected it. All she wanted was to remind Owen that he had another duty, to his family and especially to his daughter. She trusted that same sense of honor to tell Owen the right thing to do here.

They entered the barn in silence, broken only by the cheerful welcoming whicker of the horse in the first stall, who stuck his chestnut head over the low half-gate to give them a curious look. The whole place smelled like sweet oats and clean hay, woodsy with sawdust and the evergreen boughs that hung along the main corridor of stalls. Some stalls were decorated with silver tinsel and multicolored twinkle lights, and Libby noticed that each stall had a hand-lettered sign out front with the horse's name and notes about medications and special feeding instructions.

"I'm going to look for Peony's stall," she told Owen, hiding a smile when he fell into step beside her.

"It's at the other end of the barn. I'll meet you down there in a sec—just let me ask if we can push my appointment back so I can watch Caitlin's riding lesson."

"Great idea," Libby said cheerfully, tucking her hands in her pockets and sauntering down the wide corridor. It was nice to be right.

It was even nicer to settle her elbows on the rough wooden crossbeam of Peony's stall door and watch as Caitlin rubbed an oval handleless brush over the mare's dappled coat with an expression of deep concentration. Red dirt and sawdust particles puffed off the horse with every swipe of the bristles.

"Looks like she really needed that brushing," Libby commented, smiling when Caitlin lit up like a candle.

"She gets very dirty out in the pasture," Caitlin said disapprovingly. "Sometimes she rolls around on her back like a dog. Right after we wash her, even! But she doesn't do it to be bad. She can't help it. She's a horse. And she's a good girl. Aren't you, Peony?"

Something about the way the little girl spoke to the horse, tender and nurturing, tugged at Libby's heart. "She *is* a good girl."

"And so are you," Owen said, stepping up behind

Libby to lean one shoulder on the wall beside the stall. "I'm going to watch your lesson, too, if that's okay."

All but vibrating with excitement, Caitlin nevertheless shrugged. Her small features were carefully blank when she said, "Sure. If you want."

"I do." Owen was firm, and Libby was glad he wasn't fooled by Caitlin's elaborate nonchalance.

Caitlin might not be the type of kid who bounced around and waved her arms when she was happy, but from the way she started talking a mile a minute, filling them in on every detail of her grooming routine and what she was learning with Peony, Libby could tell her spirits were high. Cheeks flushed and eyes bright, Caitlin led the pony out of the stall with one small hand conscientiously clutching the reins and keeping them from dragging on the ground so Peony wouldn't trip on them.

Following her out of the barn and down the hill behind it, Libby saw the covered ring for the first time. "This is a nice facility," she commented, impressed with the scope of the sawdust-floored arena with its sets of bleachers so viewers could see over the white oval fence.

"From what I understand, they've put a lot into fixing the place up to accommodate the therapeutic riding program." Owen shaded his eyes and pointed to the left. "There's an open ring over there, smaller and a little less fancy. That's where we've done most of my exercises so far."

"Has it been as touchy-feely as you were worried about?"

"Actually, no." Owen looked thoughtfully down at the cane he was barely leaning on anymore. "We haven't talked about feelings at all, except physical feelings. The exercises work my muscles for real—I'm sore after every session, but I know I'm getting stronger."

A complex rush of emotion squeezed Libby's heart, but "That's wonderful" was all she allowed herself to say.

So you'll be leaving us soon, was all she could think.

At least we still have Christmas, she told herself. *Focus on that. It's the only future you have with this man, who deserves so much more than a woman who's been lying to him since before they even met.*

The sound of Caitlin's paddock boots was muffled on the mixture of sand and loam that carpeted the arena. Owen breathed in the now familiar smells of dust and horse, overlaid with Libby's sweet vanilla scent and the new addition of evergreen boughs bundled into a giant wreath hanging over the arena doors.

Just ahead of them, Caitlin stopped abruptly, blocking the doorway with Peony's placid bulk. Peering over her shoulder, Caitlin gave them a mischievous grin and pointed up. "Ha ha, caught you!"

Libby blinked, as clueless as Owen felt, but when her gaze followed the path of Caitlin's pointing finger, he saw her chest heave in a quick, sharp breath. Craning his neck, Owen peered up at the circlet of greenery trimmed with red and gold bows. "What's up? It's just a wreath."

Clearing her throat, Libby said, "It's not the wreath. It's what's hanging in the middle of it."

Owen looked closer, frowning at the cluster of white berries and teardrop-shaped leaves dangling in the center. "Is that . . . ?"

"Mistletoe!" Caitlin crowed gleefully. "Real life

mistletoe. It's not plastic and if you eat it you'll be sick, the horses, too, so that's why it's up high. Also to catch people and make them kiss! And now you have to kiss Miss Libby!"

Beside him, Libby went still. She wasn't even breathing.

The air between them suddenly felt charged with electricity, like the sky before a thunderstorm. Caitlin had presented him with the possibility he'd been trying to avoid thinking about for days. And now that he'd flashed on the vivid image of himself wrapping Libby in his arms and tasting her candy sweet mouth, he couldn't stop imagining it. Everything low in his body tightened and pulsed, filling him with an animal hunger that howled for satisfaction.

But Owen had worked hard to become the kind of man who could control his animal urges. The beast inside, who'd had free rein when he was a young man angry at the world—that beast was chained now. Owen let it out in the heat of battle, to lead and inspire his men, to keep them safe and whole. The rest of the time, Owen kept the leash taut.

He slowly forced his shoulders to relax, releasing the sensual tension that had held him captive for the space of a heartbeat. He turned to Libby with a half smile, intending to make light of the moment. But when he looked down at her flushed cheeks and bright eyes, Libby didn't look embarrassed. And she didn't look upset or angry or reluctant, either.

She looked as hungry as Owen felt.

He drew in a sharp breath when Libby went up on tiptoes and pressed her lips to his.

Chapter Fifteen

"It's Christmas. We can't disappoint your daughter," Libby whispered against Owen's lips as they parted in surprise. She meant to give him a quick peck, just a brush of their mouths for show more than anything else, but the instant they touched, her mind was swept clean of anything except her need for more.

She wobbled, her knees turning to jelly, and Owen's strong arms came around her shoulders to steady her. His back hit the side of the arena enclosure, his cane falling away, and Libby found herself half leaning on his chest with her arms locked around his neck. Their lips sought and clung together in a sweet, almost chaste kiss that held the promise of so much more. When Libby breathed, she shared Owen's breath. When he breathed, she felt the rise and fall of his powerful chest under her. The nape of his neck was warm beneath her stroking fingertips, and she couldn't stop herself from stretching her fingers up into the short scruff of his buzzed hair.

Desire rolled through her core like a powerful wave, surging and devouring and pulling her under the surface. Owen made a sound deep in his chest that she felt more than heard, and the kiss turned deep and ravenous for a shuddering instant before he stiffened and gently put her back on her feet.

The distance between their heated bodies was only a few inches, but it suddenly felt like an unendurable separation. Libby leaned toward him, her gaze locked on his tempting mouth, but Owen's steady hands on her shoulders kept her from coming closer. She drew in a breath, flavored with cold winter air and the dusty warmth of the barn instead of Owen's smoky essence, and her head cleared.

"I'm sorry!" she gasped, feeling a flood of embarrassed heat scorch her cheeks. "That . . . got a little out of hand."

"Don't apologize." Owen's voice was low, intimate, and it made other parts of Libby's body go hot.

"That was a good one," Caitlin commented, sounding impressed. "Most people just kiss on the cheek or the back of the lady's hand like a princess or something."

Libby had to laugh, covering her eyes with one of her unkissed hands. "Oh my gosh."

"Glad you approve," Owen said to his daughter as he stooped to retrieve his walking stick. "Now what about this riding lesson I've been hearing so much about?"

Owen followed Caitlin further into the arena. Grateful for the way he'd managed to redirect Caitlin's attention, Libby hung back a moment to collect her wits—and to cement the memory of Owen's kiss in her mind. Her fingertips drifted up to trace her lips, sensitive and a little plump from the pressure of his mouth, and she shivered in the weak winter sunlight filtering through the trees. She needed to remember how it had felt to be the center of Owen's world for that too short moment, because it could never happen again. She didn't deserve it, and he wouldn't want her if he knew the truth.

Blowing out a breath, Libby pulled up a determined smile and plastered it on her face before marching into the arena to spend a torturous hour sitting close to Owen's side and watching Caitlin ride her pony around the ring.

For the first half hour, every movement, every breath, every accidental brush of Owen's arm against hers, had Libby's pulse racing. But eventually she managed to force her attention off of the tension between her and Owen by focusing on Caitlin with all her might. The little girl displayed a fierce concentration while on horseback. She listened to her instructor's comments and directions as if the fate of the world hung on her ability to urge Peony from a walk to a trot while doing something called "posting."

"She's got so much focus," Libby observed to Owen in an undertone while Caitlin set her jaw and worked to catch her horse's rhythm while lifting herself out of the saddle in time with Peony's strides. "I haven't spent a ton of time around kids her age, but aren't most of them more scattered than this?"

"Not necessarily." Owen leaned forward, resting his elbows on his knees and keeping his unwavering gaze on his daughter. "I was an unholy mess after my mom died, too much energy and too many rules, but if it was something I cared about—I could lock in on it for hours without getting bored or distracted."

It was the first time Libby had heard Owen talk about his childhood. Intrigued, she pushed for more. "What kinds of things made you lock in?"

Owen laughed a little, but it wasn't a completely happy sound. "There was a fire station down the street from the house where I grew up, and I used to sneak off and hang out there. Looking back, the guys who manned the truck might not have loved having a kid underfoot all the time, but they were cool. They'd let me climb around the fire truck with them, inspecting the rig. The best were the days when they decided to wash the truck. I'd come home soaking wet and get the hiding of my life from Dad, but it was worth it."

Libby's heart clenched. "Was he worried when he didn't know where you were?"

"Nah." Owen's hands curled into fists, then flexed open again as if he didn't know he was doing it. "My old man was a cop. All the men in our family were, going back generations. He took that dumb rivalry between cops and firefighters seriously. Hell, probably half the reason I ran off to the firehouse was because I knew it would piss him off. But when I was there, it was funny— I'd forget all about whatever was going on at home. There was something about being around those guys, who'd go from relaxed and joking around to being ready to risk their lives at a moment's notice."

"So you wanted to be a fireman when you grew up."

"Probably it's more accurate to say I didn't want to be a cop," Owen said, shaking his head at his younger self. "But not for any good reason. The force is a calling, and the men and women who serve that way are amazing. It would have been an honor to serve with them, but I didn't see it that way at the time. All I could see was that it was what my dad expected of me. What I wanted didn't factor into the equation at all, as far as he was concerned. So of course, I had to rebel."

"You don't have any regrets, do you?" Libby was wistful. She'd give anything to be able to live a live without regrets or shame. "It seems like you felt the calling to serve and protect people—just in a different way, in the army."

"I don't regret joining up. The service took a hotheaded idiot of a kid and turned me into someone I can face in the mirror every morning."

A sudden flash of insight hit Libby. "You think if you're not in the army anymore, you'll go back to being who you were before you enlisted? I don't believe that. The things we do and see and experience—those things change us for good. Or bad, sometimes, but permanently."

Heaven knew, she wished that wasn't the case. But she knew that it was. The lies she'd told, the lie she was living, had tarnished her forever.

"Nothing is permanent," Owen countered. "The only thing you can count on is that everything changes over time. And since I got my medical discharge, I've definitely felt different. Like a boat without an anchor, set loose to drift. The only thing giving me direction right now is the idea of getting back where I belong."

Libby glanced over at him. His eyes were trained on his daughter, his entire body canted forward as if he were riding the horse along with her, and Libby's heart fluttered up into her throat. "Maybe you belong here."

She's married. She's not free. Separated isn't the same as divorced.

Owen kept the litany going in the back of his mind. It was the only thing preventing him from snugging her close to his side, reeling her in for another of those mind-tilting, addictive kisses.

He reminded himself that Libby wasn't for him—no matter how much this conversation made him wish otherwise. And no matter how much it seemed like Libby might want the same thing. He couldn't lead her on. There could be nothing more cruel than letting her think there was any possibility of a future with him.

"I wouldn't begin to know how to make a life some-place like this," he told her. If there was a note of regret in his voice, he couldn't help that. Part of him wished he had what it took to be a husband, a father, a family man—but all the softness had been burned out of him years ago, and he was better off without it.

But despite her outward softness, there was a core of steel to Libby too. A stubborn light glinting in her eye, she tilted up her chin and said, "There's nothing to know. You don't have to qualify or pass some test. You just stay. The rest will work itself out."

Something sharp slid into Owen's heart like a bayonet, piercing him through. "I can't stay," he snapped back. "That's not who I am."

Libby stiffened at his harsh tone, but she didn't back off, and against his will, Owen felt a tendril of respect uncurl in his gut.

"But maybe you want to stay," Libby replied, her hazel eyes dark with understanding. "And that's what scares you. Because you don't know who you are without the army—and I'm telling you, the army might have made a man out of you, but so will being a father to that little girl."

Before he knew what he was about to do, Owen was on his feet. Without glancing back at Libby, he started climbing down off the bleachers. *Running away,* said the taunting voice in the back of his head—the voice that sounded an awful damn lot like his father's. *Running away like you always do.*

Libby called after him, regret clear in her voice, and Owen paused long enough to say over his shoulder, "One kiss doesn't give you the right to tell me what to do with my life, Libby. Tell Caitlin I had to leave for my physical therapy appointment. It's time I got back to work."

Nash poked his head in the door and scanned the Firefly Café for glossy black hair and a red-lipped smile. There—back corner, lounging in the red vinyl booth and wearing a denim jacket and a bright purple headsscarf over her curls. Ivy Dawson tended to stick out in a crowd. She lived her life in vibrant color, making the rest of the world look like shades of beige. Nash had been drawn to her from the first moment he set eyes on her at a bar in Atlanta.

It wasn't the kind of place he usually went. There were more motorcycles than sports cars out front, and inside, the place was loud, smoky, and more than a little rough around the edges.

She'd laughed at his button-down Oxford blue shirt, he remembered, and accused him of slumming it. He'd denied it, but there was a grain of truth there. Nash Tucker didn't spend a lot of time in biker bars listening to honky tonk music and drinking cheap beer.

After the scandal of his parents' forced marriage and his father's desertion, Nash had learned early on that the smoothest path through life involved making no waves and breaking no rules. He got good grades, played varsity baseball, went to a good college, and did his level best to never be the reason his mother came home from church or a PTA function with furious, humiliated tears sparkling in her lashes.

It was a small town, and people had long memories. Nash understood why his mother had left it behind—even though it had been weird to come "home" from college on breaks to a condo in Atlanta instead of the big white house he'd grown up in. There was something peaceful about the anonymity of a big city after the scrutiny of small town life. Nash had pretended to be happy to be done with Sanctuary Island, because that's what his mother wanted.

Story of his life. He knew what was expected of him, and he didn't rebel.

At least, not often. That night out at the Lucky Strike had been one of Nash's secret rebellions . . . and it had brought him Ivy.

Who was giving him a very unwelcoming glare from her corner booth. Ignoring her for the moment, Nash stepped into the café and smiled around at the people waving and grinning at him. He shook hands and asked after families and caught up with old friends from high school, but all the time he made his way steadily toward the back of the restaurant where Ivy was sitting.

When he'd finally clapped the last acquaintance on the back, Nash slid into the booth across from Ivy without waiting for an invitation. From the way she frowned, he had a feeling he would've been waiting for a long time.

"Make yourself at home," she said, sarcasm oozing from her tone like bittersweet honey.

"I am at home," Nash pointed out, kicking back and stretching his arms across the back of the booth. "This is where I grew up. What I don't understand is what you're doing here."

"You said you were never going to come back to Sanctuary Island. I figured that made this the best place in the world to avoid you."

Nash winced. "Okay, I guess I deserved that."

To his surprise, Ivy shook her head regretfully. "No, you didn't. That was mean. Even if it was basically true, it's only part of the truth."

"What's the rest?"

She shrugged, the quick, restless movement he remembered from all their arguments at the end. "The way you talked about your hometown, you made it sound impossibly idyllic and perfect. I guess I wanted to see it for myself, to see if Sanctuary Island was as big an illusion as you turned out to be."

Nash ignored the jab, intent on keeping Ivy talking. "But then you stayed here. You got a job. You put down roots."

"Don't act like me putting down roots is such a shock," Ivy bristled.

"You never wanted to before," Nash felt compelled to point out. "Isn't that basically why we broke up? I wanted to settle down, and you didn't."

Two blotches of red appeared on Ivy's pale cheeks, as if she'd been slapped. She'd always hated how her skin telegraphed her emotions that way, but Nash was grateful for it. Sometimes it was the only warning he had before the storm broke.

This time, the storm was delayed for a few seconds by the ancient waitress, Flo, slamming down Ivy's order and tersely offering to refill her coffee before she zoomed off to deliver more plates.

Ivy didn't even glance down at the slice of pecan pie as big as her head. "That might be what you told yourself about our breakup," she hissed, "but there was a lot more to it than that, and I think you know it."

"Honestly?" Nash crossed his arms over his chest. "I don't. I never really understood why we broke up, except that you got pissed at me and stopped taking my calls. And then you disappeared and no one seemed to know where you'd gone, only that you'd left Atlanta."

Her eyes narrowed as she leaned in, nearly planting her elbow in her pie. "And exactly how hard did you try to find me, Nash? How many people did you ask? Because I'm betting it wasn't very many. I'm betting you didn't want anyone to know I'd dumped you and moved away. That would tarnish your perfect image."

"You're so stuck on that." Nash shook his head in aggravation. "I don't get it."

"Because it's a state of being for you, not something to get," Ivy retorted. "But I'm not interested in living a life that's all style and no substance."

"Really? You dress like you care a lot about style."

Smoothing a satisfied hand over the fuzzy angora sweater that clung lovingly to her curves, Ivy tossed back her curls. "So I like to look good, and I like to have a good time. That doesn't mean I can't be serious about some things. The things that matter."

"I thought I was one of those things that mattered."

She looked away. "You made it clear, over and over, that it wasn't mutual."

"I don't even know what that means." Nash's stomach curdled, his chest going tight. "It was good between us, Ivy. You know it was."

Ivy tapped her fork against the pie plate and gazed at him. There was a sheen of something like pity in her wide eyes, and it was the worst look Nash had ever seen on her expressive face. "I liked you, Nash. Loved you, even. But you weren't ready for anything real back in Atlanta, and you still aren't. Despite what your poor wife might have thought when she agreed to marry you."

"Libby and I are separated," Nash blurted out in a last ditch effort to salvage this conversation. "That's what I came over here to tell you. It's official—but we're still friends. We're going to get a divorce soon."

"That's too bad," Ivy said, heartless and firm. "Libby seems like a very nice woman. And I'd like for you to be happy, Nash. I really would."

The only person who's ever made me happy is you.

But the words stuck in his throat, sharp as stones, and Nash couldn't force them out. Maybe Ivy was right. Maybe he was too hung up on what people would think or how it would look, but he'd learned the importance of toeing the line at a very young age. It was hard to overcome the habits of a lifetime.

"I want you to be happy, too," he finally said, low and hoarse. "I wish I was the kind of man who could make you happy. I think I could, if you'd let me try."

For a brief, heart-stopping moment, Ivy hesitated, as if she were wavering. But when she spoke, there was no hesitation in her tone. "We did try, Nash. And we discovered that I need someone who's willing to put himself out there, to tell the world how he feels about me—even if I don't fit his image of the perfect ladylike wife for perfect Nash Tucker."

With that, Ivy got up and tucked a ten-dollar bill under her plate. She walked out of the cafe, leaving Nash sitting defeated at the corner booth, staring at her untouched pecan pie. Sighing, he pulled it closer and picked up her discarded fork. No point letting good pie go to waste.

But even the taste of brown sugar, buttered pecans, and flaky crust couldn't sweeten the bitter disappointment and regret filling Nash's belly. He wasn't thinking about the conversation they'd just had, though. His mind took him further back, to the night when Ivy had asked to meet his family and he'd told her he was never going home to Sanctuary Island.

"Why not?" She'd blinked those big eyes up at him from where her head was pillowed on his bare shoulder.

Twitching a corner of the blanket higher to cover their naked, entwined bodies, Nash had smoothed his hand through the tousled waves of her hair and shrugged. "It's a small town, and my family is kind of a big deal there.

If I go back, I'd have to face all those people who knew me as a kid, who knew my parents—the expectations they had for me. It's too much. Too many people whispering about how I'm not living up to my potential or how they always knew I'd never amount to much. Can't we just stay here, doing our own thing, where no one will judge us?"

She'd gone still and quiet under his stroking hand, and he'd blinked drowsily into the darkness and slipped into sleep without finishing the conversation. But it wasn't long after that night that Ivy packed her bags and left the apartment she'd practically moved into with him, and now Nash wondered . . . did Ivy think he was ashamed of her? Did she think that was why he wouldn't take her home to meet his family?

Chapter Sixteen

Libby waited until the end of Caitlin's lesson only to be told by a barn worker that Owen would be catching a ride home with his sister and having dinner over there. Aching with regret and hurt, Libby climbed into her car and started the drive back to her grandfather's house alone.

She hadn't meant to upset Owen so much, but at the same time, she couldn't be sorry for pointing out that there was another path he could at least consider. One that might not let him be a hero to his men, but would make him the hero of his daughter's story . . . and who had more of a claim on Owen than Caitlin?

Libby was still turning it over and over in her mind obsessively when her cell phone rang. A sharp pang of foreboding pierced her chest when she glanced down at the screen and saw her boss's name flash across it.

Pulling over to the side of the narrow country road, Libby stared out over the expanse of brown cordgrass waving out toward the ocean as she steeled herself. Then she answered her phone.

"Mr. Downing? Hello."

"Great news," her publisher said briskly. "I've secured us some extra publicity for the Christmas article you're doing with that war hero."

A chill skittered down Libby's spine. "Extra publicity?"

"On Christmas day, I'm bringing a camera crew from the *Good Morning Show* to your house to shoot some video of the meal, maybe a couple of sound bites from the soldier and the kid. Rhonda Friend is coming in person to do the interviews."

He actually sounded pleased. Libby felt faint. "Mr. Downing, I can't agree to this."

"It's only B-roll for a short follow-up piece," Downing said, impatient. "Not an in-depth documentary or something. Just wear something pretty, smile a lot, and fake it. You're good at that."

"I'm really not, though," Libby protested. "Writing is one thing—I can use my imagination. But no amount of imagination is going to make this meal anything but a disaster. Having a TV journalist there to document the whole thing is going to be *terrible* publicity."

"There's no such thing as terrible publicity," Downing countered ruthlessly. "All publicity is good publicity. That said, I expect you to carry this off. Remember our deal. I looked into that uncle you told me about. Ray, wasn't it? With early onset Alzheimer's. A diagnosis like that, at his age—just tragic. And it means round-the-clock care for the rest of his life. That kind of thing is pretty pricey, Ms. Leeds. I would keep that in mind when Rhonda Friend shows up with her cameras."

Downing hung up before Libby could control her quick, shallow breaths enough to answer. A camera crew scanning around, zooming in on every tiny expression and catching her every mistake—and there were sure to be plenty of mistakes. Libby had been practicing, but every time she set foot in the kitchen there seemed to be some sort of catastrophe.

There has to be a way out of this mess. Slumping, she bonked her forehead on the steering wheel hard enough to honk the car horn. The noise startled her into sitting up, blinking and dazzled by the brightness of the fading afternoon light.

Across the amber sea of dried grasses and spiky underbrush, the sandy beach spread out in a wavy line along the shore. The sky and the water were the palest of blues, almost gray—a perfect backdrop for the band of horses grazing at the edge of the beach. Their shaggy winter coats looked soft, their tangled manes and tails blowing in the salty breeze off the ocean.

The leader of the band, a stallion who stood taller than the mares around him by at least a hand, was staring back at Libby. His regal head was pitched high, scenting the wind as if her car honking was a signal of potential danger to him and his herd.

Libby sat frozen, caught by the wild beauty of the stallion and his strong protective instincts. He'd do anything to keep his family safe, she knew it in her heart. How could Libby do any less?

Half an hour later she was standing at the door of her grandfather's study and calling up the memory of the proud tilt of the stallion's head to bolster her courage.

Deep breaths, she told herself as nerves prickled along her hairline and down the slope of her back. Pressing her palms flat to the heavy oak door, she pushed her way into the quiet, bookshelf-lined room.

Dabney Leeds' inner sanctuary was full of antique furniture and carpeted with fading Persian rugs. Oil paintings of ships at sea and fog wreathing the Blue Ridge Mountains hung on the walls, but she had to squint to make out the lines of the art because the heavy velvet drapes were closed over the floor-to-ceiling windows. An unlit Tiffany glass lamp sat next to her grandfather's leather reading chair by the fireplace, which was cold and empty.

Libby frowned into the dim room. "Grandfather?"

Something stirred in the reading chair, and as her eyes grew accustomed to the shadows, she saw the old man huddled in his chair with a book open on his lap and a dark wool plaid blanket covering his legs. "Yes. What is it?" he asked, his voice creaky as if he hadn't spoken in a while.

Worry clutched at Libby's chest and she forgot her nerves. "Is everything all right?" she asked, hurrying into the room and pulling a spindly, straight-backed chair over to sit beside her grandfather.

"Of course." He scowled irritably and picked up his book, as if he wanted to make sure she saw that he'd been reading.

Except Libby was willing to bet he hadn't turned a page in ages. "It's dark in here. Can I turn on your lamp for you?"

"I can manage it myself," he said crossly, reaching across to the side table with a trembling hand. "I'm not an invalid, you know."

"I do know that," Libby assured him, sitting on her hands to keep herself from fussing with his blanket or trying to help with the lamp. "You're amazingly self-sufficient, and you've done so much to take care of me since I got here. Won't you let me take care of you, even a little?"

A tiny bit of softness relaxed Dabney's pinched mouth, but it tightened up into a dissatisfied purse as he said, "I haven't done the best job of it so far, hiring that French lunatic. What a disaster! Nearly ruined the whole thing."

He pressed a fist to his sternum as if he didn't realize he was doing it. Concerned, Libby inched her chair further into the circle of mellow, warm light cast by the stained-glass lamp. "You thought she would help, though. The fact that you tried means a lot to me."

"There's no point to trying if you fail."

The harsh words shoved Libby back in her chair like he'd pushed a hand against her forehead. "Do you really believe that?"

Dabney settled deeper under his lap blanket, a morose expression pulling at his lined, weathered face. "When you get to be as old as I am, missy, you'll see the value in not wasting any effort."

Libby was starting to get a better idea of how her grandfather had alienated his entire family. It made her think twice about asking him for help on Uncle Ray's behalf, especially knowing how much Ray would hate it. She bit her lip.

Maybe if she made it seem like the money was for her, she'd feel less guilty about ignoring her uncle's wishes. "Grandfather. There is a way you could help me."

"Oh?" He perked up a little, and Libby's heart constricted. Yes, he could be grumpy and demanding, critical and too quick with a harsh word—but how could anyone miss the fact that Dabney Leeds would do anything for the people he loved?

"Yes," Libby said with more confidence. "There's this health issue that . . . that I have. It's ongoing and—oh, don't worry, it's not life threatening! But it does require specialized treatment. Expensive medications. That kind of thing."

The concern faded from Dabney's face to be replaced by a disconcerting look of calculation. "So that's why you agreed to this charade. You need money."

"That's part of it," Libby said honestly, surreptitiously crossing her fingers that he wouldn't ask too many questions about the medical issue.

"But now that you're here, and you see how I live and how important our family is on the island, you think maybe there's an easier way to get that money." Dabney planted his feet on the floor and clutched at his cane to help him stand up. "Well, too bad. I'm not giving you a red cent just so you can scoot on out of here and never speak to me again!"

"Grandfather!" Libby reached out to steady him, her skin prickling with humiliation and regret. "That's not what I meant—I don't want to leave, and I certainly have no intention of cutting you off."

"Well, I'm not giving you the chance," Dabney yelled,

jerking free of Libby's helping hands and hobbling to wrench open the door. "You're sticking around through Christmas, like we agreed, and that's final."

She flinched at the slam of the door behind him and all the air that seemed sucked out of the room with him. Shoulders drooping, Libby pressed her hands to her eyes and wondered how that conversation went so very wrong.

Owen had never understood people who refused to apologize for anything. He'd known a lot of guys like that in the army—men who thought that saying they were sorry, that they'd been wrong, was the same as admitting a weakness. Owen's father had been like that.

But in Owen's experience, a sincere apology could clear the air and give two people a whole new foundation to build on. It was a mark of strength, not weakness, to own up to mistakes and commit to doing better. And it had the added tactical advantage of taking most people off guard. Owen had no issues with apologizing when he'd screwed up.

And today, he'd screwed up big time.

The ravaged muscle in his upper thigh knotted with pain as he stumped down the hall toward the light spilling out from under the study door. He'd worked hard in his physical therapy session. Maybe a little too hard. It was possible he'd been punishing himself.

Grimacing, Owen kneaded at the clenched muscle, but he didn't falter in his mission. He had to tell Libby he was sorry for biting her head off and shutting her out.

But when he shouldered open the study door, all he

could manage to say was, "What's wrong? Are you all right?"

Libby lifted her head from her hands, tear tracks shining on her cheeks for a moment before she turned away to hide her face. "I'm fine. I mean, I'll be okay in a minute."

You don't have to stay, said her hunched shoulders and averted gaze. But Owen watched her carelessly scrub the backs of her hands over her damp cheeks and he could no more have left the room than he could have stopped his next heartbeat. The aches and pains in his leg and hip vanished in the rush of adrenaline that got him across the floor and next to Libby in seconds.

"Please don't cry," he said, low and sincere. He reached out a hand to smooth her tousled hair, but drew it back before he could touch her. If she was crying over what he'd said to her . . . "I hate how I talked to you, back at the barn. I'm the one who invited you into my family drama and took advantage of your generosity in helping us through the holiday. You have every right to your opinions."

Libby's shoulders straightened and she lifted her face to his with a defiant tilt of her chin. "I'm not crying over you," she told him with great dignity. "Well, okay, that didn't help—but I know the stress you're under. The choice you have to make is pulling you to pieces. I get why you're on edge about it."

"None of that excuses the way I spoke to you," Owen said firmly, ignoring the ball of relief expanding under his lungs at the fact that she'd stopped crying. "But if you're not upset about our fight, what's going on? If there's any way I can help you, I will."

To Owen's dismay, that made the moisture well up in Libby's eyes all over again. She made a face and dashed at the tears caught in her lower lashes. "Oof. Once I start, it's hard to stop. Thank you, Owen. You don't know how much that means to me. But it's just . . . what did you call it? Family drama."

Flipping his cane up and around like a baton, Owen used the crook end to hook the leg of the armchair and drag it closer. He sat down, close enough to Libby that their knees kissed. "My guys tell me I'm a pretty good listener."

"Oh, it's only . . ."—she ran a distracted hand through her hair, tumbling the curls around—"grandfather. He's so stubborn and so sure everyone in his life wants to leave him. Which, to be fair, a lot of people in his life *have* left—but that's partly because he runs them off!"

Owen frowned, juggling the family relationships in his mind. Wasn't Dabney Leeds *Nash's* grandfather, making him Libby's grandfather by marriage only? But maybe that didn't matter to someone as loving and family-oriented as Libby. "What did he do this time?"

"Oh, it's all a mess." Drooping like a poinsettia after too many days without water, Libby rested her elbow on the arm of her chair and propped her forehead on her palm. "Family secrets and longstanding fights . . . I hate secrets. How have I gotten myself embroiled in so many of them?"

Was there more than the secret of her separation from Nash? Owen understood their reasoning for keeping it from Dabney Leeds, up to a point, but not if it was upsetting Libby to this extent. "Tell me what to do."

Despair shook her voice. "I'm not sure there's anything anyone can do. Some problems are too big, too entrenched to solve. Families can get like that, don't you think? Hard as rock, unchangeable."

Owen thought about his family—the years he'd spent estranged from his father, and how distant he'd allowed himself to become from his sister, even though she'd done nothing wrong other than to exist as a reminder of the family Owen had left behind. "But families can change," he said slowly. "In the most unexpected ways, and in the blink of an eye. Andie and I lost touch for a long time, but a daughter I didn't even know I had brought us back together. And now that we're talking again . . . it's rough, but being honest with each other is the only way we're going to keep this going."

"I want to be honest with everyone," Libby cried. "I feel so . . . trapped." Another tear slipped unnoticed down her flushed cheek, and Owen couldn't hold back. He reached out, cupped her soft jawline and brushed the tear away with his thumb. Libby caught her breath with a sweet gasp that went to Owen's head like a shot of whiskey.

"So be honest," he told her, leaning in close. "Get yourself free of whatever's holding you down. There's a whole world waiting for you."

A spasm of something like fear tightened Libby's features, but it was the pure longing in her eyes that wrapped itself around Owen's heart and refused to let go. "I want to," she gasped. "Oh, please believe me, I do want to. But there's more at stake than just what I want for myself. There are other people to consider . . ."

Fire lit under Owen's breastbone, tightening every muscle and filling his lungs. "Oh, yeah? What about what I want, then?"

Libby's lips parted, and Owen surrendered to his burning need to kiss her senseless.

Chapter Seventeen

Desire stole Libby's mind. She forgot how to breathe. She forgot that she needed to breathe. All she knew was the deep, consuming passion of Owen's mouth against hers, his fingers sliding into her hair and raking gently across her scalp, the crush of her soft curves against his hard-muscled chest.

Owen Shepard was everything she'd ever wanted in a man, a combination of elements from every girlish daydream and every adult fantasy Libby had entertained in her entire, fairy tale–loving life—except Owen was the real thing.

And of course, she'd ruined her chances with him before she'd even met him. The memory of her deception was like a dash of cold water in the face. Libby pulled back, regret and shame heavy on her chest.

She saw that same regret and shame reflected in Owen's deep blue-green eyes. "Damn it," he cursed, drawing himself up rigidly straight. Libby missed his hands on her as soon as they were gone.

"My self control is usually better than that," Owen told her, anger at himself roughening his voice.

Fretful and full of remorse, Libby wrapped her arms around her ribcage. "Don't blame yourself. Please, Owen. You haven't done anything wrong."

His jaw went as hard as granite. "It doesn't matter how much I want you—and I do want you, Libby. But we can't always get what we want. I know better. You might be separated, but you're still married in the eyes of God and the law. It *was* wrong."

His lip curled, all his scorn and recriminations directed inward at himself, and Libby couldn't stand it. He'd offered to help so many times—maybe that would extend to not blowing her story publically and maybe it wouldn't. But she couldn't let him hate himself for a sin he hadn't even committed.

"Owen." Libby took a deep, calming breath and forced herself to meet his dark gaze. "I have something to tell you."

His lip curled. "Is it something about how we're adults and we ought to have a better handle on our impulse control? Because I know that already."

"No." Libby clasped her hands in her lap to still their trembling. "It's about me. Who I am, I mean."

Owen's harsh expression softened. "You're Libby Leeds. And you might be stuck in a bad situation, but you're a good person."

Every word flicked over Libby's raw nerves like the tip of a whip, and she flinched. "I'm not," she said raggedly, determined to get through this. "I promise, if you listen to what I'm about to tell you, then you'll agree with me."

He sat back in his chair, one hand absently rubbing at his wounded leg. "Okay, shoot. But I reserve the right to disagree on whether or not you're wonderful."

Libby couldn't take it anymore. She met his gaze squarely and said, "I'm not married. I never have been."

Owen's hand went still, his entire body going from loose to taut in a single moment. "What do you mean?" he questioned tensely. "Who the hell is Nash, then, if he's not your husband?"

"Nash is my cousin. A cousin who, until two weeks ago, I hadn't seen in more than a decade." Libby gulped in air, hoping this would get easier as she went along. "Don't blame him, or my grandfather, for the deception—I begged for their help."

Shaking his head as if he had water in his ears, Owen knit his brows. "I don't get it. I mean, I'm glad—I think?—but I don't get the point of telling everyone you were married when you aren't."

"It's all gotten so out of hand," Libby said, knowing that was a pathetic excuse. "I guess I should start at the beginning. My parents died in a car crash when I was about Caitlin's age—that part is true. Before that, we lived here. But after they died, my uncle Ray became my guardian, and I moved to New York to live with him. He's estranged from Grandfather, so until two weeks ago, I'd never been back to Sanctuary Island . . . except in my dreams. It's always represented home for me, and a couple of years ago when Uncle Ray first got sick, I started fooling around with an idea for a novel based on my memories of growing up here. I wrote a bunch of

short fiction pieces imagining how my life might have
gone if I lived here. I imagined a home and a family, a
loving husband and a warm kitchen, a chicken coop out
back—it was a fantasy. Just for me, you know? But I put
the pieces up on a blog, and somehow people started
reading them. I don't know why they caught on, and it
wasn't until an editor at the magazine called me out of
the blue that I even realized people thought . . . it was
all true."

Every one of Owen's limbs had stiffened until he
looked like a bronze statue of an avenging warrior, furious eyes burning in his impassive face. "But it wasn't."

A tight, painful lump choked its way into Libby's
throat. "No, it wasn't. And I wanted to come clean right
away, to explain everything to the editor . . . but Uncle
Ray had gotten worse. We went to a couple of different
specialists, and they all confirmed the diagnosis of early
onset Alzheimer's. He needed a lot of help, and we were
okay on our own for a while, but ultimately he needed
a lot more care than I could give him. I wanted to hire
a nurse, but the apartment was too small—no place to
put her—and in one of his lucid moments, Uncle Ray
basically demanded that I find an assisted-living facility for him. He hated being dependent, hated feeling like
he was holding me back and keeping me at home with
him, and no matter how much I argued or pointed out
that I hadn't exactly been a party girl before he got sick,
he wouldn't listen."

"So you let him go." Owen's statement was neutral,
not a hint of judgment, but the guilt and doubts that
still haunted Libby about her decisions swirled to the
surface.

"I had to respect his wishes," she said, hearing the pleading note in her own voice but unable to cover it up. "He has so few choices left, so little ability to decide how he wants to live as his mind lets him down more and more every day—how could I ignore him when he was so clear about his wishes?"

"You couldn't. But let me guess at the next part." Owen's mouth was stiff, barely moving with his words. Only his eyes, bright with anger and betrayal, gave away his feelings. "The assisted-living place was pricey. And the editor made you an offer you couldn't refuse."

"Of course I could have refused. I'm not trying to make excuses for what I've done—I made the choices all along the way, and I'll live with the consequences. But if you'll let me, I would like to explain why I did what I did."

Owen leaned forward to rest his elbows on his knees. His hands were curled into fists, but he appeared to make a conscious effort to relax them. "Fine," he said shortly. "Explain yourself."

It was a clear challenge, and Libby did her best not to rise to it. Defensiveness wouldn't help her here. Besides, she had no defense. She'd done wrong, and she knew it.

"I accepted the editor's offer because I needed the money. I looked at every assisted-living place and nursing home in driving distance of Queens—it had to be close enough for me to visit—and . . . Owen, you wouldn't believe how sad most of those places are. Under-funded, understaffed, joyless, and hopeless. I couldn't bear to see the man who took me in and raised me like I was his own locked up in a place like that. But

Sunnyside Gardens is different. Every resident gets a private room—at most places, they have to share—and not only that, but at Sunnyside, they're allowed to keep pets. For Uncle Ray, that was huge. He couldn't remember who I was, most days, but he never forgot his cockatoo, Buster."

The lump in Libby's throat broke open, strangling her with a sob. "He loves that stupid bird. And I absolutely believe that taking care of Buster is helping Uncle Ray. That one chore, and the joy he feels when Buster perches on his shoulder and nips at his ear—those things are like pathways back to who Uncle Ray really is. It's so important—and Sunnyside was the only place that not only allowed but encouraged pets. The nurses there are incredible. They sit and talk with him, they play with Buster and help keep his cage clean, they call me every couple of days with updates on how he's doing. I couldn't put a price on that kind of care."

"But there is a price," Owen guessed quietly. "And it's a steep one."

Libby nodded, her heart feeling as fragile as a cracked crystal vase. "A price I had to pay, because Uncle Ray never made a lot of money and he refused—categorically refused—to let me ask his family for help. He doesn't want his father to know what's going on, and he would absolutely hate knowing that I'm here, and that I almost caved and asked Grandfather for money. But I don't know what else to do. This has all turned into such a huge mess. I never wanted to build my life on a lie, but somehow, that's exactly what I did. And even though I told myself it was a victimless crime, that I wasn't hurting anyone by writing those stories about my imaginary husband and our imaginary, perfect life together—I hated it."

Owen stood in a rush of controlled power and unconscious grace. The banked fires in his eyes flared to furious life. "You did hurt people with your lies, Libby. You hurt all the people who read your column and believed in you. But what I don't think I can forgive is that you hurt my daughter. Caitlin is slow to trust. I should know. But she trusted you almost immediately, and you got her hopes up sky high about this fantasy Christmas of yours."

His jaw clenched, his fingers white-knuckled on the handle of his cane. "Turns out, everything about you is a fantasy. A fairy tale you wrote, casting yourself as the heroine, and somehow you got the whole world believing it. But real life is no fairy tale, Libby. In real life, people get hurt. It's hard to tell who's the heroine and who's the villain. And there's no happy ending."

He strode toward the door, and words fluttered up into Libby's mouth like birds, flapping frantically to get out. But she swallowed them down and kept her lips tightly shut and let Owen Shepard walk out of her life. Because now he knew the truth, and it was his choice whether to forgive her or not.

How could Libby expect Owen to forgive her when she couldn't forgive herself?

Alone in the study, Libby sighed and allowed her shoulders to slump in despair. But despair wasn't going to get the twinkle lights on the tree or get the menu finalized for the big meal on Christmas Day. There was a lot to do, and not a lot of time to do it in.

Get up, Libby told herself firmly. *Get. Up.*

And with a deep breath in, she did. But all the joy had gone out of the season. Her soul felt as barren and bleak as the steel gray sky over the skeletal pines outside the study window.

What was the point of all this anymore? She'd utterly failed to put her family back together—and in the process, she'd managed to make a good man feel like a bad person. And then she'd made him hate her.

Maybe the best thing she could do for everyone was exactly what her grandfather expected of her. Maybe she should leave and let them all forget she ever existed.

"I just can't believe she'd do a thing like this," Owen finished his rant to Andie while his sister calmly stacked dirty dishes in her sink.

"I'm not sure why you're so shocked," she finally said, wiping her hands on a towel printed with sunflowers. "You hardly know this woman."

"That's true." Owen frowned. It didn't feel true, though. "I guess I thought we shared something."

"Maybe you did. Just because she was lying about one thing doesn't mean she's lying about everything."

Owen paused, narrowing his eyes on his sister. "Wait a second. Who are you, and what have you done with my rule-following, law-loving, truth-telling sister?"

"Shut up. I'm still me, just . . . with a few more shades of gray."

"Ugh, if that's some subtle reference to your sex life with Sam . . ."

Andie lobbed the dishtowel at Owen's head, laughing when he ducked. "My sex life is none of your business, thank you very much. But I guess you could say that Sam is at least partially responsible for my new perspective. He never lied to me about who he was, but there was a big secret he was keeping when he first showed up on Sanctuary Island. When I found out about it, I had a choice. I could either follow the letter of the law . . . or I could recognize that human beings are complicated, and sometimes they do the wrong thing for the right reasons."

Owen thought about the way Libby's bottom lip had quivered when she talked about her uncle's terrifying disease. He couldn't imagine what it would be like to lose himself like that, bit by bit and day by day, until the man Owen had worked so hard to become was gone. "I get why Libby started down this path. What I don't understand is why she couldn't tell me the truth from the start. I would've helped her."

"She couldn't know that for sure," Andie pointed out. "And it's not all about her. It sounds like she was juggling a lot of different people's wishes and best interests . . . while putting her own dead last, most of the time."

There were scuffs in the linoleum under Owen's boots, and the wooden table he occupied in the breakfast nook was scarred and had a distinct wobble. But the kitchen in Andie's small house on Sanctuary Island felt cozy and warm, welcoming in a way that reminded Owen of what it had been like when their mother was alive. Some of it came from the rekindled family connection, but a lot of it was about how happy Andie was here.

"You made the right choice," Owen told her. "This is a good life you've built here with Sam and Caitlin."

Andie sank into the chair across the table from him, stretching out her hand to prod his arm. "Thanks. I want you to have a happy life too, you know. For a while there, I wondered if you might find it with Libby Leeds."

"Even though she was married—or so we thought? Scandalous."

"Hmm. I never totally bought into that marriage to Nash Tucker, anyway," Andie claimed, sitting back in her chair and crossing her arms over her chest decisively. "Nash has the hots for my best friend, and she's not the kind of woman a man gets over."

"Wait. Are you saying you knew the marriage was a sham?"

"No, just that I wouldn't have given them good odds on making it to the end of the year still hitched. And as events have proved, I was right. So tell me this, Owen. Are you actually angry at Libby for deceiving you . . . or are you running scared because now you know that you have a real shot with her?"

Owen sat up straight. "Holy sh—don't hold back, sis! Tell me what's really on your mind."

The smug satisfaction of an older sibling who still knew how to rattle her baby bro brightened Andie's smile. "That's pretty much it. Did you even stay to hear her whole explanation, or did you jet out of there as if she'd lit your socks on fire?"

Owen pushed back from the table, jittery enough to haul himself to his feet and try to pace around the cramped kitchen. "I heard her out . . . mostly."

"Oh, yeah?" Andie looked unimpressed. "So, you asked her what you asked me, about why she didn't confide in you sooner?"

The expression on Owen's face was obviously answer enough.

"I see," Andie said calmly. "And you probably also thought to inquire as to whether she's still set on going through with this crazy charade."

Owen stopped dead. "What do you mean?"

Andie gave him a slightly pitying glance. "What I mean, my big, dumb idiot brother, is now that Libby's secret is out, does she plan to stay on Sanctuary Island and go through with the whole Christmas dinner thing? Or is she heading back up north instead?"

The idea of it cut Owen off at the knees. "Heading back . . ."

Andie pressed her lips together sympathetically, but she didn't mollycoddle him. "Back to where she lives. Queens, isn't it? For all you know, she could be on the ferry over to the mainland to catch a plane right now."

Chapter Eighteen

Libby settled her wooly cap more firmly on her head, tugging to make sure it covered the tops of her cold ears, and let herself out the back door. The pines creaked in the wind, rustling and whispering to each other in the gathering dusk. There was something peaceful and melancholy about them, Libby decided, walking briskly to get her blood moving.

She wrapped her arms around herself, slapping at her puffy-coated sleeves, and marched deeper into the woods away from her grandfather's house. Every step farther from the deep gloom of that broken home, every breath of sharply cold air, cleared a little more of the fog from Libby's brain.

Never before had Libby come face-to-face with the depth of her family's unhappiness. A terrible rift had pulled her family to pieces before Libby was even born—maybe she'd been naive and arrogant to think there was anything she could do to fix that. But maybe she could fix other things.

Libby paused, her booted steps cushioned by the bed of fallen pine needles carpeting the frozen ground. Her breath fogged in front of her face, and the tip of her nose tingled with cold. She glanced up through the waving branches at the monochrome sky, the clouds heavy with the promise of snow. The whole world felt hushed, as if it were waiting for something.

She breathed in, tasting the possibilities like snow-flakes on her tongue. She could run away, leave her misdeeds and the people she'd wronged behind her—but she'd carry her guilt with her wherever she went. Her other option was to stay and try to make things right. Or if not right, at least better.

Caught on the edge of the decision, Libby stood still and shut her eyes tight, trying to listen for an answer on the chill wind.

"Libby!"

Owen's calling voice reached her, sending her heartbeat into a frantic gallop. Her eyes popped open in time to see him striding through the trees, tall and broad-shouldered and sure. A man on a mission.

"Libby," he repeated, relief clear in his ocean-blue eyes when they found her. "There you are. I couldn't find you back at the house. I was worried you'd left town."

"I thought about it," she admitted, breathless at his nearness. Her hungry gaze roved over his leanly mus-cled form, committing him to memory. His russet hair caught the fading light, tickling her palms with yearn-ing to run her fingers through the short bristles. Tiny lines fanned out from the corners of his eyes, from laughter or from too much squinting against the glare of the harsh desert sun. His skin still carried a deep golden tan, though the other legacies of his time in Afghanistan, his visible wounds, were fading. He didn't even have his cane, Libby noticed with a pang of concern.

"Don't leave," Owen said, reaching out to clasp her by the upper arms. Libby fought a gasp, and the urge to go boneless in his grasp.

"Why not? I'm the villain, remember? The only happy ending is for me to go slinking off in disgrace. Or for me to get my comeuppance."

Libby tried to smile a little to show she knew how much she deserved it, but Owen didn't even see it. He was too busy shaking his head. "You don't get off that easy."

Shame burned through Libby. Running away would be taking the easy way out, she saw with a sick lurch to her stomach. "You're right," she said numbly. "You were right about everything. I can't leave like that. I have to stick it out, and take whatever's coming to me."

"That's not what I meant. Don't stay to punish yourself, or because you hope I'll punish you."

Frustrated, Libby pulled away from Owen's hands. "What else can I do? What more do you want from me?"

Hands flexing as if he wanted to grab her and pull her close, Owen clenched his jaw. "Just stay. I'm not saying I forgive you—I need some time. But I know this: You can't change what you did in the past, but it doesn't have to overshadow your entire future."

Libby shivered as a single, perfect snowflake fluttered between them. That sense of infinite possibility shot through her again, energizing every nerve and prickling over her skin. She looked up to see more snowflakes drifting down, swirling in the wind. A couple got stuck in Owen's unfairly long lashes, making tenderness catch at Libby's throat.

"Maybe we'll get a white Christmas after all," she said huskily, wrapping her arms around herself.

"There's still time," Owen agreed, his eyes watchful.

"I got everyone's hopes up about this Christmas, including mine." Libby stuck out her tongue to catch a snowflake and grinned at the dot of frozen water instantly melting in her mouth. "You were wrong about one thing. I haven't hurt Caitlin with my lies. Not yet. If I pull off this Christmas the way I imagined, none of this ugliness will ever touch that little girl."

Determination made Libby restless. She started walking again, Owen at her side, as she thought. Owen was right. Maybe Libby had hurt some people—but somehow, she understood with a pang, the person she'd hurt the most was Owen himself. And maybe there was no way to make it up to him . . .

But she could try. And the fact that Owen was here, beside her, walking through the first snowfall of the year under the wide canopy of pine boughs, gave Libby hope.

They walked in silence, their matched steps muffled by the thin layer of snow accumulating on the ground. Libby wasn't sure where they were going. All she knew was that as long as Owen was with her, she wanted to keep walking. She wanted to keep whatever fragile peace they'd built between them, and hold it safe against her chest like the baby chick she'd dreamed up to live in her fantasy chicken coop.

Without meaning to, they stumbled across what looked like a footpath through the trees. Maybe a deer path, Libby thought, or one of the meandering trails beaten down by the wild horse bands as they foraged across the island and searched out fresh water and shelter from the storms. But then the path widened, the snow gathering in a pair of grooves like tire tracks, but smooth instead of ridged.

"I thought your grandfather owned all this land," Owen said into the stillness of the winter forest.

"So did I. But I don't know where these tracks lead. Should we follow them and find out?"

Owen rubbed absently at his healing leg. "Walking is good therapy. Or so they tell me."

"How is physical rehab going?" Libby asked delicately, aware that Owen's progress back toward full health—and reinstatement in the armed forces—was a sore subject.

"Better than I could have hoped. I think I told you I was skeptical about the whole equine assisted–therapy thing. I don't know what I thought it was going to be like. Hug a horse, let the vibes of being around a big, gentle creature magically heal you." He made a wry face. "But it's not like that at all. There's good science behind it. Sitting on a walking horse, keeping your balance as he paces forward—that works the same muscles in your pelvis as walking. But gently, without putting stress on them while they're healing."

"That's wild. So you've been strengthening the muscles that will help you walk while sitting on a horse. I hope Windy Corner can get enough clients and grants to keep going. They could do a lot of good for a lot of people. I mean, look at Caitlin."

Owen stuck his hands in his jacket pockets. "Yeah, maybe I shouldn't be so dismissive of the magical healing properties of horses. Those riding lessons sure seem to have done wonders for my daughter. At least, from what Andie has told me. Not that I was here to see it for myself."

"But you're here now," Libby said, trying to be comforting.

"Right. I'm here now, finally getting my chance to screw up with my kid." Owen's jaw clenched before he shook his head. "Maybe I always would've screwed up, maybe I wouldn't have been any better at this if I'd been in Caitlin's life right from the jump—but I'll never know. Caitlin's mother took that choice, that chance, away from me. It's not the same and I'm not saying it is, but can you see how a woman keeping relevant information from me might bring up some bad stuff?"

Libby's lips went numb from how hard she was biting them. Shame scoured through her chest, sending prickles of heat over her scalp and twisting her stomach into knots. "I'm sorry. I didn't think about that before, but I see it now. I hate myself, Owen. If there were any way I could go back in time and make different choices, I would."

"I'm not trying to make you feel like crap," Owen told her, the words slow and deliberate, as if he wanted to be sure she understood. "I wanted to explain why I went off half-cocked back there. I tore into you without trying to understand what really went down—no army

officer worth his salt strikes first and finds out the details after. And I know you, Libby. I should have realized you'd have a good reason for telling this lie."

Gratitude flooded her, but Libby shook her head. "I
don't even know anymore. Maybe there's no reason good
enough to justify being untruthful."

"Maybe it's not up to us to judge whether it's good
enough or not. But I'd like to know all your reasoning, just
the same."

"I already told you about Uncle Ray," Libby said,
fingers twisting nervously inside her woolen mittens.
"That's basically it. He's my whole reason. He was my
whole family for a lot of years. I would've done anything
to help him."

"Understandable. But what I don't get is why money
was an issue." Owen swept an arm out, indicating the
gently rolling hills and acres of tall, stately pines around
them. "Your grandfather—Ray's father—is obviously
pretty wealthy. Why didn't you go to him for help?"

Emotion choked up into Libby's throat, but she forced
herself to say, "I tried. Today, actually. Even though
Uncle Ray made me swear I never would. He didn't want
his father to know anything about his condition. They've
been estranged for years, I'm not entirely sure why, because Ray would never talk about it. He didn't tell me
anything about the rest of my family, I guess because it
was such a source of pain for him. But when I got here
and met Nash and Grandfather, I started to wonder if it
might be possible to heal that pain. And after everything
that's been happening between you and me, I wanted so
badly to be able to come clean—and I thought if Grand-

father would agree to pay for Uncle Ray's care, then I'd finally be free to tell the truth."

"Makes sense. What went wrong?"

Defeat and remembered disappointment weighed on Libby's shoulders. "Grandfather. He's so stubborn! He got it into his head that if I had the money, I'd leave him."

"Sounds like you wouldn't be the first member of his family to desert him," Owen pointed out. "Maybe for completely legitimate reasons, but still."

"I know. And I feel for him," Libby said, squinting through the snow at the vague outline of a building in the distance. "But with his attitude, maybe it's no wonder he's driven all of his family away. I wanted to believe there was more to him than selfishness and bitterness, but after today, I'm not so sure. What's that building over there?"

Owen lifted a hand to shade his eyes. "Not sure. Some sort of outbuilding or shed. I guess it's not the chicken coop you wrote about."

"Er, no. Sorry. That coop is another thing that exists only in my dreams. I've always wanted to keep chickens, so I invented a whole flock of them."

"What's the big attraction with chickens?"

Libby laughed, her breath puffing out of her on a white cloud. "I don't know. There's just something so cozy and friendly and funny about chickens. The way they squabble and peck; their silly, sweet faces. When I was in Queens, keeping chickens seemed like the ultimate symbol of being settled and happy in a small town. If I lived here for real, a chicken coop would be my first project. Once you have chickens, you know you've got a home." She paused, thinking about it. "I also happen to love fresh eggs."

"I'm with you on that. When you're out on a mission and it's been weeks of MREs and nothing fresh, you start to dream about real scrambled eggs. Too bad there isn't a real henhouse behind your grandfather's place."

They'd gotten closer to the mysterious structure in the woods as they talked. It was bigger than Libby had thought at first, a one-story rectangular structure with wide double doors that reached almost all the way up to the sloping metal roof. Excitement sparked in Libby's blood. "Oh, my gosh. That building—maybe it's storage! Grandfather put away a lot of my grandmother's things years ago, and now he says he can't remember where. Can you imagine being so uncaring about your family's history that you forget what you did with it?"

"Maybe he doesn't want to be reminded of the past."

"I'd give anything to have a few of those memories. But for all I know, Grandfather threw away all my parents' things, and Grandmother's." Libby shook her head in disbelief, hurt all over again at the thought that she might never find a single memento from her late parents. When she considered that, it was hard to keep sympathy for her grandfather's losses in her heart. "I've been searching everywhere for Grandmother's nativity set, one of the few memories I still have from my childhood on Sanctuary Island—but I didn't know about this shed. Maybe it's in there! Come on, we have to check."

Snow started falling in earnest as they followed the tracks up to the shed. By the time Libby was close enough to reach out and test the strength of the shiny padlock holding the thick wooden doors closed, the snow was so thick she could barely see the outline of the shed's roof stretching up against the sky.

"L-Locked," she said, disappointed and shivering. "I don't suppose picking locks is part of basic training."

"Not as such, no," Owen replied with a ghost of a grin as he fingered the padlock. "But it sure was part of a misspent youth rebelling against my cop father. You sure you want me to break in?"

Another shiver took Libby, frigid wind biting through her coat and hat to chill her to the bone. "D-Don't d-do anything that m-m-makes you uncomfortable," she chattered out. "I c-can ask Grandfather about it later, c-come back on my own."

Owen raked his gaze over her, taking in everything from the snow-dampened tendrils of hair clinging to cheeks that felt raw from the wind and cold. "We're breaking in," he decided. "You need to warm up, and I'm not sure how far we are from the house."

I love a man who takes charge, Libby thought a little dazedly as she watched Owen fiddle with the lock. He worked patiently, not even seeming to feel the cold on his bare hands, and Libby couldn't suppress another shiver at the thought of those strong, sensitive fingers touching her as carefully as Owen touched the lock.

She blinked, and when she opened her eyes again, some time seemed to have passed. Owen had the lock open and was pushing apart the sliding doors with a mighty heave. "Come on," he said, "let's get you inside. You're freezing."

"I feel warmer," Libby told him, stumbling a little on feet gone numb.

"Yeah, that's not actually a good sign."

Owen's muscular arms came around her from be-hind, holding her up and reeling her in close to the solid, heated wall of his chest. Libby sank back with a sigh of pure animal pleasure in the warmth, her eyes drifting closed as the world swirled around her dizzily.

She blinked again and realized Owen had lifted her into his arms and carried her into the shed. Disoriented, Libby shook her head to clear it. "Why did you stop? What's the matter?"

Peering up at Owen's still face, Libby saw that he was staring over her head at something. She craned her neck to see, but the angle was wrong and it was dark. "What's going on? Is there something in here?"

Owen's voice was strange when he replied. "The answer to a mystery."

"What?" Libby wriggled a little, curiosity piqued. "What mystery?"

Responding to her unspoken desire to be put down, Owen shifted her in his arms as if she weighed no more than a snowflake and let her feet touch the floor. He turned her until her back was against his chest, his hands on her shoulders as he bent close enough to whisper in her ear. "The eternal mystery. Santa Claus is real, and I know who he is."

Chapter Nineteen

Owen felt more than heard Libby's gasp as she took in the majestic red sleigh parked in the center of the large shed. Light from a window high in the wall slanted over the gold-painted trim and gleamed on the dull brass of the jingle bells trailing from the brown leather reins.

"Santa's sleigh. In my grandfather's shed." Libby sounded as if she couldn't believe her own eyes.

"Maybe your grandfather isn't as uncaring and cold as he wants people to think."

She made a tiny sound deep in her throat that tugged at Owen's heart. Pulling away from him, she stepped closer to the sleigh and ran her hand over the smooth varnish. Someone loved this sleigh and took great care of it.

"We might have stumbled onto someone else's property by mistake," Libby pointed out uncertainly. "I don't think there are any fences along the property line, and I don't exactly know my way around."

"Why are you so reluctant to admit your grandfather might be the town's mystery Santa?"

He saw the movement of Libby's throat as she swallowed. Her eyes looked damp in the dim light of the shed. "Because if he cares this much about his neighbors and the townspeople, but doesn't care enough about his own family to hold onto them . . . I don't know what that means."

"Maybe it means that people are complicated. Contradictory and unexpected. I kind of like that idea. It gives me hope."

Libby didn't reply. She was too busy climbing up into the sleigh to sit on the tufted cushion of the seat, stroking her hand along the well-conditioned leather. "Whoever owns this sleigh loves it. He keeps it safe and secret all year round. He guards it like a piece of his own heart."

Owen watched as she leaned down to pick up the wine-colored velvet sack the Santa had reached into during the parade. He'd drawn out toys and candy, tossing them to the jumping, excited children with a big, booming laugh. Libby didn't laugh as she opened the bag and peered inside.

"Empty?" Owen guessed, stepping up to the opposite side of the sleigh and vaulting lightly into the seat. It was a relief to sit and rest his leg after all that walking, but not as necessary as it would have been even a week ago.

"No." Libby's voice was odd, hushed and awed as if they were in church. "There's a box at the bottom."

A tingle of anticipation raised the hairs on the back of Owen's neck. "Well. Aren't you going to open it?"

Libby set the sack on the seat between them and pulled down the sides to reveal a heavy lacquered chest about the size of a briefcase, but deeper. "It's not wrapped. I doubt it's a gift for me."

"But it might give us a clue about who the Santa is."

Delicate fingers stroked the lid of the chest, tracing the initials carved there. "E.C.L. My initials."

"See? It *is* meant for you," Owen teased.

She shot him a brief smile that faded into seriousness as she took a breath and lifted the lid of the box and gasped. The box was full of small things wrapped in white linen and stacks of yellowing papers tied with ribbon, and folded on top was a handkerchief embroidered with tiny purple flowers and green twining vines.

"I remember this," Libby cried, picking up the fine cloth with reverent hands. "This was my mother's. Grandmother stitched the lilacs herself, because they were my mother's favorite flower. I'd forgotten all about that."

Libby brought the thin cotton to her face and inhaled deeply, her eyelashes fluttering shut as she was transported into a memory Owen could only imagine.

"For years," he said, "I kept this silk scarf of my mother's hidden under my mattress. Every time I touched it, I remembered her smile. The way it felt when she hugged me."

"Why did you have to hide it?"

Owen tensed for a moment, then forced himself to relax. He was a grown man, not a little boy. "My father kept all of Mom's things, hoarded them like a dragon sitting on treasure. The scarf she wore to church every Sunday was the one thing I managed to steal for myself."

Libby sucked in a breath. "That sounds really hard, Owen. Not being able to share your grief with your father. Hiding it from everyone."

"It was the same for you," Owen said, his heart breaking open at the clear sympathy in Libby's warm hazel eyes. "You were ripped away from everything you knew and sent to live with a man who wouldn't even talk about your family."

No wonder Libby was such a dreamer. She'd been telling herself stories all her life because her entire childhood on Sanctuary Island must have seemed as unreal and distant as a fairy tale.

"I guess we have that in common." She smiled a little, ducking her head to peer back into the open box. "I wonder what else is in here."

"More family things?"

"My family's things," Libby agreed, eyes widening. "Which means . . . Grandfather really is the town Santa Claus. I can't believe it."

"Maybe there's more to him than meets the eye."

"I was so angry with him." Libby carefully refolded the handkerchief and placed it back in the box, smoothing it with shaking fingers. "I was ready to do exactly what he yelled at me about, and walk away. I'm glad I didn't."

Owen's heart jumped. He'd come that close to losing her. "What stopped you?" he asked hoarsely.

Pink flooded Libby's cheeks, but for once, she didn't evade his gaze shyly. She met his stare head on and said, "You did. I hurt you, and I wanted the chance to make it right. Running away doesn't solve anything."

A rush of emotion hit Owen's bloodstream like the

adrenaline of an oncoming firefight. He stared into Libby's eyes, her warmth and softness so close, his palms itched to reach out and touch her. "The army taught me to stand my ground, no matter what. Which is not to say that I feel no fear. Fear is normal, a healthy response to danger. The hard part is being able to control your re-action, to be the guy who runs toward the threat instead of away from it. Don't ever call yourself a coward in front of me again, Elizabeth Leeds. You're as brave as anyone I ever served with."

The flush mantling Libby's cheeks went darker red, but she still didn't back down. "I don't know about that. If I were really brave, I would have kissed you by now."

The words trembled between them for a hushed, expectant moment, and then they were in each other's arms. Owen honestly didn't know who reached out first, and he didn't care. All he cared about was the sweet-ness of Libby's mouth, the brush of her lips against his skin, and the stroke of her fingers in his hair. Desire roared through him, heat and lust tangled with tender-ness until Owen barely recognized it. He'd never felt anything like it before.

Self-control was a distant memory as Owen covered Libby with his body, cradling her against the leather cushions of the sleigh's bench seat. He couldn't even re-member why he'd wanted to stop himself from doing this, from getting his hands inside Libby's winter coat to shape the curve of her waist. He couldn't understand why he'd tried to keep himself from mouthing at the juncture of her neck and shoulder where the warm vanilla scent of her was strongest.

He didn't want to remember anything but the sounds
she made when he touched her. The fierce clutch of her
thighs around his hips as they thrust together, caught up
in the heat of their bodies and how close they'd come to
pushing each other away.

Libby writhed in his arms, her kiss-swollen lips
parted on a soundless expression of shocked pleasure.
He couldn't get enough of her unselfconscious, uninhib-
ited reactions. Every touch, every kiss, every caress of
his hands over her bared skin seemed to surprise and
delight Libby.

Owen's hard, raging hunger receded to the back of
his mind as his focus narrowed to one thing: Libby's
pleasure. He watched her moan and quake under his
touch, greedy for her sighs and the way her fingers went
white-knuckled against the leather seat. There was
nothing in the world but this woman in his arms, this
woman who made Owen wonder what it would be like
to have a home . . . this woman who was still searching for a home of her own, every bit as much as Owen
ever had.

He tasted her lips, savoring the plush, trembling
softness, and closed his eyes as her cries quieted to
quick, panted breaths. Owen rested his forehead against
Libby's and tried to calm his throbbing pulse. This
wasn't the time or place for anything more—and he still
wasn't sure he was the man for Libby.

God, how he wanted to be, though.

Owen forced himself to move, to pull away enough
so that every breath he took in wasn't heavy with the
vanilla sweetness of Libby. His knee jostled the heavy

box on the seat beside them and it rattled, making Libby sit up with a gasp.

"Don't drop it! There's something in there that sounds breakable."

"I've got it," he assured her, putting a steadying hand on the box. "Don't worry."

Libby subsided back against the cushion, her heavy-lidded eyes and flushed cheeks making Owen feel about ten feet tall. "Okay. Yay. Because I'm having a hard time worrying about much of anything right this minute."

Primal satisfaction flooded Owen, lowering his voice to a pleased growl. "Good."

Licking her lips, Libby lifted tentative hands toward Owen's waist. "But what about you? Are you—I could . . . shoot. This is hard."

Owen couldn't help it. One of his eyebrows shot up, and he barked out a laugh that had Libby scooting up in the seat and babbling, "I mean, not hard! Or maybe it is, I don't know. But that's sort of my point! I could find out, or help you out, if you wanted . . . oh, my gosh, please say something."

"I want you," Owen said bluntly, his smile fading and leaving behind nothing but desire and intent. "But this isn't an equation we have to balance right now. Not without talking a little more first."

Because the more Owen's head cleared, the fog of lust dissipating, the more he wondered just how experienced his shy little dreamer was with the opposite sex. The way Libby had responded to him had looked a lot like beginner's innocence, every sigh and moan flavored with surprise at what her body was capable of feeling.

Libby made a face that almost confirmed Owen's guess—simultaneously relieved and disappointed. "You know I'm not great with the talking. But I can try, if we have to."

"We don't have to do anything." Owen felt he had to clarify. The wind picked up outside, whistling past the shed in a cold fury and making Owen glance up at the snow-darkened window overhead. "Except wait out this storm and try not to freeze to death."

"I don't think I'll ever be cold again." Libby's eyelashes swept down shyly as she shifted around to right her clothes. Owen felt a pang of loss when she zipped up her pink coat once more, but it couldn't be helped. They had to stay warm. There was no telling how long the storm might last, and he'd rather not call anyone and make them take the risk of driving in this weather to try and save two people who were perfectly safe . . . as long as they could manage to keep their clothes on.

Chapter Twenty

Libby couldn't catch her breath. She'd never felt like that before—completely out of control, and loving every second of it. Although, okay, it was a little scary to fall to pieces in front of Owen, to be so exposed to his sharp, heated stare.

And now, when it was clear that Owen had no intention of going further, she didn't know how to feel about it. For a few brief and glorious minutes, she had felt closer to Owen than to anyone in her life before. But now they were back to being two separate people. The distance between them, while small in physical terms, felt impossible to bridge.

Owen had touched her, so sweetly and deeply and passionately . . . but he didn't want to be touched in return. Libby's cheeks flamed in embarrassment and she glanced to the side, hoping to hide her expression as she bundled herself back into her coat. The layer of padding felt like insulation against the unbearable intimacy of this moment, even more than the cold.

It would be so easy to back away. It was awfully tempting to put on a smile and pretend she was worldly and sophisticated enough to think nothing of what just happened. But Libby was tired of taking the coward's way out. She didn't want to lie anymore, not even lies of omission. Besides, Owen had said he wanted to talk about it. It was time Libby took him at his word and believed in him.

"So." The word croaked out husky and thick, and Libby cleared her throat. "Where do we go from here?"

"Honestly? I think we're stuck." Owen turned from his study of the weather visible out the one window in time to catch Libby's wrinkled nose. "Oh, you mean . . . where do *we* go."

He gestured between their bodies, sitting side by side in her grandfather's old-fashioned sleigh, and Libby lifted her chin. "I don't want any more misunderstandings or confusion or hidden agendas. I want everything out on the table so we know where we stand."

And, because Rome wasn't built in a day and neither was a woman's self confidence, she added, "Um, is that okay?" and instantly wanted to smack herself in the face.

But Owen didn't laugh at her. In fact, his eyes softened. "Of course it's okay. It's good. We should talk."

Libby waited, silence falling over the shed like snow, burying them in a soft, white blanket. *At least we know the shed is well sealed and insulated,* she thought wildly. *And there are definitely no crickets in here, because if there were, we'd hear them chirping.*

"Why is this so difficult?" she blurted. "I'm pretty sure we like each other. That ought to be enough to get a conversation going."

Owen's mouth twisted in a rueful smile. "I've run ops against insurgents without blinking, but there's something about the phrase 'we should talk.' It seems to freeze a man from the inside out."

"It's not any easier for me, if that helps. But I think we have to try."

His deep breath lifted his chest, reminding Libby of the powerful musculature of Owen's solid frame. "In boot camp, they teach you how to keep going, how not to freeze up. And it might sound simplistic, but a big part of it is to really just *keep going*. Get your body moving and you can bypass your brain, at least long enough to let higher reason take over from the fear response. I suggest we do the same. We should talk while we go through the rest of these boxes and things for supplies to see us through the storm—blankets, warm coats, things like that—and the movement will have the added bonus of keeping our blood pumping, which will keep us warmer than sitting here like lumps."

"I see why your men follow you," Libby said, jumping down from the sleigh. "A man with a plan is very compelling."

Owen shrugged, but there was amused tilt to one corner of his mouth. "What can I say? I like a plan the way you like a story."

"A man with a plan and a woman with a story." Libby's heart sank a little. "That doesn't exactly sound like a perfect match."

Maybe it was time to get her head out of the clouds

and see what was waiting for her back in real life, she thought as she watched Owen lever himself down to the floor of the shed. He was gentle with his injured leg, but more confident in its strength than he had been only a few days before.

"Perfect is overrated," Owen said firmly, pointing to a stack of cardboard boxes in the corner of the shed. "My old CO had a saying: The perfect is the enemy of the good. Meaning, if you've got a workable strategy that advances your mission, go for it. Don't wait around for something perfect to come along. You can miss out on a lot in life by holding out for some impossible dream of perfection."

"Dreams were all I had for so long," Libby murmured, kneeling on the dusty floor and dragging one of the boxes toward her. "Your CO sounds like a very wise man."

"He is." She could hear the smile in Owen's voice, even though his face was hidden by his upraised arms as he reached to pull down a box from the top of the stack. "He retired a few years ago, but we keep in touch. I learned a lot from him."

"Like what else?" Libby asked, intrigued.

"How to walk tall and carry myself with pride, and how to be humble enough to admit it when I needed help or when I didn't know something. How to apologize, how to lead by example. How to be a man, I guess."

Libby tugged the folded flaps of the cardboard box open and paused. "The way you talk about him, he sounds almost like a father to you."

"He was. I guess I was looking for that, after I left home so young. A shrink would have a field day with me joining up the way I did, rejecting my dad and everything he wanted for me. Whatever motivated me back then, I have no regrets. Joining the army was the best thing I ever did. It made me who I am. And it got me out of a situation, off a path, that was leading nowhere good."

Owen paused, the muscles in his shoulders bunching with sudden tension where he was bent over the open box. "Except that path led to Caitlin. So I can't regret the time I spent with her mother, either."

"Kids change everything," Libby said softly, her throat aching with sympathy at the lost, stunned expression in the depths of Owen's eyes whenever he talked about Caitlin.

"Not just about the future, either." Owen went back to rifling through his box, bending his head down so Libby couldn't read his expression. "Caitlin—being around her, trying to get her to open up and talk to me, trying to figure out how to build a relationship with her . . . it's hard. One of the hardest things I've ever done, and I'm in the damn special forces. An elite solder in the armed forces, and one little girl's got me stymied. It makes me rethink everything about my relationship with my dad."

She made a cautious hum to show she was listening. Thirsty for any drop of information Owen spilled, Libby didn't want to speak, to break whatever spell was making him talk like this. Every word gave her a new, deeper insight into this man she'd let into her heart.

"I spent a lot of years angry with my dad for the way he shut down after Mom died," Owen said slowly, his movements halting. He looked up at Libby, letting her see the naked emotion written all over his features. "Dad turned our home into a training program for the police academy, except unlike real cadets, we got no breaks. No downtime. No encouragement. Only discipline, criticism. Coldness."

"That sounds like a harsh way to grow up," Libby said, her heart squeezing at the idea of Owen, younger and smaller and more innocent, looking to his father for comfort after the death of his mother, and finding that all softness and warmth had died with her. For the first time, Libby realized that in his own way, Owen was as much an orphan as she was.

"I rebelled every way I could think of, while Andie tried her best to be the perfect kid." Owen shook his head "I've held onto my anger for a long time. Nothing got me past it—not even learning the meaning of true self-discipline in the army. But now, with Caitlin, when she looks at me with those big eyes and I know that I'm all she has in the world . . . it's a lot of pressure. And I get how my dad crumpled under that pressure and fell back on what he knew. I don't like it and I never will. But I can understand it a little better now."

Libby's heart started to pound in her chest. "Does that mean you intend to do better by Caitlin than was done by you?"

"I know what you want me to say." Owen pulled a blanket out of his box and shook it out, revealing a hand-stitched quilt that tugged at the corners of Libby's memory. "You want me to say I've realized that I can be the father Caitlin needs, and I'll stick around and prove it. But it's not that easy, Libby."

"I never said it was easy," she protested. "But I still

think what Caitlin needs more than anything is you, in her life. And I think maybe you need her every bit as much."

"Maybe I do." Owen stood from his crouch and swirled the quilt out to drape over Libby's shoulders in one graceful, economical motion. "But this isn't about what I need. It's about what I owe. To my men, my country, the army. And what I owe my family—Caitlin is happy here. She has Andie, who loves her like her own. Maybe what's best for Caitlin is to stay here with her aunt instead of with me. I know maybe that's hard for you to hear, growing up the way you did."

Libby paused, searching her own feelings as she clutched the quilt gratefully around her. "No. My uncle loved me. Still does, when he remembers who I am. I was lucky to have him, and if you don't want Caitlin or can't commit to being there for her, then you're right— she is better off with someone who loves her and is able to make a home for her. But Owen, I know you do want your daughter. I watched the way your face lit up when you talked about her, before you even met her. And now, when I see you together, the tentative steps you're taking toward each other—you can't tell me you don't love that little girl."

Shadows moved across Owen's face as he turned aside. His voice was wrecked when he admitted, "More than my own life. But that doesn't mean I'd be a good dad. I don't have a lot to go on, here. And I *am* a good officer. That's what I know. It's all I know."

Libby bit her lip. She didn't want to argue. She couldn't argue—she was sure Owen was a huge asset to his team, and that they'd welcome him back with open arms the minute he was fit for duty. And the knowledge that arguing for Owen to stay could be motivated purely by her own desire for more time with him made Libby want to keep her mouth shut.

But the memory of Caitlin's wide, brilliant smile when she saw that Owen had skipped his rehab to watch her lesson forced Libby to speak up. "When you first joined the army, you didn't know how to be an officer, right?"

Owen cut her a sidelong glance that said he knew where she was going with this. "That's true. But I had good teachers."

"All I'm saying is, if you put your mind and heart into it, I know you'll figure out this fatherhood thing. And if it were part of your army training, you wouldn't have let fear or uncertainty hold you back. That's what makes you a hero. Deny it all you want," Libby said stubbornly, crossing her arms over her chest at Owen's shaking head. "You'll never convince me you aren't a hero. But my point about Caitlin is that there's more than one way to be a hero."

Owen turned away abruptly, reaching for another box and signaling the end of the conversation by saying, "Let's hope there's another blanket in here. Now that the sun's gone down for real, I'm starting to feel the chill."

Suppressing a sigh, Libby scrambled to her feet and held out a corner of her quilt. "Come here, I'll share."

That got him to look at her . . . and what a look. Owen's eyes went from shuttered to blazing with heat in a single heartbeat, and Libby shivered convulsively at the fire-bright desire in his stare. "Sharing a blanket with you would definitely warm me up, but it wouldn't get us any closer to that conversation we got sidetracked from."

The dark promise in his voice rubbed over Libby's skin like velvet. "Let's keep looking," she suggested breathlessly, going back to staring blindly down into her box, which seemed to be filled with crumpled newspaper.

Doing her best to focus on the task at hand instead of the wall of heat and solid muscle at her back, Libby started to dig through the papers. Her fingers closed around the top clump of paper and lifted something surprisingly heavy. She could feel pointy bits poking through the newspaper. For some reason, her hands were trembling as she started unwrapping it.

Libby unraveled the paper, which was wound carefully around a small object, no larger than the palm of her hand, but dense enough to have heft to it. Little by little, the paper fell away to reveal a tiny china cow, painted white with big, black splotches across its withers.

Behind her, she distantly heard Owen say, "Oh, of course. Any port in a storm, I guess," in a resigned tone, but she couldn't look away from the cow figurine in her hand. She stroked its perky ears and short, curved horns—the pointed tips she'd felt through the paper. With a gasp, Libby dove back into the box and pulled out another newspaper-wrapped object.

By the time she finally let herself believe it, Libby was sitting on the shed floor in the midst of a menagerie: three cows, two standing and one lying down; a pair of white curly sheep with sleepy eyes and black legs curled under them demurely; a camel in mid-stride; a long-eared donkey with a sweetly dopey expression.

"We found it," she murmured, her voice almost choked by tears of gratitude and blessing. "My grandmother's nativity."

"That's not all we found."

Libby twisted around and blinked away the tears blurring her vision to see Owen standing with his arms out at his sides, wearing a sheepish smile and a red velvet suit trimmed in white fur. Between one blink and the next, her overwhelmed tears turned to laughter.

The Santa suit hung on Owen's trim frame, making him look like a little boy playing dress up. "It's warm," he said defensively, cinching the leather belt in as tight as he could. It still draped over his lean hips but at least it gathered the extra material at his waist.

"It's wonderful," Libby told him, completely sincerely. "You look great."

"Thanks. But it's not actually what I was talking about. Come see."

With a last, lingering caress to the manger animals from the nativity, Libby got to her feet and went to see what else Owen had found.

"This was in the last box," he said, his voice gentle. "It was underneath the Santa suit."

He handed her a leather-bound three-ring binder that looked like a scrapbook, thick with pages Libby couldn't wait to flip through. "Is it family photographs?" she asked eagerly.

"Turn it over."

Libby flipped the binder and blinked down at the

word RECIPES embossed in the brown leather cover. "Oh, my gosh. Owen."

Her knees went watery, but Owen was there to put a steadying arm around her shoulders and steer her back to the sleigh to sit down. Libby settled back against the cushion and opened the heavy binder over her knees.

Page after page of yellowed, stained index cards, preserved in their individual plastic sleeves. Libby's breath caught at the spidery, handwritten titles of some of the dishes: Sweet Potato Pone, Grandma Helene's Buttermilk Biscuits, Daddy's Fried Chicken. Some of the cards were notched and creased, the writing faded and blurry, but still legible. And the newer cards . . . that was Libby's mother's handwriting. She recognized it from someplace deep in her memory, deeper than conscious thought.

"This is . . ." Libby looked up at Owen where he stood beside the sleigh, watching her with a tender expression warming his ocean blue eyes.

"It's a treasure trove," he agreed. "I'm no gourmet chef, but every one of those recipes I looked at sounded like something I'd love to eat. I think we might have found a way to pull off this Christmas dinner."

But Libby shook her head. "No. I mean yes, we will definitely be using these recipes for Christmas. But what I wanted to say was, thank you. It feels like you've given my mother back to me. At least, a part of her, a memory I didn't know I had. I'll be forever grateful."

Owen's gaze sharpened in intensity, and Libby gladly parted her lips for his kiss an instant before he brought their mouths together. In the brief flash of time before the brush of his lips and the velvety rub of his tongue robbed her of thought, Libby made a vow to return the favor, if she could.

I'll do whatever I can to give you back your family, Owen. Even if I'm never going to be a part of it. Maybe that's the only way I can make things right between us.

Chapter Twenty-One

Everything changed after that night, Libby thought as she took up her rolling pin and whacked at a stick of butter to soften it. All she had to do was close her eyes to relive the experience of lying for hours wrapped in Owen's arms, sharing body heat and whispered memories and confidences to keep warm.

And then, when the storm finally blew itself out somewhere around dawn, they'd hauled open the storage shed's heavy doors to step out into a winter wonderland. White snow dusted the world, lying in smooth drifts and crusting the tops of tree branches like the sugar Libby sprinkled over the lattice-top crust of her mother's caramel apple pie. Owen had taken Libby's hand and led her home, a sack of precious treasures over his red-clad shoulder, the handsomest Santa Claus in history.

Libby tossed the softened butter into her bowl of measured-out granulated sugar and took a wooden spoon to it, creaming the two together. A tiny bead of sweat tickled at her forehead, and Libby blew a wisp of hair out of her eyes, but kept going even when her wrist started to ache from the repetitive motion.

"We have a mixer, you know."

The grumpy voice came from behind her, and Libby tensed. She didn't stop stirring, though. "I saw it. But the recipe says to do it by hand, so that's what I'm doing."

Grandfather stumped into the kitchen, his movements halting and slow, as if he'd passed a long and restless night. Libby resisted the urge to ask him how he was, biting back her concern. He came up beside her at the counter and watched in silence for a long moment as Libby doggedly worked the butter and sugar into a smooth, fluffy mixture.

"Your grandmother used to do it that way," Grandfather muttered, his watery blue eyes trained on Libby's hands. "She said she could never get a feel for what she was doing when she used a machine."

It was a peace offering—a tiny bit of the past handed over like a coin to a beggar—and Libby pressed her lips together. "I know. This is Grandmother's recipe. I found it last night, in the shed where you store your Santa suit and sleigh. And all of my mother's things."

Dabney Leeds reared back, his head wagging shakily. "You shouldn't have been in there."

"It was snowing and we needed shelter," Libby said impatiently. "That's not the point! The point is that you had all those things, all those memories, locked away and hidden from me. Why? All I wanted when I came here was to learn about my family, my history. You seem to want to build a relationship with me—but I don't see how that's possible when you won't tell me anything about the people we both loved and lost."

The thin, papery skin of his hand where it clutched the head of his cane showed the tension running through his stooped, creaky body. "You shouldn't have been snooping. Those are my things. My personal, private—"

"They don't belong only to you, though." Libby gave up pretending to focus on the bowl of creamed butter and sugar. "You're not the only one who misses them. There's a huge hole in my heart where my memories of my parents, my family, should live. I came here hoping to fill it. You're the only one who can help me. And instead, you hoarded those memories like a miser, like Ebenezer Scrooge—"

Libby broke off, remembering her conversation with Owen, his confession about stealing a scarf that belonged to his mother because his father had kept everything else for himself. At the time she'd been intent on learning all she could about the events that had shaped the man Owen had become, but in the back of her mind, she'd spared a moment of compassion for his father, too. He'd been misguided and cruel, but he'd been in the grip of a loss Libby could hardly comprehend.

Could she offer her own grandfather, a man who'd lost not only his wife but all three of his children, in different ways, any less compassion?

"That box of recipes, a few handkerchiefs, a bunch of ceramic figurines—they're all I have left," Grandfather said gruffly, his pinched mouth folding in on itself to hide what he was feeling.

But Libby was pretty sure she knew. And her big,

hopeful heart softened faster than butter in an over-heated kitchen. "Those things are precious, and I understand why you held them close. But they're not all you have left, Grandfather."

"Nash's mother calls sometimes," he shrugged, his unsteady gaze wavering off to the side. "She's got her own life. Too busy to come home for holidays."

"That's not what I meant. And I don't mean me, either—although you do have me, Grandfather, and Nash too. We want to be your family, if you'll let us. But I wasn't talking about Nash's mom." Libby took in a deep, fortifying breath. "I was talking about your son. Ray."

His voice went cold and hard as the frozen surface of Lantern Lake. "I don't have a son by that name."

"Yes, you do, and he needs you!" Libby dropped the rolling pin onto the counter with a loud clatter. "He's your family. We neither of us have so much family left that we can afford to cut anyone off. I don't know what happened between you, what happened to tear this family to shreds . . ."

"I'll tell you what happened. Your grandmother died, and my ungrateful children used it as an excuse to abandon me when I needed them most."

Libby gave him a narrow stare. "Really. And it had nothing to do with you trying to control them and tell them how to live their lives."

"It's a father's responsibility to take care of his children and help them make good choices," Grandfather sputtered. "I wanted my family around me. And I wanted them to avoid doing things that would make their lives harder. Is that so wrong?"

"What's wrong is holding a grudge against your only living son because he refused to fall in line and obey your decrees."

"Ray was always reckless. Headstrong and independent. The fights we used to have . . ." Grandfather's gaze turned distant, his eyes wet and red. "Your grandmother played peacemaker. But without her—maybe I went too far. Said things I didn't mean. But that doesn't mean I deserved to lose everything."

A chill ran over Libby's scalp. It was so similar to what Owen had said about his own father's abrupt personality shift after losing his wife. "Grief makes us do crazy things. It changes who we are and how we see the world. But you weren't the only one suffering, Grandfather. Surely you can see that Ray, and your other children—they'd lost their mother. Maybe they didn't mean what they said back then, either."

The old man's jaw hardened as he turned to leave. "It's been decades. Plenty of time to take it back, if that's what Ray wanted to do. He's always known where to find me."

"I can tell you where he is." Libby bit her lip when her blurted words caused Grandfather to pause. Maybe this was a bad idea. So much pain, so many years of regret and bitterness—could she really have the audacity to think she could change any of that for the better? "But it might be hard for you to hear."

"Nothing is harder than not knowing where your son is or how he's doing."

The raw emotion in Grandfather's voice made Libby swallow hard. Clearly, Dabney Leeds had not managed to cut Ray out of his heart, even if he'd wanted to.

Which was going to make it even harder to share the difficult news about Ray's condition. But it had to be done. This family didn't need any more secrets.

Gathering her courage in both hands, Libby lifted her eyes to meet her grandfather's wary, hopeful gaze and told him the truth.

"Good for you," Owen said. His voice was strained by the odd position he'd contorted himself into while wrapping white twinkle lights around the banister railing of the front staircase. "If you ask me, the old man needed to hear that. He's had a lot of loss, but not everyone in his family is actually dead and beyond help."

Libby unwrapped a shepherd and tenderly placed him with his flock on the foyer table that held her grandmother's nativity. She didn't allow her hands to shake with nerves—these heirlooms were too precious for that. "But then he stalked out of the kitchen without saying a word. That was days ago, and no one has seen Grandfather since! It was too much for him to take, or something, and now he's gone into hiding and my boss is arriving in two days with the camera crew, so there's no time to convince Grandfather to help me with Uncle Ray, which means I have to go through with Christmas dinner and it needs to not give anyone food poisoning and . . ."

"Hey."

A pair of warm, strong arms encircled Libby's waist from behind, encouraging her to lean back against a tall, hard, masculine body. Instinctively, Libby melted. Not everything in her life was going wrong, she remembered, as gratitude fizzed through her veins like sparkling apple cider.

"Everything is going to be okay," Owen said, low and husky. His breath fanned the hair behind Libby's ear, sending shivers up and down her spine. "You've got a great menu planned, guests coming over to help distract the TV people . . . and you've got me."

Joy bloomed in Libby's heart. Turning in his arms, she pressed up against his chest to loop her wrists behind his neck and flutter a kiss across his mouth. "I do have you, don't I," she said, wistful hope turning her voice breathless.

For now.

Instead of answering, Owen deepened the kiss, turning it hungry and ravishing between one heartbeat and the next. Libby's body awoke, clamoring for more of the pleasure he'd shown her in the Christmas shed.

In the days since the snowstorm, they'd been run off their feet getting ready for the holiday. In and around Owen's daily appointments at the therapeutic riding facility and Libby's ongoing campaign to show Caitlin the best Christmas of her life, they had decked the halls of Libby's grandfather's house from top to bottom.

Twinkle lights, pine boughs, red velvet ribbons, and gold-glittered berries draped every available surface. Ella Fitzgerald and Nat King Cole crooned carols from the stereo at all hours to accompany the near-constant delicious smells wafting from the kitchen, where Libby was teaching herself to cook from her mother's and grandmother's handed-down recipes.

The last few days had shown Libby that she didn't

need to go to culinary school to learn how to make tasty food that people wanted to eat. All she needed was a few good recipes and the guts to try.

Not that everything she'd tried had turned out well. There was the time she forgot the baking powder in the lemon cake, and it turned out flat and hard as stone, or when she put a cup and a half of salt instead of sugar into the peppermint brownies. . . . Libby moaned as Owen cupped her jaw and angled her head for a deeper kiss.

Focus on this, she told herself fiercely as desire weighted her limbs and molded her to Owen's form. *Don't think about anything else.*

Easier said than done as the front door opened and a blast of frigid air blew into the hallway. Canine nails clicked quickly down the hall as Grandfather's loyal bulldog, Pippin, came running to see if his master had returned, barking his oddly high-pitched bark all the while.

Pippin scrabbled for purchase on the hardwood floors, skidding and nearly braining himself on the doorframe before he realized it was only Caitlin.

"Pippin!" she cried, kneeling down to give the disappointed dog a hug that he leaned into, his overlong tongue lolling out of his wide, panting mouth. "Ew, you're all slobbery."

Owen dropped his hands from Libby's shoulders and stepped back, which Libby tried not to take personally, while down the hall, Nash poked his head out of the dining room where he was supposed to be polishing the silver.

"What's all the fuss about—oh, hey there, sprout. Are you here to help Miss Libby cook again today?"

"We're making spinach casserole," Caitlin told Nash proudly. "From scratch."

"How did you get over here?" Owen wanted to know. "Did you ride Peony?"

Caitlin's face lit up the way it always did when anyone mentioned horses. Of course, Owen's gentle teasing had the same effect, so it was hard to know what was making her eyes so bright as she said, "No! It's too cold out. The horses are all snug in the barn."

"So is Andie here? I should go say hi."

But before Owen could make a move for the door, Caitlin shook her head. "No, Aunt Andie had to work. Ivy gave me a ride."

Nash was out of the dining room and across the hall to pull the front door wide before Libby could blink.

"Hey, Libs?" Nash said over his shoulder as he snagged his coat from the rack by the door. "Would it be a big deal if I invited one more guest to Christmas dinner?"

Libby clapped her hands, delighted. "Of course not! The more the merrier. Tell Ivy we'll look forward to seeing her tomorrow."

"The more the merrier?" Owen muttered as they followed a bright, chattering Caitlin down the hall toward the kitchen. "I got the biggest turkey they had at the market, but I don't know how many more people we can squeeze around the dining room table."

"Ivy is Nash's long lost love," Libby explained. "And I screwed everything up for him by coming here and asking him to play house. The least I can do is let the woman come over for some turkey and stuff—oh, no."

Caitlin had stopped dead in the kitchen doorway, forcing Owen and Libby to nearly crash into her. But the reason for her shock was only too obvious as they took in the sight that greeted them.

There was the stepladder Libby had gotten out for the express purpose of boosting Caitlin up to help with cooking tasks at the high kitchen counter. She'd set it up a few days ago and hadn't put it away, since Caitlin had been coming over every day.

Unfortunately, Libby hadn't considered what a temptation it would be to leave a stepladder out by the countertop that also held the roasting pan and rack where she'd unwrapped and left the twenty-pound turkey to defrost.

"I thought Pippin was slobbering an extra lot," Caitlin said, looking up at Libby tearfully. "Miss Libby. Look at the turkey."

"I see it," she said faintly, almost unable to believe her eyes. Her perfect, pristine bird, that she'd planned to get up at one in the morning to start roasting so it would be golden-brown and juicy in time for a mid-day meal, had been torn to shreds. The white, dimpled skin hung in strands around the carcass, which looked like it had been picked clean by an army of scavengers. It was almost impressive for one elderly bulldog.

"He got up on my ladder!" Caitlin sobbed. "I'm sorry. It's my fault."

"Hey, no." Libby had drifted into the kitchen to inspect the remains up close, but she turned back at that.

"It's really not your fault at all. It's mine, for being careless and leaving the turkey out where Pippin could get to it."

Caitlin's thin shoulders shook, the girl heading toward the kind of meltdown that couldn't be reasoned with. Andie had confided to Owen that these recent intense emotional outbursts were reassuring, in a way—they were a more natural, healthy way of processing than the total withdrawal Caitlin had used in the past. But when Caitlin wailed like that, it was hard to see it as progress.

Owen stood behind his daughter, an agonized expression on his face. His big hand hovered an inch above Caitlin's back, as if he were afraid to reach out to her. Libby remembered the way Caitlin had pulled away from him before, and she knew Owen was remembering it too.

She started to hurry back, intending to give Caitlin a hug if the kid would allow it, but before she took two steps, Caitlin had turned and thrown herself at her father. Her skinny arms went around his waist, her red face buried in his stomach, and Owen closed his eyes as if he'd been hit with the butt of a rifle.

But he didn't hesitate. He dropped to his knees to pull Caitlin into his arms, that same hand that had hesitated to touch her now cradling her carroty-red curls against his shoulder. Owen whispered soothing words Libby couldn't quite make out, but she knew the tone well enough. And she recognized the way Owen's hand stroked down Caitlin's back, tender and careful as if he were handling something infinitely precious.

The knot of upset and tears that had choked into Libby's throat at the sight of her ruined hopes for a perfect Christmas dinner melted, along with every bone in her body. Only the swelling of happiness in her heart was enough to keep her upright.

Caitlin quieted, her sobs trailing off into hiccups and sighs. Owen bent his head to bury a kiss in her messy red hair, and when he looked up again he caught Libby's eyes. Her breath hitched and her heart swelled at the naked love shimmering in Owen's gaze.

"Is Libby mad at me?" Caitlin asked in a small voice, her face still pushed into the curve of Owen's neck.

Libby smiled tremulously when Owen immediately said, "No, sweetheart. No one is mad at you. You didn't do anything wrong. But even if you had, we'd forgive you."

Knees weakening, Libby groped for the edge of the counter behind her. Owen never dropped his gaze. His warm, reassuring voice was steady and clear. "We all make mistakes now and then. And we all deserve forgiveness."

Libby's vision blurred with tears, emotion filling her heart to the brim and running over. Owen nodded slightly, his face serious, and a weight Libby had been dragging around for what felt like years suddenly lifted from her shoulders.

Owen forgave her.

Filled with renewed energy, Libby whirled to face the task of disposing of her poor turkey. She rolled up her sleeves and got to work, her mind already racing with ideas for how they could replace the centerpiece of the holiday meal with less than two days to go.

It was a daunting idea, but for the first time, Libby found herself believing what Owen had tried to tell her earlier.

Everything was going to be okay. It might take a Christmas miracle—or two—but it would work out. Libby believed that with all her heart.

Chapter Twenty-Two

The morning of Christmas Eve brought a new bank of storm clouds rolling in with the dawn.

Libby, who had already been up for a couple of hours by the time the sun refused to show its face, kept the radio tuned to the local station in hopes of a weather update. Maybe her Christmas miracle would take the form of a snowstorm that would keep travelers—like her boss and the camera crew—from boarding the ferry to Sanctuary Island. That would work.

Closing her eyes and sending up a quick prayer, Libby took a moment to massage a cramp out of her aching lower back. *In my next article,* she thought absently, *I'm going to write about what hard work it is to put on a multi-course dinner for a dozen people.*

Of course, unless she went through with this crazy charade, she wouldn't be writing any more articles. She'd be out of a job.

As much as she'd longed to be done with the elaborate lie her career had become, the idea of being done with writing stung. Especially now that she'd learned so much about the art of the kitchen from her mother's notes on her grandmother's recipes . . . and she'd learned so much about being a family from Nash and Grandfather, and from Owen and Caitlin. She'd always treasured the stories she'd spun about her imaginary life on Sanctuary Island, but after this experience, she was sure she could give them even more depth and detail.

"Happy Christmas Eve," Owen said, slouching into the kitchen with his gaze trained on the ancient coffeemaker perking in the corner.

Libby paused in the act of cutting marshmallows into tiny cubes for ambrosia, her scissors hanging forgotten from her fingers as she contemplated the delicious sight of Sergeant Owen Shepard, sleep-tousled and heavy-lidded, with coppery stubble shadowing his jaw. The standard issue desert-tan T-shirt was rumpled over the black jeans he'd obviously thrown on to avoid shocking her with his boxer shorts. But he'd forgotten to do up the top button, and the way they slipped down his lean hips when he leaned over the coffeemaker had Libby's mind going blank with a heady pulse of desire.

Sighing to herself, she acknowledged that she'd be perfectly happy to have sleepy Owen be the first thing she saw every morning for the rest of her life.

He poured himself a cup of coffee while Libby surreptitiously ogled him. The first sip seemed to give him a boost that allowed his eyes to open fully for the first time. They immediately zeroed in on Libby, who instantly became aware of her bedraggled hair and sticky, fruit-juice-stained hands.

"Tell me you haven't been up all night," Owen demanded, a stern frown lowering his red-gold brows.

"I haven't," Libby hedged defensively. Anytime after midnight was technically a new day, right? "There's a lot to get done."

"And you can't help worrying that if you leave the kitchen for more than a couple of hours, some new disaster will explode in your face." Owen shook his head, but his expression had softened into something like fond indulgence.

"Not only that. I'm worried about Grandfather. Nash heard from him last night, and Grandfather says he's fine, not to worry about him, but I can't help it. I'm afraid he's going to miss Christmas."

As if hearing the real tears that shook Libby's voice, Owen set down his coffee mug and crossed the kitchen in two long strides to take her in his arms. Libby let herself sink into his warmth, smooshing her face into his firm shoulder while holding her sticky hands safely out to the sides.

"I'm sure he won't want to miss Christmas at home with you and Nash," Owen murmured, so strong and sure that Libby wanted desperately to believe him.

"But if he's where I pray he is, visiting Uncle Ray up in New York, he might not have a choice," she fretted, already feeling guilty for hoping a snowstorm would sweep in and bury all her problems under a thick blanket of white.

"Is it really that bad out?"

"Not yet, maybe, but the last forecast predicted a new snowfall. Six inches!"

Owen hummed thoughtfully, the vibration under

Libby's cheek making her shiver just as the jazzy, full-orchestral version of "Rudolph the Red-Nosed Reindeer" faded out and the announcer's voice came back over the airwaves.

"As we've been predicting, folks, it looks like it's going to be a white Christmas here on Sanctuary Island! And I'm not talking about the white sands of our beautiful beaches, either, or the leftover snow from last week's storm—no sir, we're getting a brand-new dusting of powder just in time to cushion Old St. Nick as he slides down your chimneys tomorrow night. Festive as that sounds, the Town Council is holding an emergency session right now to figure out how to prepare for the storm. Keep that dial right where it is, folks. We'll be updating you on the latest business closings and weather advisories as soon as we get 'em. For now, let's all keep warm by the fire with Miss Dolly Parton."

Libby stood paralyzed in Owen's embrace as the first few notes of "Away in a Manger" played on a simple piano came tinkling out of the radio. " 'Closings,' " she said, a mixture of dread and relief churning in her belly. "I wonder what that means."

"Let me text my sister. Andie's the sheriff, if anyone knows what's going down at that Town Council meeting, it's her."

Reluctantly, Libby stepped back and let Owen dig through his pockets for his phone. He thumbed out a quick message then laid the phone on the counter in favor of picking up his coffee mug once more. "Have you tried calling your grandfather?"

Guilt swamped her, drowning every other emotion under a tidal wave of regret. "He won't answer when I call. It goes straight to voicemail. Why did I have to push? Grandfather is old. His heart isn't the strongest. I knew he'd take it hard."

"Ray is his son," Owen said, his lips set in a hard line. "Your grandfather needed to hear the truth about what's happening to him. He needed to face it, even if it's hard."

Owen, who'd missed years of his daughter's life just as Dabney Leeds had missed out on his son's, had a point. But if anything bad happened to Grandfather because of what Libby had told him, she'd never forgive herself.

"I just wish I knew what was happening," she fretted. "I'm sure he went to see Ray. That's the only thing that makes sense, after what I told him. But I don't even know if Grandfather's going up there to reconcile with his son or to fight with him some more! Or maybe just to make sure I'm telling the truth. I wouldn't blame him for doubting me, after all of this."

Sniffling, Libby picked up her scissors and glumly went back to snipping jumbo marshmallows into quarters. Every other marshmallow or so, she dipped the scissor blades into a glass of water to keep them from getting too gunked up—a tip her mother had scrawled across the back of one of the three separate recipes for marshmallow cream salad—aka ambrosia—in her grandmother's recipe box.

"Wouldn't it be easier to use mini marshmallows?" Owen asked, his tone determinedly light.

Libby shrugged. "Maybe. But the recipe says to use big ones and cut them down, so that's what I'm doing."

Amusement curved Owen's beautiful lips. "You're really getting into this cooking thing, aren't you?"

"You know, I am." Libby struggled for a moment, tears closer to the surface than she'd like. "It almost feels like my mother is here, looking over my shoulder and helping me. It's like she's teaching me to cook from the beyond."

"That's beautiful, Libby." Owen stroked a hand over her hair, his fingers too nimble and gentle to catch in the tangles.

She felt a tension she hadn't been aware of flow out of her shoulders at Owen's simple acceptance. "I haven't felt this close to her in a long time. And it feels great, but it hurts a little too. Because this is all I can have of her now—and it's taken me so long to get here."

On the counter, Owen's phone vibrated with an incoming text, and Libby let out a grateful breath. She took the time to pull herself together while Owen checked his sister's reply.

"Andie says the Town Council meeting is over," he told her, voice tense. "And they voted to close the ferry down after this morning's run."

Libby sagged over her cutting board, not sure how she felt. "Oh my goodness. Well, if that's what it takes to keep people safe, that's what they have to do."

Looking at her limp hands and the half-full bowl of snipped marshmallows, Owen raised a brow. "I guess that means you can stop cooking now, if you want. No more television crew, no more boss to lie for."

"No!" Libby straightened her shoulders and dunked her scissors determinedly before picking up a jumbo marshmallow. "Maybe Grandfather won't make it home in time, but we're still having a wonderful family Christmas here if it kills me."

The silence from Owen felt taut, full of things unsaid. Libby peered over her shoulder to see him standing in uncharacteristic indecision, one hand rubbing absently at his injured leg as a frown dropped over his handsome face. "I guess Caitlin and I will do Christmas at Andie's, then."

Oh. Pierced through, Libby kept herself upright by sheer force of will. Looking back down at her work, she said, "Okay. If that's what you want. But I would love to have you here, especially with no cameras or prying eyes to put on some big act for."

"I know you promised to help me give Caitlin a Christmas to remember, but you've already done that— we've built snowmen, made a gingerbread house and snow angels, decorated cookies, had homemade snow ice cream. I'm pretty sure we could take Caitlin through the drive through for a hamburger for Christmas dinner and she'd still think this was the best Christmas ever."

"I'm glad of that. But I don't want you both here to fulfill a promise," Libby said, reaching deep for the courage Owen kept saying she possessed. "It's much more selfish than that, I'm afraid. I want you here because it won't feel like a real family Christmas to me without the two of you. You and Caitlin—you're family to me. The family of my heart. I know that's a lot to take in . . ."

The rest of Libby's words were lost, swallowed by Owen's mouth as he grabbed her and whirled her into his arms, bending her back in a low dip and kissing the breath out of her. Shocked and off balance, Libby clutched at his shoulders and kissed him back with everything she had, pouring every drop of love from her overflowing heart into this man who was so much more than the handsome hero of a story she'd made up. Owen was real, haunted and flawed and perfectly imperfect. He was here, in her arms, and he was kissing her as if he'd never let her go.

She held on with all her strength and wished that it meant what she wanted it to mean—that Owen was starting to love her back.

Hearing Libby tell him that he and his daughter were the family of her heart brought out something wild and primitive in Owen. He had to touch her, had to possess her and claim her and mark her somehow.

A hard tug at his hair shocked Owen out of free fall. Maybe Libby was the one marking him, with her sticky sugar-coated fingers. That was okay too, Owen decided, loving the way her eyes went hot and dark when he lifted her right hand to his mouth and sucked her index finger between his lips. She tasted like sugar and cream, with the bright tang of crushed pineapple and mandarin oranges, and an underlying richness that was all Libby.

From the front of the house came the distant chime of the doorbell. It barely registered in Owen's brain, busy as he was with cataloguing every sigh and shift of Libby's sweetly rounded body against his much larger, much harder one. The sound of footsteps descending the staircase from the second floor let Owen put it out of his mind completely. Nash would answer the door and deal with whoever it was. Owen could concentrate on mapping the velvet of Libby's mouth, testing the plush plumpness of her bottom lip with the barest edge of his teeth, enjoying the way she jumped then moaned.

Voices in the hallway and a quick knock at the kitchen door had Owen growling low in his chest at the interruption. When Nash stuck his head in, wild-eyed and shocked, it was all Owen could do not to snarl at the man.

"Crap, get a room," Nash hissed when he saw them, making a slashing motion with one hand as he darted a quick look over his shoulder. "Only don't, because guys, I hate to tell you this but we have company."

"Is that my favorite writer in there?" boomed a hearty male voice from the hall. It was unfamiliar to Owen, but from the way Libby went cold and stiff in his arms, she knew exactly who was out there.

"Oh no," she breathed, tearing herself out of Owen's arms and frantically smoothing at her hair and clothes. Despite Owen's best efforts, her hands were still so sticky that she was messing herself up more than tidying. Owen reached out to help, but she ducked away from his touch, leaving his empty hand to grasp at thin air before falling uselessly to his side.

"Just a quick second," Nash was saying to whoever it was. "My wife is in the middle of a slightly sensitive kitchen maneuver—I don't pretend to understand it myself, ha ha—but if I can get y'all to wait in the library, she'll be with you in a moment."

His wife. Owen went cold with dread, but he couldn't let that keep him from moving forward. Calling on all his training, Owen rallied. "Calm down, Libby. Nash bought us a few minutes. Breathe, and give me a sit rep."

As he'd hoped, curiosity cut through the panic on Libby's pretty face. "Sit rep? Oh, situation report. Right. Um, well, I guess the situation is that the universe hates me? And is punishing me? Because that out there is my boss, Hugo Downing. A day earlier than planned, no less. Since he isn't alone, I can only assume he brought your old pal Rhonda Friend and her camera crew with him. And they almost caught America's Favorite Cook cheating on her husband with America's Favorite War Hero."

The guilt in her voice battered at Owen's heart, but there was no time to deal with it. "Okay," he said, going into strategic mode. "We planned for this. All we have to do is go back to the original plan, and we should be fine."

"I know." Libby finally went to the sink to wash her hands, and Owen was surprised by how much he wanted to stop her and offer to clean every one of her fingers himself. With his mouth.

Get your head in the game, he told himself fiercely. For the first time, he wondered if he would actually be able to make it through the entire holiday without betraying the fact that he and Libby were intimately, deeply, irrevocably bound together in a way he didn't even understand fully yet.

"I was just starting to let myself believe we wouldn't have to do this," Libby was saying, a heartbreaking wistfulness running through the words while she soaped up. "I hate that you've been pulled into my lies, Owen. I hate it so much. I hate that this means we can't tell Caitlin the truth yet, and Nash has to spend the holiday pretending he's not in love with Ivy, and I wish I could tell them to go to hell but there's still my uncle Ray to think about, and I don't know what Grandfather is planning to do about all that and I can't risk . . ."

This, Owen knew how to deal with. Coming up behind Libby, her cupped his palms over her shoulders and let the outsides of his thumbs stroke her neck. "Breathe," he repeated, gently implacable. "In and out, honey. Come on."

Libby drew in a shuddering breath, her head falling forward and exposing the vulnerable nape of her neck. Owen longed to set his teeth to it, to bite down ever so gently and suck a mark of ownership into her fair skin, but he controlled himself.

Pulling herself together, Libby dashed a hand over her eyes and squared her shoulders. She gave him a shaky smile that got brighter as they stared at each other silently. "You can do this," Owen finally said.

"*We* can do it—together," she corrected, but her voice lilted up questioningly at the end, as if she still couldn't quite believe it was true.

How did I get here? Owen wondered suddenly. To this place where he was contemplating lying to the entire world. He hadn't told a lie since the day he joined the army. He'd always taken the army's code of ethics seriously, and had done his best to conduct himself as an officer and a gentleman. But as he gazed at Libby Leeds, Owen knew that he'd do far worse things to keep this woman safe and happy.

"Together," he told her, snagging her clean, damp hand and bringing it to his lips for one last kiss.

The hardest thing about this situation wasn't going to be lying to the world about who Libby really was. The hardest thing would be lying about who she was to him.

Chapter Twenty-Three

Nash showed Hugo Downing and Rhonda Friend into the library with a strange sense of not having woken up completely. Surely this was a dream. And a really, really bad one, at that.

Thank goodness Rhonda had left her camera crew outside in the van for this first meeting, because Nash was pretty sure he *looked* like he was still asleep. He was wearing green and white striped pajama pants, for Pete's sake.

"Love these stately old homes," Downing boomed. He seemed to be incapable of speaking at any volume less than a roar.

"Hmm," Rhonda Friend hummed, casting an analytical eye over the antique furnishings. "It's a little dark in here. I'll get the boys to set up some lights . . . if that's all right with you, of course, Mr. Leeds."

When she turned the full force of her smile on him,

Nash blinked. It was a little like coming face to face with a shark in his living room.

He blinked, and a nearly hidden spasm of annoyance tightened the corners of Rhonda's eyes. "Mr. Leeds?"

Right, Nash was supposedly Mr. Leeds. "Oh, sure. I guess you can bring in lighting. Why not? Except won't you mostly be filming the dinner, in the dining room?"

Ms. Friend stalked a quick circuit around the library, her stiletto heels clicking on the hardwood. "Certainly. But we'll need plenty of B-roll—that's the extra scenes we film for background, to show the happy family, perfect home, et cetera, cut in between the main segment of the dinner itself. Really, it's convenient we're here a day early. We'll have lots of time to get good film."

"Wonderful!" Nash found himself echoing Hugo Downing's too hearty tone while his mind jumped forward several steps to stress out about having these people underfoot for an extra day.

"This place reminds me of my vacation home on the East Bay," Hugo Downing was saying as Libby slipped into the library, followed by Owen.

They'd managed to mostly put themselves back together, Nash noted with approval, although Libby was still nervously tucking her messy blonde hair behind her ears. Did it look weird that they showed up together? Could anyone who didn't know them tell that they were *together* together?

Striding over, Nash clapped his own hand down on Owen's shoulder and beamed a huge not-a-care-in-the-world, nothing-to-see-here grin.

"At last," Nash said loudly. "My lovely wife and her kitchen assistant, Sergeant Owen Shepard. Of course,

Ms. Friend, y'all have already met. Owen, this is Mr. Hugo Downing."

"Proud to meet you," Downing said, striding forward to pump Owen's hand briskly. "Thank you for your service. As the publisher of *Savor* magazine, I can tell you we're all behind you boys, and we're glad you made it home safely."

"Safely-ish," Owen said with a faint smile and a gesture at his wounded leg. "But I'm one of the lucky ones, I know."

In the brief, awkward silence that followed, Nash caught the stricken look on his cousin's face. She was probably imagining how she might never have met Owen at all if he'd been more severely wounded or even killed in Afghanistan. Or maybe she was worrying about what would happen when Owen achieved his goal of getting back to combat-ready status and reenlisted. Either way, she was as pale as the sky outside, except for her eyes bright with unshed tears.

While Rhonda pranced over to renew her acquaintance with Owen, who didn't seem all that stoked to see her but covered with a polite smile, Nash sidled over to his "wife" and put a supportive arm around her shoulders. Bending his head, he whispered, "Buck up, Libs. You've got to come up with a better place to keep your heart than right out here on your sleeve like this."

She took a shuddering breath. "I'll try," she murmured back. "But I wasn't ready. I thought we'd have more time to prepare . . . or even that the snow would've kept them away."

Mr. Downing apparently caught the word "snow." "Yes, yes, awful weather heading this way. We thought we'd fly in a day early and get ahead of it. Hope it's not an inconvenience."

The way he said it made it very clear that even if it was an inconvenience, Mr. Hugo Downing didn't expect to hear anything about it. "Not at all," Nash said, mustering every drop of charm he could manage. "It's Christmas! Our house is always open, but never more so than at this time of year."

"Oh, good. We were hoping you'd say that," Rhonda gushed, her scarlet smile going feline and pleased. "I'll have the boys start bringing in the luggage."

Beside him, Libby froze, and a tiny squeak came from high in her throat. Nash was pretty sure he was the only one close enough to hear it, but he hurried to reply anyway. "I thought you were planning to stay at the Fireside Inn, in Winter Harbor."

"We were. But after today, the ferry won't be making runs back and forth to the mainland," Downing explained. "And since there's no hotel on Sanctuary Island, no room at the inn as it were, ha ha, our plan was to rely on good old-fashioned Southern hospitality and hope you'd take in a group of weary wanderers for the holidays."

Nightmare. Had to be. Nash pinched himself surreptitiously, but it didn't help. This was really happening, and he didn't see that they had a choice. Turning Libby's boss and a prominent television personality and her crew out into the snow would raise more questions than anyone here wanted to answer.

"Wonderful," Nash declared grimly, giving Libby's shoulders a prompting squeeze.

"Yes, wonderful," she echoed, shaking herself into

motion. "Of course, we'd be happy to have you. We have tons of space, even with Sergeant Shepard staying here. How many bedrooms will you need?"

"Four, if possible," Rhonda answered, so smoothly that Nash started to wonder if this had been her plan all along. "Thanks so much."

Nash frowned, mentally setting up the guestrooms and counting out the number of beds . . . uh oh. His gaze flew to Libby's and he saw the exact moment she realized. They would only have enough room for their new guests if Libby gave up her guestroom. Which meant she'd have to bunk in with Nash . . . or with someone else.

Things were about to get interesting.

The rest of the day was a scramble. While Nash took their guests on an extended tour of the island—Rhonda was eager to get some of her B-roll before the weather kept them indoors—Libby threw herself into her kitchen tasks. Owen pitched in where he could, grateful for the army training that allowed him to make six beds in record time, neat and tidy as anyone could want.

He also whisked Libby's things out of the bedroom she'd been using and moved them to Nash's room, trying his best to ignore how much he wished he had the right to put Libby where she belonged . . . with Owen.

But maybe this is better, he thought to himself as he firmly shut the door on the possibility of spending the night with Libby. They'd flirted with intimacy, and he would never forget the sight of her coming to pieces at his touch, but since the night of the storm, they'd been too busy getting ready for Christmas to go any further. And maybe that was good. He'd gotten in so deep with Libby, and right when his life was in the biggest transition and turmoil he'd faced since he left home as a teenager.

A decade in the army had given Owen stability, security, order. Six months without it, and he felt lost. Unmoored. How could he think about getting seriously involved with someone like Libby Leeds when he didn't know where he'd be in a month? When he didn't know if he'd be caring for his daughter as a single dad or if he'd be leaving her here with the aunt who loved her? When he couldn't even figure out what would be best for Caitlin, much less himself?

They worked through the rest of the afternoon, tidying and finishing decorating, cooking and cleaning. Through it all, there was no word from Libby's grandfather, and she got more and more despondent about it as time went on. By the time their guests returned, cold and red-cheeked and full of the wonders of the Sanctuary Island scenery, Owen was ready to call it a night. Nash seemed to agree, disappearing at once upstairs with an expression that said he'd done his time and couldn't take much more of their illustrious company.

But Rhonda Friend had other ideas.

"I've been looking forward to eating your cooking for some time now," Rhonda purred, glancing at the closed kitchen door. "I hope you're not going to disappoint us."

The kitchen door was closed because behind it, the kitchen looked as if a flour bomb had exploded. Dishes were piled all around the sink, and dirty knives and utensils covered every surface, but Libby had made it through her prep list like a champ. However, Owen had his doubts about whether she had the energy to get back in there and prepare dinner for all these people after a full day of intense cooking.

Libby wilted before his eyes. "Oh. Gosh, I wasn't really planning on—you see, the fridge is so full of things for tomorrow . . ."

"But surely that's no problem for an accomplished home cook like yourself," Rhonda said. "You must throw parties like this all the time. At least, according to your articles, you do."

"Actually," Hugo Downing said swiftly, "I was thinking tonight would be a good time for me to take everyone out to dinner as a thank-you for the generous hospitality you and your family are showing, not only to us, but to Sergeant Shepard and his family. What do you say?"

Rhonda pouted slightly, giving Owen a sideways glance that made him uncomfortable. "Is there even a restaurant worth going to on this teeny island? I'm sure Owen would prefer a home-cooked meal."

"As a matter of fact, there's a great restaurant on Sanctuary Island." Libby pulled her shoulders back, her chin tilting up determinedly. "And I'd love to take Mr. Downing up on his kind offer. As much as I hate to disappoint you, Ms. Friend, I'm not a professional chef. I've been cooking all day, and I have to be honest, the idea of someone else bringing me food while I get to sit down and do nothing is pretty appealing."

Owen was so proud of her in that moment, he could have kissed her. It went against her grain to stand up for herself and say what she needed when someone else wanted her to do something. But like Owen had been saying all along, Libby had guts.

"The Firefly Café sounds awesome to me," Owen put in. "Try the fried chicken, Mr. Downing, it'll knock your socks off. But as it happens, I was planning to spend tonight at my sister's house with my daughter. Libby, Caitlin specifically invited you to come along too. I think she's got a gift for you that can't wait until tomorrow."

Delighted curiosity lit Libby's beautiful eyes. *I want to make her look like that fifty times a day,* Owen caught himself thinking.

"Oh, I'd love to get a look at your sister's house and meet your family," Rhonda said instantly, the words like a bucket of ice water dumped over Owen's head.

"Sorry." Owen did his best to actually sound like he meant it. "But my sister's place is tiny. It really couldn't handle all of us. So if you and your crew wouldn't mind having dinner without us tonight . . ."

Rhonda frowned, sharp eyes narrowing, but Mr. Downing came to the rescue with a bluff, cheerful, "Of course we don't mind! We know we showed up when you weren't expecting us. We completely understand. And we'll meet your sister and daughter at Christmas dinner tomorrow, won't we, Sergeant?"

"Yes, sir," Owen said, resolutely not making eye contact with Rhonda Friend, who seemed to want something from him that he wasn't prepared to give. "But for now, we'd probably better get going, Libby. My sister is expecting us."

They had almost escaped, shrugging into their coats and wrapping scarves around their necks, before Rhonda said, "Don't you want to wait for Mr. Leeds? Surely he's invited, too."

Under his guiding hand, Libby stilled like a rabbit

scenting a predator. She let out a high, slightly nervous laugh. "Oh! Gracious, I must have inhaled too much powdered sugar earlier. We can wait for Nash, right, Sergeant Shepard?"

"I told Nash about the plan earlier," Owen said as smoothly as he could. "He's going to drive separately so I can spend the night at my sister's, if I want to. We can play it by ear if we have two cars."

"Good idea," Libby said, clearly relieved. She blinked at him gratefully before saying good night to everyone and slipping outside, probably to text Nash and fill him in.

Owen gave one of Rhonda's crew guys the directions to the Firefly Café, then followed Libby with a wave to Downing and Rhonda, who still looked suspicious—or at least annoyed at not getting her way.

Outside, the frigid air was heavy with the scent of an oncoming snowstorm. Owen inhaled deeply, savoring the shock of it in his lungs. He let it out and gestured Libby silently toward the car. Her gaze flicked back toward the house, then she started walking. The only sound was the crunch of their boots over the hard-packed snow on the walkway.

Once inside the car, close and relatively safe from prying eyes, it took every ounce of Owen's hard-won self control not to reach for Libby immediately.

It helped that Libby started babbling the instant her door shut and the engine started up. "Thank goodness you were there! I don't know what I would have done if you hadn't been. A whole extra meal with them! All evening having to watch my every move, my every word, in front of that awful Rhonda Friend."

Owen laughed as he shifted into gear and started driving. "Wow. I don't think I've ever heard you say anything negative about anyone before."

"All evening to watch her make eyes at you."

Owen had no idea why the sulky jut of Libby's lower lip made him want to take a bite out of her when Rhonda's perfectly practiced pout had left him cold.

"Good thing we avoided *that*," he said calmly, the small indication of Libby's possessiveness making him feel warmer than the hot air pumping from the car vents.

"I'd much rather spend the evening with you and Caitlin. But are you sure it's okay to spring this on your sister at the last minute?"

"I'm not springing it on her," Owen assured her. "Caitlin texted me earlier today, I just hadn't had a chance to talk to you about it yet. She and Andie have cooked up some scheme, between the two of them, and it has something to do with horses."

"Horses!" Thoroughly intrigued, if the light in her eyes was anything to go by, Libby tapped the corner of her phone against her chin. "I wonder what it could be. Oh, by the way, I told Nash what's going on and he said he had other plans tonight anyway, so it'll be just us."

"Just us," Owen repeated, a slow smile uncurling as he let the thought wash over him. Just us. Just him, and Caitlin, and Libby, at his sister's house.

Just family.

Chapter Twenty-Four

"Okay, now you can look!"

Caitlin's excited voice had Libby laughingly pulling off the knit cap that had been tugged down to cover her eyes. The first thing she saw was Caitlin's fiery red hair under a wool hat, with a navy blue duffel coat on over her flannel nightgown and a pair of stout paddock boots on her feet.

Oh, Libby realized. *Paddock boots instead of snow boots because . . . we're in the barn.*

"We're at Windy Corner," Caitlin squealed, clapping her mittens together. "You didn't know where we were going, did you? It's a big surprise. No one is usually supposed to be here this late at night, but we have special permission. For a special treat, I mean, a present. A Christmas present."

"For me?" Libby glanced at Owen, still mystified. The secret smile he gave her didn't clear anything up, but it did send a shock of heat to the furthest reaches of Libby's body.

"Yes, for you, duh," Caitlin said, rolling her eyes impatiently.

"Tell her why," Andie prompted from the doorway of the barn, a secretive smile the twin of her brother's curving her lips.

"Oh, right." Caitlin was all but dancing in place, obviously wanting to get this part over with so she could unveil the present, whatever it was. But she cleared her throat and said, very nicely, "Miss Libby. Tonight is for you, to thank you for the candy houses and the snow ice cream and all the other stuff you've done for us. This has been the best Christmas ever!"

Libby's heart clenched, too much happiness and pleased surprise wrapping around her chest and squeezing tight. "I'm so happy to hear you say that," she managed, even though part of her wanted to caution the girl, "It's not Christmas yet! Thank me after we get through tomorrow unscathed."

"It's going to be even more perfect later," Caitlin pronounced, grabbing Libby's hand and towing her enthusiastically down the empty barn hallway.

Owen followed behind, a bemused look on his face, as they hurried down the hall. Several horses stuck their heads out of their stalls, as if wondering what the ruckus was all about so late at night when the barn was usually silent.

Caitlin stopped in front of the last stall on the left, dropping Libby's hand to do a quick twirl in place. "Ta da!"

Poking her head in, Libby saw that the stall was empty. Clean, fresh hay was scattered across the floor and a couple of large, square bales of hay were snugged up against the walls and covered in a blankets. Glittery tinsel garlands wreathed the walls, and a picnic basket and thermos sat next to the hay bale.

"Surprise!"

Libby blinked. "You . . . got me a stall at the barn. Thank you?"

She hadn't managed to decide whether to be offended at being equated with a horse—horses were Caitlin's favorite creatures on earth, after all—by the time Caitlin rolled her eyes again.

"No! It's not to live in. It's only for tonight, because tonight is a very, very special night."

"It's Christmas Eve," Owen guessed, snapping his fingers as if he'd just remembered.

Caitlin beamed. "Yeah. And Miss Jo says that on Christmas Eve, an amazing thing happens."

"What's that?" Owen dropped to his haunches, putting him at eye level with Caitlin.

After a conspiratorial glance up at Andie, who was leaning on the stall's open door and smiling, Caitlin whispered, "At midnight, the horses will talk."

"Wow," Libby said, her heart thrilling in her chest. "That sounds amazing."

"It's going to be." Caitlin nodded confidently as she pulled off her mittens and hat. The barn was warm and dark, Christmas lights and an electric lamp the only illumination in the stall. "I'm going to stay up all night until I hear them. As long as . . ."

The little girl paused, her confidence evaporating like snow under the sun.

"As long as what, sweetheart?" Owen asked, his voice soft and gentle.

Caitlin pressed her lips together and peered up at her father from under her pale, redhead's lashes. "Aunt Andie has to work tomorrow, the early shift. She can't stay up all night. So. I was wondering . . . will you stay with me?"

Libby's heart jumped into her throat. She saw the movement of Owen's strong, brown throat as he swallowed down some overpowering emotion that Libby could only guess at. But she knew what a big step this was for Caitlin and Owen's relationship.

Libby backed up a step, meaning to leave the two of them to talk in relative privacy, but Caitlin turned those pleading eyes on her. "You too, Miss Libby! I want you to stay and hear the horses talk!"

Throat too full to allow for speech, Libby only nodded. She could feel her smile trembling at the corners.

"We'd love to stay with you," Owen said gruffly, standing up and moving to rummage through the picnic basket. "What do we have here?"

"It's an old Scandinavian legend," Andie explained, her eyes soft as she watched her niece explore their provisions with Owen. "It has to do with Jesus being born in a manger, among the animals. According to the story, the birth happened at midnight precisely, and the Lord gave the animals voices to speak in human tongues. They used their voices to sing praises until the shepherds arrived. And the only ones who heard them were Mary, Joseph, and of course, the baby Jesus."

"That's beautiful." Libby's head was full of it, the image of the exhausted, elated mother and her newborn babe, the stoic father standing by, and the magical moment of the horses, cows, oxen, sheep . . . suddenly opening their mouths and speaking.

"I don't know how popular a myth it is anymore, generally," Andie was saying. "But apparently the story still thrives among horse people. Jo says everyone she knows who owns a barn has spent at least one sleepless Christmas Eve in the stables, hoping to witness magic."

Libby glanced back at the two ginger heads bent close together over the open picnic basket, and felt as if she'd swallowed a flock of fireflies. "I think we've already seen our moment of magic tonight."

After hours of reading aloud to each other from the books packed at the bottom of the picnic basket, sampling the delights of crustless peanut butter and jelly sandwiches and apple slices, and singing carols to keep each other awake, Caitlin had finally given in to her obvious sleepiness and agreed to take a short nap. Of course, she extracted a promise from her father first to wake her up the minute the horses started chatting.

Owen had sworn faithfully, taking this vow as seriously as any other in his life. His daughter had asked him for something, for the first time. And maybe it was a silly promise to give, based on a legend and predicated on a myth, but when Owen looked into Caitlin's deep, wounded, earnest eyes, he remembered what it was like to believe in something with his whole heart. He remembered the hurt of others disregarding or belittling that belief.

And he remembered the way Libby had spoken to Caitlin the night they met, at the Christmas Village nativity play, when she'd reached out to the girl by taking her seriously—and she'd gotten through to Caitlin.

So he'd promised that when the animals spoke he'd wake her, straight-faced and meaning it with his whole heart, and Caitlin had curled up in the red plaid blanket and fallen asleep leaning into his side. The slight, warm weight of her there anchored Owen to the world in a way he'd never experienced before.

From her spot perched on the other hay bale, Libby smiled at them. "She lasted longer than I thought she would."

A sudden rush of tenderness seized Owen's throat. "She's a fighter."

"Like her dad."

They were keeping their voices quiet to let Caitlin sleep, but Owen could still hear the thread of sadness under Libby's soft words. He glanced away, out into the darkness of the night barn. "I guess that seems strange to you, that anyone would want a life like that."

She didn't pretend not to know what he meant. "The life of a soldier is almost impossible for me to imagine. And I admire you so much for the way you seem to deal with it."

"Every soldier is affected by his or her service. Of course we are. And I have exactly zero judgment for the ones who come home haunted by what they've seen and done—PTSD is real. It's a problem, and it needs to be taken seriously. But it's not necessarily the default. Movies and books and the media make out like every single soldier comes home from war too messed up to function, and that's not the case. Transitioning back to civilian life has its challenges, sure, but . . . sorry." Owen stopped, grimacing. "I don't mean to get up on a soapbox here."

"No, it's okay." Libby pulled both her legs up onto the hay bale and rested her crossed arms on her raised knees. "This is fascinating. And I think I get what you mean. Treating all returning war vets like ticking time bombs isn't fair. Also, maybe it makes it harder to diagnose and help those vets who really are suffering if we assume everyone has the exact same problems."

"I'm not saying I've never had a flashback or a nightmare," Owen clarified, the need for honesty thrumming through him. "Or struggled with some of the same stuff I've seen buddies go through when they get sent home. I guess all I'm saying is it's a spectrum, and as hard as my service was—I'd still do it over again. Which is exactly what makes me feel like I need to go back. I can handle it. Not everyone can—and that doesn't mean I'm better than them, by the way. The guys I know who've had the toughest time since they got back are some of the best soldiers I've ever seen. Men I trusted with my life in combat, and they never let me down once."

"I'm not surprised. Having PTSD doesn't mean someone is weak."

"Exactly." Relief that she understood nearly took Owen's breath. "And not getting it doesn't mean I'm stronger. But maybe it does mean I have a responsibility to keep fighting when others can't."

Libby smiled again, that same edge of bittersweetness twisting at her lips. "That's what makes you a hero, I guess."

Something surged through Owen, an emotion so fierce he couldn't have named it with a gun to his head. "I'm not a hero."

The words were almost growled, low and throbbing, and Caitlin stirred against him restlessly. Libby, however, didn't even flinch.

"Trust me," she said quietly. "I know stories, and you're the hero of this one."

Despair had Owen closing his eyes briefly. "You want to make me a hero, but one day you're going to figure out that you made it all up in your head. I'm not a hero, Libby. I'm just a man. A regular guy who wants to do the right thing."

Libby rested her chin on her crossed arms, tilting her head slightly. "See, that would be exactly my definition of a hero. Which makes me wonder what you think a hero is, if not a man who wants to do the right thing."

An image of his own father, crisp and stern in his police dress uniform, took over Owen's mental vision. The podium, the medal, the mayor's commendation . . . the first time he'd seen Dad smile since Mom died.

"A hero is someone who puts his duty before everything else in his life," Owen said slowly. "Someone who sacrifices his own desires in service to the greater good."

"That's certainly one definition," Libby said contemplatively. "Although that also sounds kind of like somebody with something to prove."

Owen frowned. "What do you mean?"

"Some sacrifices are noble," Libby said, shrugging. "Obviously. But sometimes people can appear to be sacrificing for the greater good when actually everything they're doing is about pumping themselves up to look big and important. If ego is what's most important to you, you're nobody's hero except your own."

Her words filtered into Owen's deepest memories and rearranged them, shuffling them like cards and dealing out an entirely new hand. Feeling as if one of the silent, nonspeaking horses had kicked him in the chest, Owen tipped his head back against the stall wall and laughed. "Has anyone ever told you that your ability to cut through the bull is kind of devastating?"

Libby blinked, eyes wide and innocent. "No? I don't mean to be devastating."

"I know. That's part of what makes it so rough. But don't worry, I love it."

I love you.

The words tickled the tip of his tongue, trying to leap free, but Owen swallowed them back. He couldn't do that, he couldn't drag Libby in any deeper, when the future was so uncertain.

But he should have known that Libby—his brave, reckless Libby—wasn't going to live her life in fear of the future.

"I love *you*," she said, three simple, straightforward words that could change Owen's life forever, if he let them. "You don't have to say it back or feel guilty, I just wanted you to know. And I want you to know that's not why I think you're a hero. I think you're a hero because whatever choices you make are about what's best for others, not for yourself. It's inspiring and humbling, and so, so sexy. And if you've made up your mind to go, I won't be the one who begs you to stay. I'll be the one who trusts that you're doing the right thing, because I don't think you know how to do anything less."

Talk about humbling. Owen shook his head, feeling the weight of his sleeping daughter pressing him into the hay bale and keeping him from striding across the stall to show Libby exactly how much he wanted to do the wrong thing with her.

"I can't move without waking Caitlin," he said hoarsely. "So I'm going to need you to come over here. Because I have to kiss you. Right now."

A beautiful flush pinked Libby's cheeks as she uncurled herself from her hay bale to snuggle up next to Owen. He got his free arm around her slim form, feeling whole and right for the first time all night, even before he put his mouth on hers.

The kiss was slow but not hesitant. Owen savored every second of it, the dangerous intimacy and undeniable connection he felt every time Libby turned her face up to his. He could kiss her forever and never get tired of it, he thought hazily.

But eventually, they both had to breathe. Owen pulled back, tilting his head down to press their foreheads together.

"I've never known anyone like you," he said helplessly.

Her fingers tightened where they clutched at his waist. "Ditto. Despite what you think, I'm not delusional enough to believe the fairy tales are true. I know real-life heroes are thin on the ground. But on a night like this, it's hard not to sense magic in the air. It's hard not to believe in miracles."

Owen breathed in, the scents of sweet hay, contented child, and warm woman filling his lungs. "Libby, I hope you know how I—"

"Please don't." Libby shook her head and sat back. "I didn't tell you I loved you to make you feel bad or to force some kind of confession in return. I just . . . there have been enough lies and secrets between us already. I couldn't bear another one."

Before she could move further away, Owen reached out and cuddled her back against his side. She was tense for a moment before settling close with a sigh. Owen pressed a kiss to the crown of her head and laid his cheek there to feel the rise and fall of her breath. "You're wrong, you know."

It was a mark of how relaxed she was that Libby didn't stiffen. "Oh? How's that?"

"I'm not the hero of this story," Owen whispered. "You are."

He felt her smile against his shoulder, right before she yawned. "Oops."

"Go to sleep," he told her. "It's okay. I'll keep watch."

"Are you sure?" she asked, already nuzzling her face against the shoulder she was using as a pillow.

"I don't need much sleep."

She roused slightly, blinking up at him. "Hey. Wake me up if any animals start talking, okay?"

With his arms and his heart full of this woman and this child who believed in miracles, Owen could do no more than nod. "You got it."

Satisfied with that, Libby put her head back down. At once, her breathing evened and deepened into the rhythms of sleep, and Owen let himself fall into the patient stillness and alertness of keeping watch.

Guarding the two people who meant most to him in the world, Owen knew there was no greater gift he could receive that Christmas.

Chapter Twenty-Five

"But we all fell asleep, so we missed it when the horses talked!"

Caitlin was so aggrieved, so mad at herself, she couldn't stop telling people about their failed Christmas Eve experiment. Even the fascinating topic of what she'd gotten for Christmas couldn't derail her for long, although she'd been pretty excited to show off the new jodhpurs and paddock boots under her Rudolph the Red-Nosed Reindeer sweater.

Every time Caitlin brought up their missed chance at hearing the horses speak, Libby felt guilty for falling asleep. But she also felt like she'd be miserable right now if she hadn't gotten any sleep at all the night before.

It was stressful enough to wrangle eight guests around an elaborately decorated holiday meal, complete with silently filming camera crew, an empty place setting for her absent grandfather, and a variety of secret relationships to hide. She'd been up since five as it was, doing last-minute prep and cooking. Exhaustion pulled at every muscle and made her bones feel weighted with lead, but they were seconds away from the first course being finished and so far, all the cameras had gotten was a half-hour diatribe from Caitlin about how much it sucked to fall asleep when you didn't want to.

Libby let herself be momentarily distracted by the memory of waking up on Owen's shoulder with a crick in her neck and a pervasive sense of safety and happiness. Owen had smiled down at her, not a trace of weariness on his handsome face, even under his coppery morning stubble. Libby was pretty sure he hadn't slept a wink, but when Caitlin roused a few minutes later and cried out at the sight of the sun rising outside the stall's back window, Owen had apologized gravely for failing her.

When Caitlin dragged herself out of the stall to visit Peony and see if she would maybe consent to speak even though Christmas Eve was technically over, Owen had lowered his head to whisper in Libby's ear. "I know I shouldn't lie to her. But I don't want her to stop believing in magic."

Libby had curled her arms around his neck and climbed into his lap with her heart beating the "Hallelujah" chorus behind her ribs. "Merry Christmas," she'd whispered back, then kissed him.

But now was not the time to get distracted. Now was the time to move onto the next course and pray her luck held. Trying to maintain her poise when all she wanted was to run into the kitchen to check on things, Libby smoothed her black-and-red checked dress—patterned to hide food splotches—and stood up to gather the empty soup bowls.

"Can I take that?" she politely asked Mr. Downing, who dabbed at his mouth and nodded.

"Wonderful," he told her. "Top notch. I never had an oyster soup like that, but I'll be asking you for the recipe for my personal chef."

Libby glowed under the praise until she got to Rhonda Friend, who had barely touched her soup.

"It's very rich," Rhonda commented, nudging the bowl away from her as if the calories were contagious.

"Cream does tend to be rich," Libby agreed, smiling around her clenched jaw and taking extra care with the almost full bowl.

"Here, let me help you clear this course," Ivy Dawson said, every inch the perfect guest.

"Oh, I can manage," Libby tried, but Ivy insisted, and it was easier to give in than to squabble about it in front of the cameras bristling from the four corners of the dining room like one-eyed black beasts.

After a quick, surprised "Oh!" when Ivy got a look at the disaster that was the kitchen, the silence that reigned as they stacked up the soup bowls felt as thick and stilted as the awkward conversation around the table.

Libby opened the fridge to get the ingredients she'd prepared for the salad course, and groaned when she encountered the solid wall of casseroles, mixing bowls, and other dishes. She was going to have to excavate to get to the pomegranate seeds and orange sections she'd carefully removed from their skins yesterday.

Pulling out the biggest casserole, the one right in front, Libby turned to put it on the counter and almost dropped the pan when Ivy was right behind her.

"You startled me," Libby said, trying to laugh it off.

"Sorry. I just wanted to say, while we have a minute alone—I know."

Libby's heart, which had started to slow after her moment of startlement, began to pick up speed once more. Edging past Ivy, Libby looked for a place to put the spinach casserole, but the counter was already packed with cutting boards, dirty dishes, and bags of flour and sugar.

"I know about you and Nash," Ivy spelled out, while Libby tried unsuccessfully to wedge the casserole onto the counter between the salad spinner and the food processor. "Nash came to see me last night, and he explained a few things."

Sweat prickled at Libby's hairline, and her palms got clammy enough that she worried the casserole would slip out of her hands. At her wits' end, she kicked open the back door and set the casserole dish down on the top back step. It would stay plenty cold out there, she reasoned, slamming the door shut and turning back to face Ivy.

"I see," Libby settled on, not sure how to respond without knowing exactly what it was that Nash had told Ivy. No wonder he'd been trying to get a word with her all morning, but Libby had been like a whirlwind in the kitchen, and then the camera crew was setting up and she had to shower or risk showing up on national television with a stringy ponytail, no makeup, and the jeans and sweater she'd slept in the night before.

"Don't be angry with Nash," Ivy said, a pleading note entering her sweet drawl. "I already knew some of it. Andie told me you and Nash weren't really married, but she couldn't explain all the reasoning behind it. I still don't think I've got it all straight, but at least I know now why Nash went along with it."

Libby raised her brows, relief filtering in and calming her heart rate. "Then you know everything. I'm glad. I hated asking him to lie for me, especially when it became clear how much he cared about you—and how much this whole deception was ruining his chances with you. But now you know the truth, the two of you can work out your differences and get back together! Well, once the camera crews are gone. If you don't mind waiting a few more hours."

"No," Ivy said sharply, shaking her head of smooth, retro, coal-black waves. Her red lips were turned down at the corners, and as Libby watched, tears welled at the corners of her eyes. Careful not to smear the black wings of her eyeliner, Ivy dabbed a finger at her eyes. "I mean, I won't do anything to blow your cover in front of the cameras. But I'm not sure what Nash told you, if you think this lie was the only thing keeping us apart."

Libby shifted her weight uncomfortably. "I guess . . . I don't know that much about your relationship. Only that Nash is deeply in love with you, and I suppose I assumed . . . well, hoped, that you felt the same."

Sniffing, Ivy shook herself like a cat coming in from the rain, her lushly curved body doing a quick shimmy that made the metallic green threads in her tight sweaterdress catch the light. "Come on, they're all waiting. Let's get this salad course underway."

Unhappy but not sure how much to push, Libby subsided. They worked side by side arranging orange wedges
and slices of pale green avocado on mounds of butter
lettuce, ladling over her grandmother's homemade poppy-
seed dressing, and scattering pomegranate seeds across
the plates like tiny rubies.

As they loaded up their arms with plates and prepared to head back into the dining room, Ivy suddenly
said, "I do love him, you know. I always have. But all
this sneaking around and cloak-and-dagger stuff is
pretty familiar. He's never been one for proclaiming his
love from the rooftops, and I just can't go through that
again. When we were together before back in Atlanta,
it was so good between us . . . as long as it was only the
two of us. Or if we were with my friends. But every time
I asked to meet his friends, or if he had a work function
where everyone else was bringing a plus one, he just . . .
faded away. He'd smile that charming smile and change
the subject, and I let him. For a long time. Longer than
I should have."

She looked down at the plates in her hands, blinking
quickly. Libby's heart went out to her. "You don't have to
tell me this if you don't want to."

Ivy sniffed once then tilted her chin at a proud,
determined angle. "He was obviously ashamed of our
relationship, on some level. And I get it. I'm not exactly
the pearl-wearing, white-gloved debutante who'd fit
right into a rich, old southern legacy. But I can't be anyone's dirty little secret. I deserve better than that. And
it's not that I don't believe him when he comes to my
house and pours his heart out to me in private, but I've
heard that before. Plenty of times. And at this point, I

won't feel like my heart is safe with him until he's ready to tell the whole world how he feels."

With that, Ivy swept out of the kitchen, and Libby could only scramble to follow her. They went around the quiet table, setting down plates, and Libby couldn't help but notice the way Nash tried to catch Ivy's eye and the way she avoided looking at him. Libby's heart hurt for them both, but when Rhonda Friend cleared her throat, Libby's gaze snapped back to the reporter in terror that she might have given something away.

Rhonda had a predatory air about her, like a lioness who'd spotted a lame gazelle, as she lifted one hand and signaled at the nearest cameraman. "Before we move on to the salad course, I have a surprise guest to introduce."

Under the table, Nash kicked at Libby's ankle, and she kicked him back. She had no idea what this was all about. Across from them, Owen scowled slightly, obviously as mystified as anyone else.

Standing smoothly, Rhonda straightened her black, sequined sheath dress and raised her voice, "You can come in now."

For a heart-stopping moment, Libby dared to hope that somehow Rhonda had found Dabney Leeds and helped him get home for a dramatic family reunion moment, but the person who entered the dining room was a woman. Young and fair-skinned with dark brown hair and eyes, the woman stepped up to the head of the long table as if she were preparing to address Congress.

She wore a no-nonsense suit in navy blue wool with a silvery gray shirt underneath. The only concession to the season was the glint of a gold pendant in the shape of a snowflake winking at her open collar.

"Um, hello," Libby said, remembering her hostess duties but unsure what to say. "Would you like some orange and avocado salad?"

"Happy holidays," the woman replied briskly, her gaze scanning the table and seeming to size up every one of the guests. Her eyes softened when they landed on Caitlin, making Libby think she had hidden depths of emotion. "And thank you for the invitation, but I'm not here for supper. I'm here to give Sergeant Owen Shepard some good news."

At the mention of his rank, Owen straightened his shoulders as if unconsciously. He was also wearing his dress uniform, looking so handsome and strong and yes, downright heroic in it that it was all Libby could do to keep from lunging across the table and kissing him.

"I'm Sergeant Shepard. Would you like to step outside, ma'am? I hate to interrupt Christmas dinner with my personal business," Owen said, a muscle ticking behind his jaw.

"It's no interruption," Rhonda protested, rounding the table to stand with the mystery woman and, not coincidentally, making sure to put herself in the camera's frame. "What, are we worried the salad will get cold? Relax, Sergeant, this is my gift to you. I'm sure everyone here can't wait to watch you open it."

Beside her, the unknown woman arched one perfect dark brow so slightly, Libby almost missed it. But that moment, along with the bone-dry tone of her voice when she spoke, gave Libby the impression that this woman wasn't pleased or impressed with Rhonda's attention-seeking shenanigans.

"My name is Hannah Swift," she said crisply, wasting no more time and addressing Owen directly. She didn't look at the cameras even once, although she clearly knew they were there. "I am the founder and president of The Hero Project, a national charitable organization whose mission is to provide service, care, education, and help to those wounded in the line of duty, from military veterans to cops to firefighters and more."

Without knowing why, Libby's fingers gripped the edges of her straight-backed wooden chair and held on tight.

"Thank you for everything you do," Andie Shepard said into the brief pause that followed Hannah Swift's introduction. Andie's voice was thick with emotion, but it didn't shake at all. "Your organization has helped hundreds of people to overcome and learn to live with their injuries, both mental and physical."

Hannah Swift put a hand to her face and whispered, "Your check is in the mail!" without ever cracking a smile. Libby liked her all the more for being able to make such a deadpan joke. "No, really. Thank you—I know that you serve and protect your community as sheriff. And you, Sergeant Shepard, were placed on the Permanent Disability Retired List six months ago following a catastrophic injury to your left leg and hip. At that time, the military doctors determined that you would never walk normally again, that your disability was, in fact, permanent—but I am here today to tell you that is not the case."

Across the table, Owen went entirely still, his blue eyes going as opaque as the ocean before a storm. Libby couldn't catch her breath. The inside of her head was all white noise and static, until she heard the words she'd been dreading for weeks: "Sergeant Shepard, it is my very great honor and joy to inform you that The Hero Project's medical team has informed me that your progress since you began your therapy at the Windy Corner Therapeutic Riding Center has been nothing short of amazing. Congratulations, you beat all the odds—with continued hard work and the help of a local therapeutic riding program, there is reason to hope that you will soon regain full use of your leg."

Owen was better. He was going to be completely healed. Joy and gratitude welled up in Libby's heart, even as it splintered apart with the knowledge that this meant Owen would be leaving Sanctuary Island—leaving her—very soon.

"Of course, the requirements for active military service are somewhat more demanding than what we civilians would consider a complete recovery," Hannah Swift continued. "But when you're ready, we would be happy to facilitate a consultation with the military hospital that treated you, and help get you reinstated in the Army."

"It's a little more complicated than that," Owen said slowly. "We'd have to present evidence before the Army Physical Disability Review Board, get my status changed from PDRL to TDRL—that is, Permanent Disability Retired List to Temporary Disability Retired List—before anyone will even think about looking at my case for reinstatement."

Interest honed Hannah Swift's gaze, turning her from

a serious, pretty women to a charismatic bombshell. Her fingers twitched, and Libby got the distinct impression the woman wished she had a pad and pencil so she could take notes. "That's fascinating, Sergeant. I'd love to talk further about this, if you'd be agreeable. My contacts at Windy Corner say you're eager to get back out there."

"What does she mean?" Caitlin's whisper was louder than a shout in the pregnant pause after Hannah Swift's announcement, as she tugged on Owen's sleeve. "Get back out where, Daddy?"

Owen tore his gaze from the woman watching him with calm understanding in the depths of her dark eyes. That woman was offering him everything he'd been working toward for months . . . and instead, he looked down at the little girl who'd just called him "Daddy" for the first time.

"She said you beat the odds," Caitlin pursued, her nose wrinkled in the same look of confusion that Andie used to get when they were kids. "Is that like beating someone in a race?"

Owen stared down at her. He couldn't find the words. He couldn't make his mouth open and shape itself around the truth. Out of the corner of his eye, he saw Libby's hand dart up to cover her own mouth, and Owen's lungs squeezed tight.

On the other side of Caitlin, Andie leaned over to wrap one arm around the girl's thin shoulders. "No, honey," Andie murmured. "Remember how your dad had to walk with a cane when he first got here? This lady helped your dad get better, and now she's here to tell him that someday soon, he could be well enough to go back to work. Until now, we didn't know for sure that he'd recover all the way."

He met Andie's eyes over the top of Caitlin's head, a silent and agonizing moment of connection, before Caitlin said dully, "So he's leaving."

"Sweetheart," Owen said, putting his hand over her small, cold fingers where they still rested on his arm, but Caitlin pulled away. She wasn't petulant or obvious about it; somehow, she seemed to shrug or shift and suddenly, she'd slipped out of his hold.

"I don't want to leave you," Owen tried, sharply conscious of the many eyes watching them, including the cameras recording every instant of this gut-wrenching conversation. "That's not what it's about. But I'm needed over there, where I work."

He paused, feeling helpless and hating it, but no one jumped in. No one else could have this conversation for him, Owen realized. It was between father and daughter, and he was the only person who could even attempt to make this better for Caitlin.

What other things in life would be like that, if he was here for her full time?

Shaking off the thought, Owen glanced at Libby, who dropped her hand from her mouth and attempted a smile and an encouraging nod. He could read her broken heart in her eyes, though, and nothing about that made what he had to say to Caitlin any easier.

"I love you," he told his daughter, the words falling out of him as if they'd always been that easy to say. "Nothing will ever change that, whether I'm here with you all the time or if I only see you for visits. Nothing has to change—"

"Everything changes." Caitlin said the words to her plate, her young voice sounding as tired and resigned as a much older person's.

He waited, heart in his throat, but she said nothing else. She didn't look up, she didn't respond when Andie tried to hug her . . . just eeled her way out of the contact as easily as breathing.

"Keep rolling," Rhonda hissed at one of the camera guys, who reluctantly brought the camera back up to his shoulder and pointed it at Owen's pale, trembling daughter.

Red-hot rage blew through Owen's chest, scouring it as clean and raw as a sandstorm in the desert. Before he knew what was happening, he was on his feet, his hands curled into fists, and Rhonda was taking a step backward with eyes gone wide with shock at whatever she saw on his face.

"Well," said Hannah Swift, smoothly interposing herself between Rhonda and Owen. "I've delivered my message, as agreed, Ms. Friend, and now I think I've taken up enough of this lovely family's time. Sergeant Shepard—Owen—it was a privilege to meet you, and The Hero Project is here to help . . . no matter what you decide."

With that, Hannah Swift turned and marched out of the dining room. Her timely intervention had broken the tension, and while Rhonda hastily conferred with her head camera guy, Libby picked up her fork and said, "Dig in, everyone. There are still two courses left to go."

Owen wondered if he was the only one who could interpret the grim determination in Libby's tone. This Christmas dinner had gone from being something to dread to something he and Libby were doing together to something to get through—to survive, no matter how difficult.

Owen glanced sideways at his daughter, sitting motionless beside him with a full plate of food in front of her, and examined the empty wasteland inside his chest.

It felt possible, in that moment, that even though he'd lived through basic training, Ranger training, and combat, he actually might not survive this holiday intact.

Chapter Twenty-Six

Libby had to go by the expressions of the people around her to tell if the salad tasted all right. Every bite she put in her mouth tasted like dust and ashes. She kept going, forkful after forkful, shoveling it in and hoping for the best.

The quicker she finished her salad, the quicker she could escape to the kitchen and let herself have a short, silent sobfest while she got the main course together.

Around the table, people were trying valiantly to move on from the floor show Rhonda Friend instigated by bringing in the head of The Hero Project to tell Owen he had a real hope of becoming combat-ready. Nash was doing his level best to engage Andie's boyfriend, Sam, and Ivy in a debate about whether or not there was a Mrs. Claus. They played along gamely, obviously hoping to cheer up Caitlin, but the little girl never looked up from her untouched plate.

Seeing her like this, so wan and withdrawn, Libby

was viscerally struck by how much Caitlin had changed in the last few weeks. Libby had gotten accustomed to a lively, chattering Caitlin who was intensely curious about the world around her. Watching her retreat into herself now sent a piercing dart of sadness through Libby's heart.

Beside Caitlin, Owen wasn't much more engaged in the conversation than his daughter was. He picked at his food, his thoughts obviously distracted and distant.

Libby was in the midst of choking down her last bit of avocado when the dining room door swung open and Hannah Swift poked her head in, looking flustered for the first time. "Excuse me," she said apologetically, "but would one of you mind moving the black SUV out there? I'm not sure how it happened, but I seem to have gotten blocked in while I was here."

Libby glanced at the confused frowns around the table. Andie started to push her chair back, saying, "We were here early and we parked right next to the house, so I don't see how we can be blocking anyone in, but . . ." when the front door opened behind Hannah.

From upstairs came the now familiar rapid clickety clack of bulldog paws coming to investigate the newcomer, but instead of a despondent sigh and a slower clickety clack as a disappointed Pippin saw that his master hadn't returned, a series of deep, throaty barks had Libby jumping to her feet.

Sure enough, the next thing she heard was her grandfather's rusty voice saying, "Where the hell is everyone? And who the hell are you?"

Without waiting for an answer, Dabney Leeds swept past Hannah Swift and into the dining room as dramatically as his walking stick and the seventy-pound bull-dog cavorting around his feet would allow.

"You're home!" Libby cried, coming around the table to crush her errant grandfather in as gentle a hug as she could manage. He felt frail and birdlike in her arms, but he returned the hug with reassuring vigor.

"This must be your grandfather," Rhonda purred, frantically signaling the nearest cameraman with her eyes. "What a touching reunion. And he brought . . . a friend?"

Libby lifted her eyes from her grandfather's shoulder to peer at the open doorway. She couldn't believe what she saw.

"Uncle Ray?"

The man who'd raised her since she was eight years old beamed across the table and said, "Emily! It's been too long. How are Phil and Libby?"

It wasn't the first time Uncle Ray had mistaken Libby for her own mother, his beloved sister-in-law, Emily, but somehow, it hit Libby especially hard out of the blue like this. When she visited Ray in the nursing home, she was able to brace herself, to be ready for it to be either a good day or a bad one.

Her throat closed up, but she didn't have to try to speak. Grandfather said calmly, "Libby's perfect, Ray. In fact, she's right here and I know she'd like a hug."

Confusion beetled Ray's brows, but it was a good day, because he obligingly shuffled over to enfold Libby in a hug that smelled like her childhood: spearmint gum and dusty library books. She couldn't hold back a sob, but there was no time for tears.

"What are you doing here, Uncle Ray? I'm so, so glad

to see you, but you should be home in Queens. How did you get here?"

"Pop came and got me," Ray said. "He told me it's Christmas, and all he wants this year is forgiveness and a second chance to be a good father."

Another sob choked off Libby's airway, but she found the breath to croak, "So you forgave him? As easy as that?"

Ray blinked and, for a moment, something wise and aware surfaced in his faded blue eyes. For that moment, Libby saw the man she'd loved and relied on for so many years take possession of himself once more. He smiled at her, then glanced behind her to his father. "It wasn't easy. That fight we had the day I took off—it left scars on both of us. The one I could never get over was Pop telling me he was glad Mama was dead and didn't have to see the mess her children were making of their lives. I decided if he didn't want to see it, he didn't have to, and I never came home. But the older I get, the more I lose, the more I understand how life sends us things we can't bear sometimes."

"I was wrong to say that," Dabney said, his jaw hard with regret. "Your mother would've loved you no matter what you did or how you lived your life. Me too— but without her to remind me, I lost track of what mattered for a while."

"Family." Libby blinked away tears and tried to summon a smile. "Family is what matters."

Ray nodded, squeezing Libby close. "We forgave each other. It was time. Besides, I figured if he was going to all this trouble to help my best girl, he couldn't be as bad as I thought all those years."

The mischievous grin was one Libby hadn't seen in a long time, but it was as infectious as ever. She laughed and hugged Uncle Ray again while Grandfather harrumphed and scowled and tried to pretend not to be absolutely thrilled with himself and his family.

Until the exact moment when he noticed the cameras and the bleached-blonde talk show host crowded around his family's table. "Vultures," he snarled, shaking his brass-topped cane at Rhonda. "Get out."

"Excuse me"" She drew herself up haughtily. "My crew and I have every right to be here—"

"Is that so?" Grandfather rapped his cane on the floor, eyes snapping with the light of battle. He appeared to be enjoying himself immensely. "I didn't sign any release, and this property is in my name. I'm pretty sure that entitles me to throw you the hell off it, if I so choose. Sheriff, correct me if I'm wrong."

Libby darted a glance at Andie, whose brows were climbing toward her hairline, but before Andie could weigh in, Hugo Downing said, "Now, now, there's no need for that. I arranged this visit and the filming with my employee, Elizabeth Leeds. All aboveboard. I'm sure you wouldn't want to do anything that might jeopardize my agreement with your granddaughter."

"Oh, wouldn't I." It wasn't a question, and as Dabney Leeds turned his attention to Hugo Downing, Libby had the uncanny feeling that they were about to witness a Godzilla versus Mothra–type smackdown. "The fact of the matter is that your agreement with Libby has been . . . superseded, shall we say? She doesn't need you or your money—she has family. She has me. And I intend to do whatever it takes to make her happy, including throwing your bloated, blackmailing carcass out of my house, along with your so-called journalist friend and her crew. So get out, before I call in my flesh-eating lawyers and have them sue you all back to the crappy Rust Belt towns you were spawned in."

Purple with rage, Mr. Downing stood up from the table so fast, his chair scooted across the hardwood floor and toppled over with a crash.

"I'll fire her," he said, pointing at Libby. "Don't think I won't!"

Libby stood up too, her heart pounding hard enough to shake her whole body. "You can fire me if you want, Mr. Downing. I can understand why you would want to. But I don't think you should."

"Why is she getting fired?" Rhonda asked the room at large, her platinum bob quivering with curiosity.

"Because she's a fraud." Downing threw his napkin down in disgust. "There's your scoop, Ms. Friend. Elizabeth Leeds is a fake."

Rhonda made a gasp that sounded more delighted than scandalized, but Libby ignored her to focus on her soon-to-be ex-boss. "It's true that when I wrote those blog posts, and then the articles for *Savor*—the ones that brought in thousands of fan letters every month—I wasn't married. I didn't live on Sanctuary Island. I didn't have much in the way of family. And I didn't know how to cook. But take a look around, Mr. Downing."

Libby gazed at the people gathered around her holiday table and felt her chest swell with brand-new confidence. "That's not true anymore. I have a home here, and family. And as you tasted for yourself, I can cook. So fire me if you want, but you'd be getting rid of your top columnist right when I'm about to be able to write better columns than ever before."

Downing locked eyes with her across the table. He was still furious at being thwarted, Libby could see, but she could also see the wheels turning in his head. Hugo Downing hadn't become the publisher of the industry's leading food magazine by letting his emotions lead him astray. "It's not up to me to out you or not. The damage is done," he said, gesturing to Rhonda and her still-recording cameras.

A chill shivered down Libby's spine, but she didn't back down. "I'm ready to tell the world the truth. Let Ms. Friend do her piece on me. I'm done with lying."

"She won't use a single second of this footage unless she wants a lawsuit on her hands," Grandfather reminded them. "And I still want you all to get the hell out of my house."

"What about my job?"

Libby waited, heart in her throat, while Hugo Downing paused. "I'll think about it," he said grudgingly. "Come on, Rhonda. We're leaving."

"But it's Christmas," she protested. "And we're stranded on this hick island with no way off it!"

"Wait," Nash shouted, standing up. At this point, there were as many people standing as there were sitting around the table. "Don't turn the cameras off yet. I have something to say."

And in front of everyone, with the cameras rolling and a fiery red blush crawling up his neck, Nash knelt down by Ivy's chair. She put her hand to her chest as if she was about to faint, but her eyes were shining with something much more powerful than surprise.

"Ivy Dawson." Nash's voice cracked, and he winced but kept going. "You are beautiful and amazing. You are the best thing that ever happened to me twice. I've spent a lot of time in my life being watched and judged—the subject of gossip. When I first met you, everything I felt for you was so big and new, I got selfish. I wanted to keep it to myself, to have one thing in my life that was just mine. But that made you think I was ashamed of you, when there couldn't be anything further from the truth. If you could love me again, I'd spend the rest of my life bragging about you to anyone who'll listen. Will you marry me?"

"At least these two did sign releases," Rhonda muttered, frantically gesturing her cameras to keep recording.

"I can't believe you're proposing on national television," Ivy chortled reaching down to run her hands through Nash's perfect dark blond hair. "Yes, yes, yes, I'll marry you! Get up, you idiot."

They kissed, and Libby clapped. Rhonda looked as if her Christmas was starting to look up.

"I don't see you all packing your bags," Dabney barked at the camera guys, who jumped and started gathering their equipment.

"But this is gold," Rhonda wailed.

"Gold you won't ever be airing," Dabney said stoutly. "I'll expect you to hand over what you're filmed before you leave the premises."

"Damn it," Nash said, tearing away from his kiss with Ivy, looking mussed and flushed with triumph now instead of embarrassment. "I thought I was proposing on national television! It still counts, doesn't it?"

In answer, Ivy pulled his head down for another kiss,

this one sultry enough to make Libby's eyes sting. Clearing her throat, she trained her eyes determinedly on her grandfather and her uncle.

"How did you get back here, anyway, Grandfather?" she asked. "Is the ferry running again?"

"Yes, the ferry has been reinstated for a single run this evening, but that's not how we got home."

"We flew!" Uncle Ray said, in such happy, wondering tones that for a brief moment, Libby pictured her grandfather and Ray in the old-fashioned sleigh they'd found in the shed, flying through the air towed by eight magical reindeer.

"We hitched a ride on Miles Harrington's helicopter," Dabney explained, shooting a triumphant glance at Hugo Downing. The mere mention of one of the most powerful billionaires in New York had Rhonda Friend practically drooling, but Downing hustled her along. He knew when it was time to retreat.

"Head down to the docks, the ferry building has a small waiting room," Grandfather was saying jovially, magnanimous in victory, with the whole dining room in chaos. Libby tried to get her uncle to sit down, but after so many years apart he wanted to stick close to his father and she couldn't blame him. Andie and Sam had hopped up to help the camera guys get their things together while Grandfather gloated. Nash and Ivy were and still making out, and when Libby looked around the room to find Owen, he was in a corner, deep in conversation with Hannah Swift.

Probably discussing how to go about getting his Permanent Disability status revoked so he could be reinstated for active duty, Libby realized with a pang.

But one person was missing from the hubbub. Libby whirled in place, searching the room wildly, but it was no use.

"Caitlin is gone!" she cried.

Owen felt as if he'd been poked with a cattle prod. He swung into action immediately, his gaze locking with Libby's panic-stricken eyes. They turned as one and ran for the back door while Andie shouted, "I'll look around front. Nash, Ivy, can you check upstairs?"

Owen was through the kitchen and down the back steps in the blink of an eye, numb to the cold air until he wondered if Caitlin had bothered to grab her coat when she snuck off. That thought made him put on an extra burst of speed as he spotted the trail of small footprints in the snow.

"She went this way." The trail led toward the pinewood behind the Leeds house, and Owen ran for it. The only sound was Libby's fast, shallow breaths at his back.

Once they hit the cover of the trees, the snow thinned out. He couldn't tell which way Caitlin had gone. Pausing in the middle of a copse of evergreens, Owen held up a hand to ask for Libby's silence. He breathed in, the cold air like chugging a glass of icy water, chilling him from the inside out.

Or maybe that was his fear. Because Owen was discovering that none of his training, none of his experience with overcoming fear was helping him now that his fear was all for his daughter.

"How long has she been gone?" he muttered, all of his senses trained on listening to the world around him, hoping for a sign of which way Caitlin might have run.

"I don't know." Libby's reply was equally soft, but he clearly heard the distress in her voice. "There was so much going on in there, she could have slipped away any time."

"She was right next to me." Self-loathing sat like a stone in the bottom of Owen's belly. "How could I have lost her when she was right there, beside me?"

"You didn't lose her," Libby argued at once. "She was upset and she ran off. Kids do that."

"Caitlin did it when I first met her," Owen admitted. The remembered pain of that moment was nothing compared to the all-consuming desolation he felt now.

"She's come a long way since then."

"Until today. When I sent her backsliding into insecurity and distrust of the very people who are supposed to take care of her."

"Stop it." Libby's voice had lost all softness and her eyes were fierce when she grabbed Owen's arm and forced him to look at her. "You standing here and punishing yourself isn't going to get Caitlin back. Focus, Owen."

She gave him a little shake, and somehow it snapped him out of the state he was in and brought his head up. Behind Libby, at the edge of the woods where the snow had drifted a little deeper, Owen thought he saw a strange shape pressed into the white powder.

"What's that?" he asked, pointing and loping toward the shape.

Libby grabbed his hand when she saw what he was looking at, the strength of her grip taking him by surprise. "Oh. Owen. It's a snow angel."

The three of them had spent a happy afternoon after

the first snowfall teaching Caitlin how to lie down in the snow and brush semicircles with her arms to make the impression of wings, and with her legs to form an indentation in the shape of an angel's robe. The part Caitlin had needed help with was getting back up without stomping all over the middle of her new creation, and it seemed she hadn't learned how to do it on her own since that first day. Because there in the middle of the snow angel were several sets of small boot prints.

And leading away from the angel, down a gentle slope that had hidden it from Owen's view before, were Caitlin's prints.

He and Libby took off again, skidding down the hill and following the trail along the slight valley that seemed to run in the direction of the shed where they'd spent the night. About halfway there, Owen caught sight of her up ahead of them.

Shivering and alone, head down, Caitlin was trudging doggedly along with her arms wrapped around her thin chest and snow slush darkening her brown leather boots in splotches. She didn't look up when Owen shouted her name, but she didn't try to run away either. She just . . . stopped.

Unreasoning terror throttled Owen, morphing into anger a moment later. "What were you thinking?" he yelled, skidding to a stop in front of Caitlin and taking in the blue tinge to her lips.

She shrugged, chin tucked to her chest, but Owen could still make out the tear tracks drying on her pale, freckled cheeks. When she shivered again, her teeth chattering lightly, Owen cursed and unzipped the gray cashmere sweater Andie had given him that morning. He had it wrapped around Caitlin's unresisting body by the time Libby caught up to them.

But Caitlin still hadn't said a word.

Chapter Twenty-Seven

"Is she okay?" Libby gasped, falling to her knees in the snow, uncaring of the icy wet seeping through her cable-knit tights. "Oh, honey, we were so worried."

"Why?" There was no emotion in Caitlin's toneless voice. "I left. That's what people do. It doesn't matter."

"It *does* matter," Owen argued, and Libby winced. She could've told him that was the wrong tack to take, and Caitlin proved it a second later by looking up at him with an accusing glare.

"*You're* leaving. And if you go, there's no reason for Libby to stay."

The words shot through Libby like an arrow, piercing her to the core. She desperately wanted to refute it but there was a grain of truth there—if Libby's relationship with Owen ended, she'd have no claim to Caitlin at all and no reason to be part of her life . . . no reason other than love. "Even if that happened, you'd still have your aunt Andie and Sam."

Caitlin's mouth worked as if she were trying not to cry. "Not if Daddy is leaving because of me. They won't want me around anymore either if I made him go away."

Heart breaking, Libby reached for Caitlin, but the little girl shied away as if Libby had raised her hand to slap her. The full-body flinch knocked Caitlin into Owen's hip, on the injured side, but he absorbed the blow without wincing. He really must be close to a full recovery, Libby thought numbly as she picked herself up from the cold, wet ground.

"Caitlin. Sweetheart, listen to me." Owen urged his daughter to turn with his hands on her shoulders. "I'm not going anywhere."

Libby suppressed a gasp, her heart galloping. *He means something else,* she thought wildly. *That he'll always be her father, no matter where he is in the world.*

But Owen was looking at Libby over top of Caitlin's head, and there was a promise in his eyes.

"What do you mean?" Caitlin asked, baring her bruised, suspicious little heart.

"I mean I'm staying here. On Sanctuary Island, with you."

Caitlin burst into tears, and Libby knew exactly how she felt. Joy so bright it almost hurt spread through Libby like a sunrise. She wanted to believe in it, but she had to be sure. "You're not going back to the army?"

Owen's smile faded a bit, but his hands were steady and sure as he pulled Caitlin in to bury her face against his stomach, her shoulders shaking under his too-big sweater wrapped around her like a blanket. "My injuries were so severe, the military hospital put me on the Permanent Disability Retirement List without even passing my case in front of a review board. When I'm able, I'm going to petition to be moved to the Temporary Disability Retirement List, and from there I'll join the Reserves. I have to do at least that much, Libby. The rest of it . . . we'll have to see how my recovery goes. But we have time."

"I understand," she said, and she did. He wouldn't be the man she loved if his sense of honor and duty were any less developed. "What made you change your mind about going back to active duty as quickly as possible?"

"Something you said has been rattling around my brain for days now, changing an idea here and shifting a perception there." Owen's mouth twisted up in a half smile. "You told me that there was more than one way to be a hero. And I realized . . . I have a sacred responsibility to Caitlin. She's my daughter and she needs me. I'm not all she's got—a lot of people love her—but I'm the only father she has. Every other duty has to take a backseat to that, and if I insist on leaving her to put myself in danger, am I really being noble? Or am I being selfish and letting my egotistic idea of heroism take precedence over my child's well-being? Because the truth is, my men are fine. I didn't want to admit they could survive without me, but they can. They have. And maybe now it's time for me to move on to a new challenge."

Libby couldn't catch her breath. Her mind was spinning with questions and possibilities. "And joining the Reserves will let you stay home most of the time."

"Well, I'll likely be doing some traveling, because I just got offered a job."

Libby wished she could sit down without getting her

rear end as freezing cold and wet as her wobbly knees. "A job?"

He nodded, his gaze never leaving her face. "Military liaison to The Hero Project. Apparently, helping wounded veterans navigate the complex infrastructure of the U.S. military's benefits system requires special skill and experience, which I have. Hannah Swift offered me a job as a consultant. I'll be helping to advocate for returning vets, advising on reintegration to civilian life, stuff like that."

"And you already accepted." Libby really wasn't sure how much longer she could stay on her feet.

Owen frowned slightly. "Maybe I should have waited and discussed it with you first, as a family."

That was it. Libby officially didn't care about having a wet butt. She let her legs give out and sat down in the snow.

Owen's eyes widened in concern. "Are you okay?"

"Miss Libby!" Caitlin cried, spinning around and seeing her on the ground. The little girl tore away from her father and ran over to where Libby was sitting, and all of a sudden, they were both laughing and crying at the same time, with Caitlin's arms around her neck and Owen was staring down at them bemusedly.

"What are you two doing down there?"

Libby beamed up at him, knowing every bit of her heart was shining in her face and not even caring, because she knew now that Owen would take good care of it.

"We're making snow angels," she cried, throwing herself backward and pinwheeling her arms and less.

"Yeah!" Caitlin grabbed her hand and lay down next to her, making her own, smaller snow angel.

"Libby, you're going to freeze to death. And oh, man, Andie is going to kill me when she sees that sweater." Owen shook his head, laughing. "But I can't resist you two."

And with that, he stepped over Libby and lay down on her other side. Tangling their fingers together, he turned his head to smile at her as all three of them waved their arms and legs through the snow. It was cold, so bitterly cold that the snow almost burned where it touched her bare skin, but Libby hardly felt it.

Everything inside her was warm with the knowledge that she was right where she'd always longed to be—in the middle of her family.

Later, after they'd admired their trio of mommy, daddy, and baby snow angels, and made it back to the house to be bundled into dry clothes and fed hot chocolate by the rest of their relieved family, Libby left Owen to explain things to the rest of them while she went and finally got the main course of their forgotten Christmas feast on the table.

She'd spent too darn long cooking all that food to let it go to waste.

Flicking the oven on, she set the roasting pan inside with its precious beef tenderloin nestled in a rack. After the Turkey Debacle, Owen had been the one to find the perfect, time-saving (if not money-saving) solution. Beef tenderloin. Special, delicious, and perfect for feeding a big group, beef tenderloin cooked in a mere half hour—unlike their huge turkey, which would've taken hours to roast.

Libby pulled the pans of mashed potatoes and spinach casserole from the fridge, pausing as she set them on top of the oven. The spinach casserole looked as if someone had spooned up a giant bite right out of the middle. Geez. It hadn't been that long between courses that anyone needed to sneak a snack in the middle of the meal, had it?

Rolling her eyes cheerfully, she smoothed the top of the spinach casserole with a spatula and put it and the pan of potatoes on the bottom oven rack to warm. Sniffing deeply at the rich, deliciously meaty smell of the beef roasting, she reflected that Pippin might have done her a huge favor by eating that turkey.

She thought it again once everyone was gathered back around the dining room table—family only, this time. But not just blood relations. This was the family they were creating by choice, the family they'd picked and fought for and built with their own hands. And when her family oohed and aahed as she triumphantly set the plate of sliced roast beef in the center of the table, pink and juicy and drenched in fragrant cognac sauce, Libby finally understood why so many people had loved her columns. They'd been chasing this feeling, this fullness and richness of emotion. The satisfaction of nourishing themselves and each other at a communal table filled with love.

Thankfulness swelled inside Libby, an emotion too big to contain. A little might have leaked from the corners of her eyes, but when Owen clasped her hand and brought her fingers to his lips, Libby found it easy to smile through her tears.

"Okay, everybody," she said, grinning around the

table. "Dig in! Don't be shy. I'm ninety-nine percent sure it won't poison you."

Everyone laughed and started passing dishes, piling plates high with tender slices of beef, snowy mounds of buttery mashed potatoes, and sweet marshmallow cream fruit salad . . . but the star of the meal was undoubtedly the spinach casserole. No one could stop raving about it—Sam was on his third helping. Even Libby had to admit that it was very tasty.

"It's official," Ivy announced. "I'm sorry, Nash, I can't marry you. I'm marrying this spinach casserole instead."

"It's even better than the way your grandmother used to make it," her grandfather said, his voice a little thick and husky.

"It tastes like home to me," Ray put in, and Libby pressed a hand to her heated cheeks.

"That's the best compliment anyone could give me," she told him, reaching for his hand, but he evaded her in favor of forking up another bite, and maybe that was the best compliment of all.

"How did you make it?" Andie asked.

"It was surprisingly simple," Libby confessed, "once I read my mother's notes about how to squeeze the liquid out of the cooked spinach so the end result wouldn't be soggy. I'm glad you all like it."

"Are you sure you don't want to try it?" Andie asked her niece, and for the first time, Libby peered around Owen to see that Caitlin had cleaned her plate of everything except the small mound of spinach casserole in the middle. Caitlin had her lips pressed together, her brow wrinkled with worry, and Libby couldn't stand it.

"That's okay," Libby said. "It doesn't have to be everyone's favorite thing."

She smiled at Caitlin reassuringly, but instead of smiling back, Caitlin's mouth opened on a wail. "I can't eat it! I can't, I can't!"

"You don't have to," Libby said at the same time Owen asked, "Why not?"

Caitlin sucked in a deep breath. "Because I stepped in it."

Everyone at the table paused. Sam, whose fork had been halfway to his lips, dropped it with a clatter. In a flash, Libby saw exactly what had happened.

"I put the casserole on the back steps to stay cool," she remembered aloud.

"And when I ran away, I didn't see it and I stepped in it," Caitlin said, the confession building steam the longer she talked. "It was gross. I wiped off my foot in the snow but I didn't know what to do with the spinach stuff so I put it back in the refrigerator."

"Where I found it and heated it up, and served it to all of you," Libby finished faintly, staring around the table in shock.

"And we all ate it." Owen stared down at his plate, probably considering throwing up.

"I'm sorry," Caitlin cried, her lower lip starting to tremble. But before she could get going, a sharp snort had them all swiveling to stare at the head of the table.

Grandfather snorted again, then let out a cackling laugh so loud it woke Pippin from his doze beside his master's chair. "Ha! You must have the touch, little girl—you gave that casserole a special spice that made it everyone's favorite dish."

His laughter was infectious. Pretty soon, everyone at the table was roaring. Sam defiantly picked up his fork and took another bite of the casserole, and that set everyone off again.

Libby leaned over and put her head on Owen's shoulder. "Well. I should have known better than to promise the perfect Christmas."

"I don't know." His depthless blue eyes crinkled at the corners with the warm, secret smile he gave her. "This feels pretty perfect to me. But if you're not happy with it, there's always next Christmas."

Next Christmas. The words filled Libby with hope and happiness. There would be a next Christmas, and a Christmas after that, and another after that. "Plenty of time to get it right," she murmured, nuzzling a kiss into the raspy stubbled underside of his jaw.

"As long as I have you and Caitlin with me," Owen said, his deep voice resonating through Libby's entire being, "every Christmas will be perfect. I love you, Libby."

And there it was. Libby's Christmas miracle. Through eyes brimming with tears and a heart brimming with love, Libby looked from face to happy face around her holiday table. Everyone who mattered most to her was gathered together under a single roof to celebrate and be together.

In the midst of the joyous chaos of conversation and laughter, Libby closed her eyes to say a prayer and remember the people who were missing. Her own, much-missed mother and father, her grandmother. Nash's mom, off somewhere doing her own thing, and Andie and Owen's estranged father and beloved, departed mother. If she concentrated, she could feel their spirits hovering over the table with a warm, loving light, enveloping everyone present in the kind of glow that only came around once a year.

"Merry Christmas," Libby whispered, her throat aching with unshed tears. She opened her eyes and found Owen watching her, an understanding smile on his lips. Libby had to kiss that smile, and she could, so she did.

"Who needs the perfect Christmas when imperfection is so great?" Owen said against her mouth, and Libby laughed with delight.

Maybe perfect was overrated.

Epilogue

One Year Later . . .

"This is getting to be a tradition," Libby said, laughing and plucking at the woolen cap pulled low over her eyes.

She wasn't trying to get a peek, not really, but Caitlin said, "Libby, no!" and grabbed for her hand. Libby laced their fingers together, taking a moment to enjoy the trusting curl of Caitlin's small digits in her clasp.

"Fine, fine. Lead the way."

Libby let herself be drawn through the house, down the narrow hallway and into the kitchen she'd come to know so well. It smelled like the cinnamon toast she'd made for breakfast, spicy-sweet and warm.

Caitlin had instructed them both into their winter things, puffed up with the importance of her role in this Christmas surprise, so Libby wasn't startled when the back screen door banged open and Caitlin said, "Three steps down, now."

The air outside was pleasantly brisk. It had been a mild winter with no snow yet, to Caitlin's daily dismay, but Libby liked the chill clarity of the winter sunlight brightening her vision even through the loose-knit wool of her blindfold.

"Where are we going?" she asked as Caitlin led her across the backyard with careful steps.

"You'll see." Caitlin's voice pitched high with the glee of finally revealing the big gift she and her father had been conspiring over for ages. "You're going to love it."

The confidence in the formerly anxious girl's tone was the best gift Libby could have asked for. It was amazing what a difference a year of stability and solid family love could make.

Caitlin still suffered setbacks. She had nightmares, and occasional bouts of mistrust and insecurity. She needed to be reminded often that she was loved, that she was important, that her needs would be met to the best of her family's abilities. She was sad sometimes, missing her mother, and angry at other times when she seemed more aware that the life she'd had with her mother before coming to Sanctuary Island had been lacking something fundamental. She wasn't over her early childhood neglect, or her loss, and it might take a while before she could sort out her complex emotions.

For now, all Libby and Owen could do was to prove to her over and over, through their words and actions, that they loved her.

"I'm sure it's going to be the best present ever," Libby told Caitlin, putting out her free hand for balance when she stumbled over uneven ground. "Because you and your daddy are giving it to me. And no one in the world knows me better than you two."

That was certainly true, now that Uncle Ray had slipped even more deeply into the arms of his disease. Grief twisted at Libby's heart when she thought of her uncle, but there was relief, too, because she knew that not only was he getting the very best care money could buy—he was getting the love and attention of the family he'd lost for so many years. With the help of a wonderful nurse, Ray was being cared for at home, where Grandfather, Libby, and Owen could all help.

"Everyone thinks they know you, though," Caitlin groused. "Because of your columns."

Caitlin could be possessive about the people she loved. Sharing was hard for her, after so many years of never having enough for herself—enough material things like food, but especially emotional things like love.

"It's not the same," Libby reminded her patiently. "The people who read the magazine know a version of me, but it's not the real me. They don't mind, as long as they get my recipes."

After the disaster with the TV crew last year, and all of Grandfather's threats about suing Rhonda Friend, Libby couldn't take the deceit any longer. With Hugo Downing's permission, she published an extremely personal letter of apology in place of her regular column, outlining her true identity, her motives for concealing it—and the extraordinary circumstances by which she'd started to finally live the life she'd always dreamed.

The response from readers was overwhelming. There were some who said they'd never read her again, but far more were caught up in the romance and magic of her story. Once she started adding her mother and grand-mother's recipes to her columns, they were more popular than ever before.

It didn't hurt that the man she loved was an extremely handsome war hero who was currently serving as the U.S. Army liaison to The Hero Project. Owen's transition from combat to administrative duty hadn't been easy for him, but the work he was able to do with The Hero Project helped a lot of people. And the sight of him in uniform never failed to stir Libby's blood.

He looked just as good in jeans and a sweater, though, she thought dazedly when Caitlin tugged her down to remove the blindfold with a triumphant flourish. Libby blinked rapidly, and at first all she could see was Owen.

Tall, strongly muscled, wide smile and ocean blue eyes. A lock of dark copper hair, grown out past regulation length, fell over his forehead and made Libby's fingers twitch against the urge to smooth it back.

"Hi," she said dumbly, struck stupid with lust and love and happiness all over again.

"Merry Christmas," Owen returned, one side of his mouth quirking up like he knew exactly what Libby was thinking. "Are you ready for your surprise?"

His gaze was as warm as his smile, full of the love Libby had learned to count on and trust in the past year. It was hard to tear her eyes away from him, but when she did, she saw that they were standing in front of the ramshackle old barn behind the Leeds house. The barn had housed horses years before, but it had fallen into disrepair and Grandfather had it boarded up after Pippin escaped and injured himself on a fallen beam inside.

Libby had been pondering what to do about the building for months, but she hadn't made any decisions.

It looked like the choice had been taken out of her hands. "What did you two do?"

Caitlin bounded over to her father and lifted her arms with the assurance of a child who knew she would be picked up. Swinging her onto his back where she clung like a monkey, Owen swept out an arm toward the open doorway and said, "Come and see."

Libby didn't need to ask if it was safe. If it wasn't, Owen wouldn't let her or Caitlin anywhere near it. She slipped inside, blinking at the change of temperature. The last time she'd peered into the old wooden barn, wind had whistled through chinks in the walls. Now it was snug and cozy inside. A skylight had been cut into the roof, pouring in sunlight, and the hard-packed dirt floor was strewn with hay.

A few of the stall dividers remained, but the stalls were open. New wood gleamed at the back of each stall where a wide ledge had been built with a sturdy ramp running up to it. Each ledge held several square cubes, like cubbyholes.

"What is all this?" Libby asked, delight fizzing in her bloodstream as she peered into each stall, working her way toward the back of the barn where she noticed a heat lamp glowing in the last stall.

"Your Christmas present," Owen replied teasingly. "Haven't figured it out yet? I'll give you a hint. Once you've got this, you know you've got a home."

Realization flooded Libby at the same moment that she registered the tiny peeping she'd been hearing as background noise since they entered the barn. Only it wasn't a barn anymore.

"It's a chicken coop!" she cried, whirling to throw her arms around Owen. With Caitlin riding piggyback, Libby got a perfect two-in-one hug in before racing off to find the source of the peeping.

"Giddyup, Daddy, I want to see, too," she heard Caitlin say behind her as she found the wide box sitting under the orange light of the heat lamp. On a flat cushion inside were six baby chicks, fluffy and dark yellow with brownish spots. They waddled and toppled over one another on their spindly little legs, stretching their necks and waggling their stubby, fluff-covered wings. Libby was instantly and irrevocably in love.

"They're beautiful," she cooed, reaching into the box to stroke a downy back with one fingertip. "What kind are they?"

"I started with Rhode Island Reds," Owen said, swinging Caitlin down from his back so she could get a closer look. "Good layers, supposedly. I know you want fresh eggs."

"Don't worry, I'll share. Caitlin and I can learn how to make omelets!" Libby grinned at her best kitchen assistant, who beamed back a Jack-o'-lantern smile where she'd lost her front tooth before leaning over the box to watch the chicks play.

Taking advantage of Caitlin's distraction, Libby stepped up close to Owen and curled her hand around the nape of his neck to entice him down for a kiss. He came willingly, his big, warm hands shaping her waist and pulling her in close. "I can't believe you got me chickens for Christmas," Libby said, feeling choked with emotion. "I've always dreamed of keeping chickens."

"I know. But that's not all I got you."

Libby tilted her head at the nerves in his deep voice, but Owen was already reaching past her and into the box of chicks. Gently and slowly, so as not to disturb the chicks too much, Owen slid his hand under the cushion and pulled out something small and shiny. Libby's heart shot into her throat and her lungs forgot how to work.

It was a ring.

Right there, in the real-life version of the fantasy chicken coop Libby had been dreaming of since she was a little girl, Owen knelt down in the fresh hay and looked up at her with hope and love shining from his eyes.

"Libby," he said thickly. "I love you. My daughter loves you. We love your dreams and your stories and your huge, open heart that believes they'll come true. We want to help. Libby Leeds, will you marry me and let me make your dreams come true for the rest of our lives?"

Pure joy cascaded through Libby like a waterfall. She tore her stare from Owen to look across the box of baby chicks at Caitlin, who was biting her lip and trying not to look nervous. The love Libby felt in that moment overwhelmed her, as if she'd somehow let her heart escape from her chest to walk around outside, vulnerable and raw and full.

"I know you two think I've got a great imagination," she said, forcing the words out through her tight, constricted throat. "And I do. It got me through a lot of hard times. But I have to tell you that even I could never have imagined happiness like this. I could never have imagined a family as wonderful as the two of you—as the three of us, together," she corrected herself with a sob catching at her breath.

"Is that a yes?" Owen asked quietly.

Libby gazed down at her own personal hero holding a gold ring with a single diamond up to her, and she let her knees crumple. She knew he would catch her, and he did. "Yes, yes, yes," she said, laughing and crying at the same time. "My answer is yes. To both of you. To all of it. To the life I always dreamed of—but better, because this is real."

A small, red-haired object barreled into them from the side, sending all three of them sprawling to the floor in a pile of legs, hay, and laughter. Libby turned her face up to Owen's for a kiss, feeling the intimacy and heat of their connection snap into place as it always did. As she prayed it always would.

Real life was different from dreams. It took work and sacrifice, and there were things she couldn't control—things that weren't perfect. But as Owen helped her up and showed her around the chicken coop, outlining his plans for the future, Libby admired her new ring and thought about what last Christmas had taught her.

Dreams were wonderful. She'd lived on nothing but dreams for a long time. But real life, where there were surprises like a man who loved her and a little girl who needed her and a family slowly knitting itself together—real life was exactly where Libby wanted to spend the rest of her days.